Trail to Trouble

Wild Hearts Series

Valerie J. Clarizio

TRAILHEAD CONSULTING LLC

Dedication

I've been truly blessed to have so many wonderful people come into my life on both a personal and professional level, and I want you to know you are all greatly appreciated.

To my readers who take time out of their precious day to read my books and leave reviews, thank you — you are amazing.

To my Clarizio Cronies who play along with me on my social media accounts, thank you for your continued support.

Special thanks to those of you who helped me along the way to ensure that my book shines. Editor Judy Rosen, cover artist Dana from Designs by Dana, and proofreader Carol Karason — you ladies are the best.

To my family and friends, thank you for your steadfast support, encouragement, and love.

To my husband Rick, your support and belief in me mean more than I can express in words, and I'm a writer!

Desciption

Every winding trail hides a mystery, and every heartbeat hides a story.

He's never stopped loving her. She's never stopped running.

Hunter Samuelson has spent a decade longing for the woman who vanished without a trace.

Hannah Rice just wants to escape the shadows of a violent past.

When a chance encounter ignites old flames, it also awakens a deadly threat. Now, survival means trusting each other, and risking everything for a second chance at love.

A relaxing escape turns deadly in Michigan's remote wilderness...

Hannah Rice joined her friends for a hiking and camping trip in Michigan's breathtaking Upper Peninsula; a chance to heal from a near-fatal brush with a violent ex. With rugged trails, stunning views, and a skilled guide like Hunter Samuelson, the trip promises the peace she craves.

Desciption

But danger lurks in the shadows.

Their serene adventure quickly spirals into a nightmare when an unseen predator targets their group. To protect his charges, Hunter throws himself into the line of fire. His life-threatening injuries force Hannah to summon every ounce of strength to survive in the wilderness alone, and ultimately live a life on the run.

A chance encounter not only ignites old flames, but awakens the deadly threat they'd nearly died to escape years earlier. This time, will Hannah and Hunter be able to outrun the danger...or will it catch up with them?

***

USA Today Bestselling author Valerie J. Clarizio brings you the first book in the Wild Hearts Series – Small Town Romantic Suspense – heroes and heroines willing to sacrifice everything to protect those they love. A happily-ever-after guaranteed.

Looking for more steamy romances with heart-pounding suspense and characters who will live in your heart forever? Sign up for my newsletter to keep abreast of what is coming next. Start enjoying exclusive updates, sneak peeks, and special offers!

Sign up here: https://valeriejclarizio.com/newsletter-signup-page/

Prologue

*G*REEN *B*AY, *Wisconsin – April 2025*

Orion's gaze was glued to the backside of the woman pointing at the presentation screen in the front of the boardroom. She hadn't seen him sneak into the dimly lit room and continued with her marketing presentation. There was something familiar about the sway of her hips and soft tone of voice. Without a doubt, he'd heard that lovely voice before. Needing to satisfy his curiosity, he willed her to spin and face him. Who was this woman with the angelic voice?

The woman spun and swung her gaze around the table, halting on a dime when she reached him. She stumbled over her words.

His heart leaped into his throat. He'd stared into those bright emerald eyes before. The tension between them thickened, along with the air in the room. He could feel the pull when she tried to tear her gaze from him, but he held on to it for a moment longer before letting it go.

She repeated her last sentence as she returned her focus to the whiteboard in the front of the room.

The new edginess and raised octave in her tone, confirmed she recognized him.

Rather than paying attention to the presentation, Orion spent the next fifteen minutes trying to figure out how he knew the woman. He thought he knew, but the name on the cover of the presentation packet was not familiar to him. Still, he was ninety-nine percent sure he'd met her in the past when he'd worked as a camping and hiking guide. Those eyes, that voice, gave her away, yet the name she used didn't match. Maybe she was a doppelgänger of the woman from his past. He should focus on what she said rather than on her, but he couldn't help himself. Adrenaline surged through him. His immediate attraction to her was strong— undeniable. Who cared about the presentation anyway? It was just another one of the four firms competing for the marketing contract for his string of sporting goods stores.

He reread the name on the packet, Katrina Holmes. *Not familiar*. Her soft voice resonated in his head. *Familiar*. He needed another glimpse of her eyes, but she averted his gaze as she fielded questions from his staff.

Once his managers finished with their inquisition, Katrina leaned over the table and folded her laptop. That's when he saw it, the tattoo that had haunted his dreams for nearly a decade. The ink confirmed it. He was right. He knew who she was. Apprehension snaked down his spine, and anxiety coiled in the pit of his stomach. The dark shadow of the past that lurked in the back of his mind moved to the forefront.

He may have only seen part of the small tattoo stamped on her cleavage, but he was certain it was the correct tattoo. A small butterfly with bright orange wings outlined in black. But still, there was something a little off about her appearance, not to mention her name. He'd never met someone by the name of Katrina Holmes before but the tattoo, eyes, and voice matched that of a woman he'd met nearly ten years ago when he worked as an outdoor guide for his uncle in the Upper Peninsula of Michigan.

His uncle owned just over three thousand acres and offered guided hiking, camping, fishing, and hunting tours. Orion was a master hiker and he knew his uncle's property like the back of his hand. He had hiked it from the moment he could walk. According to his parents, he'd hiked those woods before he could even walk, because they were hikers as well.

He'd worked his way through college, guiding mostly city folk who wanted a sneak peek at untamed wilderness. And this woman who stood before him now had been on one of his guided camping trips. The camping trip that nearly ended his life.

Katrina flashed her gaze around the conference room. All eyes were on her. The audience looked attentive. She had this. This contract was hers for sure. No doubt. Nabbing this account would surely secure that promotion she'd been working toward. Once her boss retired in a year or two, she'd step right into his management position.

Her gaze drifted back to the vacant chair at the far end of the table. Where was the boss man? She was giving the presentation of her life and the man in charge didn't show. She'd poured her life and soul into this one—this potentially big account. Okay, the account wasn't huge, but if she succeeded at landing this one, it would be her biggest yet. At least his team looked pleased.

Refocusing on the interactive whiteboard, she verified her words were timed correctly with the video that played. Spot on. Why wouldn't it be? She'd practiced many times. So much so that she was sick of hearing it.

She looked back at her audience and panned over them. Her gaze halted on the man who now filled that vacant chair. His eyes flashed in recognition, and her heart seized. She knew him. She knew those eyes. She also knew he knew.

Her extremities quivered and her skin perspired. The words scrambled in her brain and she stumbled on them. She needed out of this room, but she wasn't finished with her pitch. The only way to get through the rest of her presentation was to stop focusing on him. Those warm eyes, handsome square jaw, and unforgettable velvety lips. But his name, Orion, didn't match what she remembered. Was it not him? No, judging from the way he studied her, it had to be.

How was she going to get out of this room without talking to him? How was she going to represent this account without ever seeing him? And how was she going to ensure that he was wrong about who she really was? She'd worked so hard for this opportunity, and now she'd have to give it up. Just like she'd had to give him and her life up almost ten years ago.

Chapter One

IRON CITY - UPPER PENINSULA of Michigan - August - 2015

Hunter sighed as he eyed from afar the group of flighty college girls he was assigned to guide for the three nights and four days.

"Why do they all think they need to embark on a rugged camping and hiking adventure during their summer vacations?"

His Uncle Lee slapped his shoulder blade. "Oh, come on, it's not that bad. Besides, they've paid your tuition and then some. Without them, you'd be working indoors bussing tables or something."

Inside work was the last thing he wanted. "I know, but good Lord, if I have to listen to one more city girl whine about bugs, the weather, or breaking a nail, I'll...well, I'm not sure what I'll do but...."

His uncle laughed. "Until you get a year-round, full-time job with your big new business degree, you're stuck here with me and the rest of the crew guiding hikers, campers, anglers, and hunters."

Hunter craned his neck to look at his uncle. "Do we have a fishing crew going out this weekend? Maybe I can take that one instead."

He'd rather that, but he always got stuck guiding the giddy girls.

The man chuckled. "Sorry. We do, but Bud's been assigned to them. Plus..."

Hunter knew what he was going to say. He'd heard it before. Problem was, he wasn't sure if he should be happy or angry about it.

"You're a good-looking guy. The girls love you. They give great reviews and that's good for business. Keeps you employed. Keeps the business running."

"You know, I think it's illegal to pimp me out like this," Hunter said.

"Except I have a rule, no fraternizing with the guests. So, that squashes that."

They shared a laugh.

Uncle Lee inhaled deeply, taking in the crisp, cool morning air, and swung his proud gaze around, taking in the fore-front of the three thousand acres of land he owned, comprising various terrains, mostly hardwoods, bordering thousands of acres of state land. It didn't get much better than that. Your own massive property surrounded by state land. Public land large enough that most people didn't venture too far in and get too close to his private land.

"Too bad it's not year-round work. It's a man's paradise up here," his uncle added.

Hunter couldn't agree more, but now that he'd gradu-

6

ated with a Master of Business Administration degree, it was time he did the responsible thing and get a real job, the kind capable of paying a mortgage. What he'd really love to do is exactly what his uncle was doing: make a decent living working in the outdoors. However, you need money to buy land and set up shop, so getting a year-round job was on his to-do list.

The giddy laughter of the girls drew closer to him. He cringed. Three nights and four days of this.

He eyed the tall, slim, blonde girl with a pink backpack gripped in her hand, made up like she was going to a beauty pageant. Eyes, cheeks, lips—the whole works. Her long, shiny hair draped over her bare, thin shoulders. *Who on earth thinks a skimpy tank top is appropriate wear for a rugged camping trip in the land of mosquitoes?* The mid-morning sun peeked out from behind a cloud and nearly blinded him as the overbearing bling on her backpack sparkled. *Great.*

Hunter shifted his gaze to the girl to the left of the beauty queen. Her hair was dark, nearly black, and her complexion was olive-toned. Just like the first girl, this one's short shorts, tank top, and lightweight, thin-soled tennis shoes were not conducive to the hiking they were about to embark on. Had they not even glanced at the standard checklist he'd sent them?

Did he dare check out the third princess in this trio? He drew in a long breath and shifted his gaze to the third woman who had just stepped out from behind the princesses. A blanket of relief fell over him. She was different. A pale, plain beauty with just a bit of makeup accenting her large eyes. Her long, brown hair was pulled back into a ponytail that swayed from side to side with each step she took. A pair of sunglasses was propped on her head.

Valerie J. Clarizio

She wore a forest green T-shirt tucked into long tan shorts that almost reached her knees, and the dark brown hiking boots she wore looked like they were made for walking. Not only that, they looked like they'd been used before. The large army-green backpack slung over her shoulder was certainly not the one she used to haul her books around campus, like those her friends carried. Super, at *least one of them shouldn't be a problem.*

Hunter glanced at his clipboard and racked his brain to remember the names of the girls walking toward him, not to be confused with the many other ladies he'd guided already this summer. *Let's see Hannah Rice, Alyssa Barnes, and Bianca St. James.* He scrambled to place a name on each of the women. The model-grade blonde had to be Bianca, that seemed like a model's name. Next, he pegged the dark-haired girl for Alyssa—another fancy name for another fancy girl. As for the natural beauty, that had to be Hannah. A regular name to suit a wholesome beauty.

Hunter flashed a smile at the ladies. "Hi, I'm Hunter, I'm your guide."

The blonde raked her flirtatious gaze over him, making no attempt to hide her interest. "I'm Bianca."

She extended her hand, and from the way she presented it, he wondered if he was supposed to kiss it, rather than shake it. *Yep, rich girl.* She released him and then gestured to the other two as she introduced them. He had placed their names correctly. After years of practice, he prided himself on his success in what he called the name game.

"Are you ready to embark on the adventure of your life?" he teased with a wink.

Though Hannah smiled along with her friends, unlike them, her smile didn't reach her eyes. *Why not?* Hunter

8

wondered. Did she not want to be here? Of the three, she looked like the one who most belonged in this environment.

Hunter pointed at the two red canoes he had loaded with camping supplies earlier in the morning. "There are our rides. Shall we?" He motioned to the shoreline where the canoes sat half in and half out of the slow-flowing river water.

The ladies slid into the life vests he had pulled from the canoes. Bianca, as he suspected, played stupid, unable to figure out how to strap herself into the vest. Playing along, Hunter reached toward her and untangled the straps before fastening the ends together over her well-endowed breasts. Then, he lowered his hands to fasten the other two sets of straps for her. Out of the corner of his eye, he caught Hannah's eye roll and nearly chuckled out loud. Bianca's behavior was nothing new to him. She was one of those women. One of those who came for an adventure but wanted to be the adventure.

"Have any of you ever been in a canoe before?" he asked.

Alyssa and Bianca shook their heads. Hannah nodded. That didn't surprise him.

Bianca tilted her head to the side. The corners of her full, hot pink lips lifted. "For safety, I think I should ride with you," she stated.

Like he didn't know that was coming.

"Okay, you'll ride up front in my canoe," he shifted his gaze to Alyssa, "and you'll ride up front with Hannah."

The ladies nodded in agreement.

After giving his guests the canoeing 101, he prepared for departure, holding the canoes as each of the women climbed in and took their assigned spots.

Before taking his seat, he stepped over to Hannah and crouched down. "You got this, right?"

It's not like the waters they would canoe were rough, but there were some rapids they'd be going through, and he wanted some reassurance they'd be okay.

Her full red lips pulled into a smile wider than they had earlier. "Yeah, I'm good. It's not my first go-around in a canoe."

Little gold flecks flashed in her emerald eyes, causing a rush of adrenaline to surge through his veins. Yep, she was in her element—confident, but not cocky.

"Great. Well, let's get to it then," Hunter replied as he shoved Hannah's vessel into the water.

He climbed into his and Bianca's canoe and paddled away from the shore.

They'd row only a little over a mile and a half today, set up camp, and hike to a small waterfall. Just a brief adventure since they started out later than they would over the next couple of days.

They paddled leisurely, soaking up the warm, bright, early afternoon sun. He loved this part of the job: being able to be outside all day long, paddling along a slow-moving river, and getting paid for it. Okay, truth be told, he'd prefer to be a white-water rapids guide, rather than a lazy river guide, but either way, he was enjoying the great outdoors. Getting paid was just a bonus.

Bianca threw a glance at him over her smooth-looking, sun-kissed shoulder. Judging from her delicate features and the way she carried herself, he presumed her tan came from a tanning bed, not the natural sun. There was no denying the woman was beautiful, but it didn't matter to him. She wasn't his type.

She looked at him again and smiled, flashing her

straight, white teeth. Her bright blue eyes sparkled with sass and challenge. He returned her smile as he rethought his assessment of her. Maybe she wasn't his type, but it certainly wouldn't hurt anything to have fun with her for a while, or would it? It was against the rules, though. His uncle preached that over and over to the staff.

"Alyssa, you have to actually paddle. I can't keep us aligned by myself," Hannah yelled.

Hunter pulled his gaze from the blonde beauty in the front of his canoe and fixed it on Hannah and Alyssa's canoe, which was headed straight for a tree limb hanging low over the river. Both ladies ducked in the nick of time to avoid getting clotheslined. Hannah growled something at her friend that he couldn't make out, but whatever it was, it caused Alyssa to paddle feverishly. It was probably a good thing they started out in the shallow and mellow section of the river today. It gave the ladies a little practice before they entered the deeper, somewhat faster flowing waters.

Once the two paddled farther away from the shore, Hannah shot him a glance and shook her head. He couldn't help but grin at her obvious frustration with her friend.

Hunter paddled up alongside Hannah and pointed to the campsite they'd use the first night.

"That's where we're headed."

This was his favorite campsite. It jutted out on a little point and reminded him of the Hamm's beer sign that hung in his grandfather's basement bar. As a kid, he'd watch that lighted, rippled water motion sign for hours on end, mesmerized by the flowing waters.

Hannah nodded and followed him to the shore. He hopped out of his canoe and pulled it up onto the rocky beach, then grabbed hold of Hannah's canoe and pulled it on shore so the women could climb out without getting their feet wet.

Side by side, they all stood on the shore for a moment, looking over the river. Off in the distance, he could hear a pileated woodpecker pecking away; more like hammering at a tree. From the direction it sounded, it was probably pounding on that near-dead white pine. He'd seen wood-peckers on it recently when he and his clients hiked by, on their way to the falls and gorge they'd be seeing today. There were so many holes in that once mighty tree, he couldn't imagine there were many insects left within its bark wall to feast on.

"These tents won't pitch themselves," he exclaimed as he bent over and pulled two tent packs from his canoe.

He carried them into the woods a few feet before plop-ping each one down on a tent pad.

"That one is yours," he informed the ladies, as he pointed at the slightly larger bag.

Hannah nodded.

"The setup instructions are in the bag. And that one is mine. I'll race you," he teased.

Bianca and Alyssa smiled, Hannah, not so much. In fact, her look bordered on annoyed. Why? He was just teas-ing. Did she not like challenges or competition?

Within minutes, he'd pitched his tent. Having done this so many times, he could do it in his sleep.

Now and then, his uncle talked about building little cabins at each of the campsites, but he always decided against it because he wanted to give his customers a more 'outdoorsy' experience. Some visitors even chose to sleep under the stars. Hunter eyed his current clients. They certainly weren't the type to sleep under the open sky. In fact, it surprised him that two of the three were here at all.

Hunter stepped up to the ladies. Overall, they were doing a decent job setting up their four-person dome tent, but if it were him, he'd be finished already, and likely the camp would be set up, too. But this, the clients being hands-on, was all part of the experience they paid for, so he let them be.

Hannah read the tent assembly instructions and directed her friends on how to set up the tent. Out of the corner of her eye, she caught Hunter's amused gaze. The look in his dark brown eyes matched his teasing tone from earlier when he challenged them to a race as to who could set their tent up more quickly. Why was everything a competition for men? Especially the too-good-looking ones. The ones who thought the world revolved around them. *Jerk.*

He crossed his muscular arms over his chest and leaned back on his heels as he watched. The corners of his mouth had lifted slightly, making him even more annoying to her.

She gave a few more instructions to her friends. Why couldn't they seem to understand her? Why were they struggling so much to set up this stupid tent? And most of all, why did her friends insist on taking this trip? They were the least outdoorsy people she knew, yet they insisted on this kind of trip. She'd grown up in an outdoors-enthusiastic family and loved the outdoors and all it had to offer, but her college roommates certainly didn't. She should never have let them talk her into taking this trip.

Bianca peeked around the partially erected tent she steadied with her hands gripped around a pole. She batted her eyes at Hunter, likely hoping to get him to finish setting it up for them. Hannah barked out her next instruction. She would be darned if she'd ask for help.

"Would you like some help?" Hunter asked.

His gaze stayed on Bianca, and his grin widened.

"Sure," Bianca replied.

"No, we got this. We're almost done," Hannah said quickly as Hunter made a move toward them.

Hunter halted.

"Just insert the ends of the rods into the loops at the base of the tent, and we'll be set," Hannah instructed.

Alyssa and Bianca did as told, and the tent pulled taut.

"There. Done," Hannah said as she stepped back and eyed their handiwork.

"Looks good," Hunter affirmed.

Without looking at him, Hannah shrugged, then she spun around and headed toward the canoe to retrieve her backpack and the bedrolls their guide had packed for them. Her friends followed.

Hunter returned to his canoe and pulled a cooler from it, and carried it over to the brown, metal, bear-proof food locker. He pulled four bottles of water from the cooler and a couple of other small packages Hannah couldn't quite identify, and he stuffed them into his camouflage backpack. After stowing the cooler in the metal bin, he latched the door.

He spun to face them. "Who's up for a short hike to Wild Canyon Falls?"

"I'm ready," Bianca responded eagerly as she stepped to Hunter's side.

"I'll be ready in a second. I just need to grab my camera from my pack," Alyssa said as she dipped her hand into her backpack and pulled out her expensive-looking camera and two lenses.

"And you?" Hunter asked with a quick glance in Hannah's direction.

Hannah nodded.

Hunter led them down the single-file trail. Beach stones lined the first several feet of the path. Most were oval-shaped, dark colored, and they looked invitingly smooth. Hannah liked rocks and shells. They were like little treasures to her and she fought the urge to snap one up. Maybe on the way back.

The path quickly transitioned to moist dirt. It had rained earlier in the day, and the trees lining the path blocked the warm sun from drying the earthy-smelling ground, causing any little slope to be slippery. Hannah figured her hiking shoes would maintain her foothold, but her friends wearing their fashionable tennis shoes, rather than practical ones, would have to be careful not to slip and fall on their rumps. She had warned them to pack shoes more suitable for hiking, but they dismissed her advice.

The ground grew muddier and more slippery as they trekked over a slight decline in the terrain. Now the girls would really have to be careful. She shook her head. This was on them. She had warned them.

Closing her eyes to envision the map she'd studied earlier, and had since stuffed in her backpack, she knew the faint trickle of water she heard was likely not the Wild Canyon Falls. It had to be from something else. Probably a little creek feeding into the falls, or from the falls.

When she reopened her eyes, she focused ahead to find a narrow two-plank walkway a short distance away. The guide walked over the planks with ease, even though there was no railing. Alyssa hesitated and glanced over her shoulder at her and raised a skeptical brow. Hannah nodded, then Alyssa turned and lifted her arms for balance, and crossed over the planks. Bianca did the same.

Hannah followed suit. She glanced down. The distance

between the walkway bridge and the ground increased with each step she took. Within a few more steps, a narrow stream flowed under the boardwalk, about four feet below the planks. She studied the clear water for a moment before continuing along. Only a few more feet to go to get back onto the dirt path—solid ground.

The trail twisted and turned. Hunter stopped and pointed at a pine tree about twenty feet into the woods. A pileated woodpecker drove its beak against the bark, carving out yet another hole in the tree that already looked like Swiss cheese. How could the poor bird pound that hard and not get a migraine?

Alyssa snapped a few photos of the woodpecker before they continued down the trail. The sound of rushing water echoed through the forest, louder and louder as they closed in on Wild Canyon Falls.

A cool breeze swept through the air as she stepped onto a flat rock formation overlooking the falls and gorge. The water flowing over the twenty-foot-long ledge was fairly clear. White foam formed at the bottom of the ten-foot falls and then flowed through the gorge with the rapid current. It was louder than Hannah had expected it to be when she'd read about the falls, especially since the drop wasn't all that far.

She stared at the rushing water, mesmerized by both the sight of it and the thunderous sound echoing off the canyon walls.

Bianca, Alyssa, and Hunter milled around the area, Alyssa taking a gazillion photos as she always did. Hannah had to hand it to her, Alyssa had an eye for taking scenic photos, and an eye for capturing beautiful moments when photographing people. Lucky for Alyssa, Bianca was along.

That woman loved having her photo taken, and as pretty as Bianca was, Alyssa's job was made easier.

Hannah thought about pulling her phone from her pocket to take some photos, but she decided against it, knowing Alyssa would make a scrapbook about their whole adventure when they returned home, and she'd make copies for both her and Bianca.

"Group photo time!" Alyssa yelled as she set up the tripod for her camera. They gathered by the worn wooden fence lining a jutting section of the rock that hung out over the falls.

Bianca fit herself under the drape of Hunter's arm, curving toward him slightly, and then placed her palm against his chest. The guy ate up her attention. Too bad for him, he'd be just another notch on Bianca's bedpost. Guilt swept through Hannah's veins every time she thought of her friend as promiscuous, but the truth was that Bianca fit the mold. Hannah edged close to Bianca's side as Alyssa prepared the camera and then hustled over and molded herself to Hunter's free side.

After Alyssa's mini photoshoot was complete, Hunter pointed to the rock wall that lined the north side of the gorge. "If you want, we can climb up there, where the view of the falls is awesome."

The incline looked steep but certainly doable since the rock formation was almost like a staircase in some areas; tall steps, but steps nonetheless.

"Let's do it," Bianca immediately replied.

Hunter gestured for them to follow. Hannah took notice of how their guide's long, muscular legs seemed to climb the tall rock steps with ease. She, on the other hand, had to use her hands for support as she climbed, pressing her palms to the surface of the next ledge to help hoist herself up. Her friends did the same.

Hannah paused for a moment, watching them all climb ahead of her. Her attention refocused on Hunter's flexing leg muscles. A shiver of thrill raked through her. The guy was like a machine. It didn't seem to matter if the next step was six inches high or sixteen inches high; he climbed effortlessly.

Ugh, what am I thinking? Haven't I been through enough with men already? They're all the same. After only one thing. Especially the good-looking, well-built ones, but the ones that know they're all that are the worst.

Refocusing on her footing, Hannah took the next step and caught up with her friends.

"You need to wait a minute," Alyssa said as she looked over her shoulder at Hannah.

Her friend had stopped and was waiting for Hunter to help her with the last step to the top of the cliff. The step looked to be about two feet in height. Hunter stood on the top ledge, reached down, grasped one of Alyssa's hands, and effortlessly hoisted her up. Hannah stepped onto the ledge Alyssa had been standing on, and Hunter reached down. She stared at his large hand. Flashbacks of her ex's harsh hand flooded her and fear shook her extremities. She didn't want to touch him. Not just him, but any man. Ever.

Reassessing the height of the makeshift step, she determined she didn't need his help. If he'd just back up, she could place her palms on the top of the ledge where he stood and lift herself up and onto it.

"Those rocks on the edge aren't the most secure and sometimes break loose when stepped on. Just grab my hand and I'll hoist you up and over them."

She eyed him for a moment, debating his offer.

"It's okay, I won't let you fall."

Great, now he thinks I'm just a chicken. That was true in a sense, but she wasn't afraid of falling. She swallowed hard; she was afraid of him. Not just him, all men. She knew she shouldn't fear him because she didn't even know him. But with all that had gone on lately in her life where men were concerned, her general impression of the bunch was not pleasant. In fact, it was downright unpleasant. Yep, she was guilty of grouping all men into the same category. Until one could prove different, that's how it would be.

She focused on his dark eyes. They softened, as if he knew there was more to her hesitation than a fear of falling.

"Hannah, I just want to help you up, that's all." His tone was gentle with a tinge of sympathy.

Her hand perspired and shivered as she reached up. He wrapped his large, warm hand around hers, pulled her to the top of the cliff, and then immediately released her. Her fingers tingled, and her stomach swirled from his touch. For a moment, she wanted to reach out and snatch up his comforting hand. Where did that thought come from? She shook her head as if that would help shake the unwanted thought from her mind. It didn't help.

It was windy atop the cliff, and the damp, earthy smell from below faded. She closed her eyes and lifted her face toward the sun. The rays warmed her cheeks and relaxed her.

"This is one of my favorite spots on the entire property. You can see so much from here," Hunter said.

Hannah opened her eyes to find him staring at something across the gorge, his hand shielding his eyes from the sun. The same hand that had left her all gooey inside only moments ago.

He lowered his hand, pulled a set of binoculars from his

pack, and lifted them to his eyes, staring through them for a moment before handing them to her.

He pointed in the direction he had glassed. "That's an eagle's nest over there. There were a couple of eaglets, but they may have left the nest. I haven't seen them for a while now."

Hannah lifted the binoculars to her eyes and pointed them in the same direction Hunter had. "I don't see it."

He stepped behind her, reached around her, and pointed. "Try there."

His warm breath tickled her neck, distracting her.

"Do you see them now?"

"No."

From behind her, he took the binoculars, crouched slightly to align with her height, and held them to his eyes. While holding them in place, he edged back.

"I've got the binos on them. Step over here. I'll try not to move them."

Hannah eased over into the crook of his arm and looked through the binoculars to find the nest. The hint of cedar in the air strengthened with his proximity to her. His stimulating, outdoorsy scent suited him—made sense to her. He smelled so good and she inhaled deeper.

"Do you see it now?" he asked.

"Yes."

She drew in another inhalation before she reached up and took the binoculars from him so she could watch the adult bald eagle. She knew it was a mature eagle because its head and tail feathers were bright white. Whether it was male or female, she didn't know because both genders looked the same.

Hunter stepped away from her. She wished she hadn't taken the binoculars from him. If she had let him keep holding them, he'd still be standing next to her. Her stomach tossed. What was she thinking? Was she just an idiot who didn't learn from past mistakes? *Stay away from men. They're no good*, she silently reminded herself.

Bianca asked for the binoculars so she could see the eagles.

"Where are they?" she asked as she batted her long, lashed eyelids at Hunter.

From a distance, Hunter pointed across the gorge.

"See that dying tree standing taller than the rest of the tree line?"

"Yeah."

"Zone in on that and then swing to the right, following the tree line. You can't miss the nest if you do that."

Bianca tilted her head to the side and pulled a frown that seemed to go ignored by Hunter.

"Okay," she replied.

Her disappointed look matched her tone. Hannah guessed her friend wanted Hunter to come over and help her find the nest like he had done with her. But instead, he directed her from afar. *Poor Bianca.* Was she losing her touch? Or was he on to her game? No, even if he was on to her game, like any other guy, he'd surely play along to get what he wanted from her. So, what was his deal?

Alyssa switched out her camera lenses and aimed at the eagle nest.

"This is awesome," Alyssa said.

"Isn't it, though?" Hunter replied. "Just wait until you see what else is in store for you guys during this trip."

"What do you mean?" Alyssa asked.

"For sure, we'll see some deer. Tomorrow, I can take you to an active beaver pond and with any luck we'll see some moose, and perhaps, a coyote or a bear, and, if we're really lucky, a wolf."

"A wolf?" Alyssa asked with a tinge of surprise in her voice.

"Well, luck would have to be on our side, but it is a possibility."

Hannah could see the wheels turning in her friend's head. A picture of a wolf in the wild would surely garner some first-place contest awards for Alyssa.

A wolf. Was she staring at one right now? A wolf in sheep's clothing. Was that who Hunter was? Being a nice guy now, but who was he really?

Chapter Two

By the time he and his crew returned to camp, it was dinnertime.

"Any volunteers to start the fire while I prepare dinner?" Hunter asked.

"I can do it," Hannah replied.

He wasn't surprised she was the one who offered. For starters, she was probably the only one who had ever started a campfire in a fire pit before, and second, he assumed the other two were used to being waited on.

She dropped her pack and rummaged through it until she pulled out a round, watertight container. It was one of those survival kits one can buy at any sporting goods store. The kind with fire starter, waterproof matches, signaling mirror, and one of those silver, reflective survival blankets. There were several other necessities in that bin. Hopefully, none they'd need, but it never hurt to have them.

Hannah retrieved kindling from the stack next to the split wood pile. A puzzled look washed over her face.

"Something wrong?" he asked.

Her brows knit. "Not really, but I don't recall seeing this

pile of wood before when I walked past here to set up my tent."

Ahh, she's perceptive.

"That's because it wasn't there."

"Where did it come from?"

Hunter grinned. "We have staff that services the campsites. They check on each site daily to make sure there's enough firewood, food, and water, and to make sure the campers and guides are okay."

He winked at her. "So, I guess our campers aren't getting the full outdoors experience since they don't have to find and split their own wood. But hey, if you don't want to use that, you can go scavenge for your own."

Hannah opened her mouth to respond, but Bianca beat her to words. "We're good, we'll use it."

A hint of sound escaped Hannah's lips, and Bianca shot her friend a silencing glare.

Hunter nearly chuckled out loud, sure that Hannah would have offered to gather her own firewood.

Once the coals in the fire pit were red hot, Hunter flipped the grate over it and set the pot of pork and beans on it.

Alyssa looked at him. Her pert nose wrinkled. "What is that?"

"Pork and beans."

"Seriously?" she asked.

"Hey, nothing but the best for my campers. And that's just not any ole pork and beans. I cut these venison hot dogs up myself to put in those beans, so technically it's venison and beans."

Alyssa's eyes widened. "Venison?"

"Yep. I'm giving the most outdoorsy experience I can. You gals paid for that, and I will not let you down."

Alyssa's olive colored skin turned pale, Bianca's hand went over her mouth, and Hannah's lips curved upward.

He figured if the girls were hungry enough, they'd eat the venison. Heck, they may actually find they like it. Hannah accepted the bowl of food from him while the other two moved with apprehension and ate in silence. The ladies were probably rethinking their choice of vacation. In fact, their choice puzzled him. They probably had enough money to go anywhere, yet they chose the remote wilderness of the Upper Peninsula of Michigan. *Odd.* There had to be something more to this story.

After they finished eating, he sent Bianca to the river with an empty pot to fetch water for washing the dishes. Alyssa took more photos while Hannah stoked the fire.

Bianca returned with the water and handed him the pot and then stayed next to him, shifting from foot to foot.

He shared a knowing glance with Hannah, then looked at Bianca. "You can't hold it for three days. You're just going to have to use the pit toilet."

The model-grade woman sucked her bottom lip into her mouth and chewed on it for a moment as she looked past him to the pit toilet shielded by one wall. The wall served as a privacy screen from the campsite, but beyond that, it was open to the great outdoors.

"How often does that motorized boat come by to check on campers?"

She wasn't the first city girl to ask that question, but it still amazed him when they did. *Did they honestly think he'd call the staff for a bathroom run? Yes, they did.*

"Unless I do an emergency call, they're done checking on campers for the day."

She eyed him intently. He waited for the customary eye-batting to start and it came quickly.

He shook his head. "Sorry, princess, this is not an emergency. Plus, there isn't much for phone reception in these parts."

Bianca bounced her gaze between her friends.

Alyssa shrugged.

Hannah offered a crooked smile. "For crying out loud, it's not going to kill you."

Hunter pulled a roll of toilet paper from his bag and handed it to Bianca.

"Fine," Bianca said.

She stomped down the path to the toilet. Her long legs carried her there quickly.

Hunter watched as she inspected the toilet. Looking for spiders and other creepy, crawly critters, he presumed. Eventually, she ducked behind the privacy wall, resurfacing moments later, she trudged back up the path.

"Now, that wasn't so bad, was it?" Hunter asked as he took the roll of toilet tissue from her and held out the container of hand sanitizer to her.

Judging from the scowl she wore, she either didn't appreciate his teasing tone, or using the pit toilet. He imagined, if by choice, she'd opt to bathe in the bottle of sanitizer, so he squirted a dime-sized amount onto her palm, saving enough for the rest of the trip.

The clear night sky moved in. The moon and stars glowed brightly, and between the sky and the roaring fire, the campsite was well lit.

Alyssa and Bianca sat on the bench opposite the fire pit from him. He watched Hannah as her eyes shifted from the spot next to him on his bench to other options for her to sit. Those choices being the ground or a large rock immediately to the left of his bench. She chose the rock. That rock couldn't be comfortable, not in the least bit.

"I don't bite," he teased, then he patted the spot next to him.

"I'm fine here," Hannah replied without so much as a glance in his direction.

Hmm. He didn't recall having said anything to make her angry.

"Okay, but if you change your mind..."

"I said I'm good," she snapped.

Yikes.

Out of the corner of his eye, he caught Bianca's scolding glance directed at Hannah.

Alyssa cleared her throat. "She's just..."

"Stop! Why can't you guys just leave it alone? I don't need you to make excuses for me," Hannah barked.

Alyssa's gaze landed on the ground.

What the hell? What set her off?

The group silenced, and everyone stared at the fire.

After a few beats, Hannah rose to her feet. "I'm sorry I snapped at you guys. I'm going to turn in."

The apologetic tone she used implied she meant it, and the fact that she'd made no eye contact with him or any of her friends let him know she was embarrassed.

She slipped into her tent, taking the tension in the air with her.

Hunter chatted casually with Bianca and Alyssa about everything and anything, ranging from their childhoods to college, and the career paths they planned to explore now that they'd graduated. Bianca hadn't worried about getting a job yet because she and her mom planned to travel internationally for a couple of months when she returned home from this trip. Looking like she came from old money, that didn't surprise him. The woman would probably marry from a list of her father's well-to-do suitors for his daughter, and Bianca's days would be spent at charity luncheons. But hey, charities were needed. She'd probably never work a day in her life.

Alyssa would soon be off to her parents' furniture gallery to help her mother in the interior design department. She seemed truly excited about it.

Hannah, what would she do? Earlier, Alyssa had spoken for her friend, mentioning that she'd earned a degree in marketing that she could do a lot with. But where would it take her?

Alyssa tapped the screen of her cell phone. "Nothing. No reception," she said with a complete look of disappointment on her face.

"Yeah, I'm not surprised. It's spotty. You should have been informed in the paperwork when you booked the trip."

She nodded. "I remember reading that. It's just...well, I'd hoped for the best."

At least the woman admitted she'd read it in the paperwork. Many did not and threw little hissy fits when their phones didn't work.

She set her phone on her lap and stared into the fire for a moment, as if mesmerized, then looked up. "It's so peaceful here."

"The U.P. is heaven on earth."

"Have you been doing this a while?" she asked.

He couldn't help but smile when he thought about how long he'd been hiking, camping, fishing, and hunting in the U.P., at his uncle's place. And how much he loved it.

"My uncle owns this property and business. I've been coming up here ever since I can remember. I've guided since I was sixteen years old. It's the best job ever."

Bianca waved her hand in a circular motion. "This is what you plan to do in the future?"

Her degrading tone let him know she'd certainly thought there were bigger and better things to do with his life. What did she know? This was his happy place. But she was right in a way. This job wouldn't pay the mortgage. Not that he had one yet, but he would someday.

"I'd love to do this my entire life, but I won't, as I plan to make use of my MBA degree soon. You know, get a big boy job," he replied with an intentional edge in his tone to inform the princess that he was educated as well as her, if not more.

With her silence, he wondered if he'd bit back a smidge too much.

Bianca pulled her cell phone from her pocket and glanced at the screen. Her shoulders slumped.

"Well, since there's nothing to do, I may as well just go to bed," she said as she rose and stretched her long, thin arms into the air.

"Me, too," Alyssa said, and then they both climbed into the small tent.

Hunter glanced around the campsite, then lifted his gaze. The constellations within view shone brightly in the clear night sky. His mom had educated him and his brother and sister well, regarding the constellations. They fascinated her. Hence their unusual names, of which none of them went by. Instead, they went by nicknames chosen with purpose.

The sound of the tent zipper pulled his attention from the star-lit sky.

Hannah caught his gaze.

"Everything okay? You need something?" he asked.

"No, just couldn't sleep. I assumed when Alyssa and Bianca came into the tent, you'd turned in as well."

He shrugged. "I wasn't tired yet, and I like to soak in the

29

peaceful night atmosphere for a while before bed. It relaxes me."

She made a move to climb back into the tent.

"What are you doing?" he asked.

"Leaving you in peace."

"That's not what I meant. Join me. Relax and enjoy," he said as he motioned to the bench across the fire pit from him.

From the edgy way she acted earlier, he figured she needed to find some sort of peace and relaxation. Maybe the serene atmosphere would help do the trick.

She closed the tent and took a seat on the bench opposite the fire pit from him and then lifted her face to the sky.

"It's so beautiful. I miss this," she said.

"Miss the stars?" he asked.

"Yeah. Going to school in the Twin Cities, with all the lights, you don't see the brightness of the stars."

That he understood.

"You said, miss. Were you not born and raised in the city?"

She focused on him. "No. Northern Minnesota."

Ah, that explained the camping and hiking experience and readiness. She wasn't a city girl. He'd suspected that.

"I'm actually from Door County, Wisconsin. We see the stars pretty well there, but not like this," he informed her, though she hadn't asked.

He raised his gaze to the stars. It easily landed on the Big Dipper.

"There's the Big Dipper," he said as he pointed to it.

"Yep, a group of stars within the constellation Ursa Major," Hannah replied.

The fact she knew her stars made him smile.

"Also known as The Great Bear," he added.

She nodded, and the corners of her mouth tipped upward.

So, she does smile.

She focused on him and sucked her bottom lip into her mouth and clamped onto it with her teeth for a couple of beats before releasing it.

"I'm sorry I snapped at you earlier."

"No worries."

"It's just...I have...never mind. You didn't deserve it, and I'm sorry."

She leaned forward slightly and wrapped herself in her arms. The story behind the sadness emitting from her gaze was likely the culprit for the need of a self-hug. It certainly wasn't the weather. It was warm, especially with their proximity to the fire.

Hannah tightened her arms around herself as she stared into the flames. The heat soothed her skin. The warm chestnut eyes glancing at her now and then over the fire showed concern, not anger, from when she'd snapped at him. It wasn't like she'd really let him have it, but she snapped at an innocent bystander. She despised the angry person she'd become.

God, she was on edge. She couldn't wait for this trial to be over. For Sebastián to be convicted and rot in jail where he belonged. But what if he didn't get convicted and went free? Would he stalk her again? Put his grubby hands on her again? Anxiety swirled in the pit of her stomach and her body quivered.

"You okay?" Hunter asked.

No, she wasn't. Far from it. But he didn't need to know that.

"Yeah."

He nodded, but the concern in his eyes deepened.

Hunter returned his gaze to the fire. She did the same, but rather than finding solace in the flames, they reminded her of the unshakable white-hot anger she held for Sebastián Garcia. During the five-hour drive from the Twin Cities to this remote area of the Upper Peninsula of Michigan, the tension in her body had dissipated more and more with each mile of distance put between her and that horrible place. Once she'd finished school and her work schedule, she'd vowed to never return to the Twin Cities again...except for when she had to testify. Then she'd never return to that godforsaken place.

She glanced around. *Wilderness.* Even considering there were bears and wolves, she felt safer here than in the city. Maybe Hunter had it right. Maybe this was the perfect place to live.

Recalling her encounter with the creep at the gas station sixty miles down the road, during the last stop she and her friends had before arriving here, she realized no place was exempt from assholes. Not even this tranquil place.

The intense, angry look the man had given her reminded her of the way Sebastián looked at her, putting her right back to the moment Sebastián laid his horrible hands on her. Dread saturated every cell of her being and her body shook. The gas station guy's creepy eye color even matched Sebastián's. Dark, almost black, with a hint of red, russet with no variation. No flecks of gold or green, just that dark brown with a red undertone. Devil like.

Now that she knew Sebastián and his true ways, she took the old saying that eyes are the window to the soul more seriously. Sebastián was pure evil, and with the swift look she'd had into the eyes of the guy at the gas station, he was too. For him to be that angry with her just because she drained the last of the coffee was ridiculous. Even the attendant noticed and rushed over to start another pot. So, the guy would have to wait a few minutes. Big deal. The man's loud and continued tongue lashing caused her to freeze in place. She'd thought about giving him the cup of coffee in her hand, but then changed her mind. Screw him and all those alike. She'd had enough of men and their stupid behavior. Maybe he was just having a bad day, but that still didn't give him the right to yell and cuss at her. Hell, she'd had a pretty tough year, and she didn't go around cussing at people. If the guy hadn't been so big, the encounter wouldn't have been so scary, but he was big and seemed unhinged, so her fear was justified.

She glanced across the fire to Hunter and felt regret. She did snap at him and for no good reason other than the asshole at the gas station, putting her in a foul mood. An all-familiar mood that she'd thought she'd been making progress on changing. She didn't like her new self, the self that Sebastián had defined for her. She needed to redefine herself, and as soon as he was convicted and sentenced, she would.

"It's nice here," she said, drawing a full smile from Hunter.

Nice, straight, white teeth gleamed in the firelight's glow.

"I love it here. I hate the thought of leaving."

"You're leaving?"

His grin faded. "Yeah. Not for good, though. I plan to come back whenever I can. I just got my master's degree in business, so I thought I'd better put that to use. I have a couple of job interviews scheduled for next week. We'll see what happens."

"Me too."

Hunter arched a brow.

"I mean, I have a couple interviews lined up as well. I just finished school. My degree is in marketing."

"Where do you hope to land?"

"I had thought that maybe I'd stay in the Twin Cities, as I enjoyed my first few years at school there, but now...let's just say I might not be suited for the city."

His brow arched again. Must be his thing.

"It's a long story," she added.

He nodded, but didn't ask for the story. Smart guy. He'd figured out she didn't want to talk about the long story.

It was getting late, and Hannah suspected Hunter wouldn't climb into his tent until all his campers were tucked in for the night. Though her mind raced and she doubted she'd be able to fall asleep right away, she pushed herself up to let him off the hook.

"I guess I'll turn in now."

"Me, too," he replied as he stood and broke up what remained of the dying fire.

Hannah made a move for her tent, paused, and looked over her shoulder. "Good night, and thank you for a good day. It was a pleasant hike to the waterfall. I'm looking forward to tomorrow."

The handsome guide smiled softly. "Me too."

She tried to pull away from his intense gaze, but couldn't. Those warm eyes of his emitted pure kindness. Still, a hint of apprehension snaked through her. She'd once trusted Sebastián, and look how that turned out.

Chapter Three

THE GLOW of the campfire died down, and the silhouettes of the guide and his target faded into the darkness. If only he'd caught up with them sooner, his work here would be done. But, they—she—the Almighty Bitch, had the luxury of a canoe and he had to follow on foot in unknown territory. Crossing over tributaries, ravines, and trudging through thick brush had slowed him down some. That, and making sure his target or the other parties hiking and canoeing did not see him, caused his travel to take even more time.

His heart raced, but Almighty Bitch was in his sight now. In the darkness of night, he'd edge closer to her and then wait for daylight to find an opportunity to right the wrong she'd done to him and others in her wake. She'd pissed him off. He was sick of her kind. The perfect and almighty. Those who looked down upon him. She'd pay and never do that to him or any other man again. A rush of adrenaline shot through him. He smiled at himself. Yes, when he was done with her, she'd never be able to look down upon anyone again. That thought was euphoric.

A knife stabbed at his brain, ruining the beautiful thought in his mind. He cupped his head with his hands and pushed with all the strength he had, as if that would help to ease the sharp pain. It didn't. With his right hand, he slapped his own head. Hard. He wanted to scream in agony, but still had enough wits about himself to know he shouldn't or the others would hear him.

The pain in his brain intensified. He squeezed his eyes shut. It didn't help, so he reopened them.

Distraction. He needed a distraction. He slapped himself again, then reached down and pulled the switchblade from his pocket, opened it, and with a small bit of pressure, dragged the sharp blade over the top of his forearm, careful not to cut too deep. Just deep enough to pull his attention from the shooting pain in his head. The last cut to his arm hadn't healed yet. The cuts were coming faster and faster.

In the darkness, he could barely see the wound, but his stinging flesh and the feel of the moisture on his arm brought relief to him. His body went languid, and he slid his back down the tree behind him until his butt rested on the ground. He closed his eyes and leaned his head back against the tree. Total euphoria as if he was on the best drug-induced high known to man, yet he didn't take drugs. Not anymore. Not since his last run-in with law enforcement. He had no chances remaining. Any other mishaps and he'd be in prison. He knew and believed it. His lawyer warned him, too. The man was confident he could get him out of the mess he was currently in, but one more misstep and he'd be done. Even with knowing that, here he was, trailing Almighty Bitch. It's like he couldn't help himself. He was drawn to her like a magnet.

Slowly, he opened his tired eyes, though he was exhausted. Life exhausted him. People exhausted him. He needed the high of teaching Almighty Bitch a lesson. That should get him through a few more days.

Chapter Four

THE PLEASANT AROMA of smoked bacon teased her nostrils. Then, the hiss of grease in a fry pan wafted into her ear canals. She opened her eyes, hoping this wasn't a dream. Surprisingly, she found herself alone in the tent. Whispers outside the tent pulled her into reality. She was the last one up. Unusual. Even more unusual was the fact that she hadn't woken at all throughout the course of the night. That was something that hadn't happened since Sebastián— dread coiled in the pit of her stomach—since he'd begun to stalk her. She swallowed hard.

She curled into a tight ball, sucked in a deep breath, and then willed herself to relax, to take advantage of a few more moments of peaceful solitude. Sebastián wasn't here. She was fine.

Maybe it was the fact that she was in the wilderness's security that helped to calm her mind and had allowed her to get a good night's rest. Guys, cowards like Sebastián would never venture into the wild. She was safe here. Safe from assholes anyhow. Though her guide was a man, she felt like she could trust him. She saw the goodness in his eyes. But she once thought Sebastián was a good person, and look how that turned out. Once he knew she wanted only friendship from him, he lost it. Called her a tease, among other horrible names. Then, stalked, kidnapped her, and...

"Hey sleepyhead, your eggs and bacon are ready," Alyssa called out, shaking her from the unwanted reverie.

The same reverie that ruined most every day and night, except for last night.

Hannah slipped out of her sleeping bag, did a quick clothing change, and poked her head out of the tent.

Her gaze landed on the tall man scooping eggs and bacon onto Bianca's plate. It looked delicious. He looked delicious. There was nothing better than a good-looking guy cooking breakfast in the wilderness for her and her friends. Yeah, they paid for this service, but it was still nice to see a man who could cook.

Maybe it was the full night's sleep that put her in this good mood and gave her a bit of a change of heart when it came to men. The mood change was welcome. She was sick of being bitter and angry, and sick of being afraid of men. She knew good men were out there. Her father and older brothers were proof, but her experience with Sebastián had changed her—damaged her.

"That smells delicious," she commented.

Hunter's warm chestnut gaze caught hers. Amber flecks flashed in his irises. Her stomach swirled. She hadn't noticed those in his eyes yesterday, but today they seemed to sparkle. Maybe it was the way the sun shone on him today that caused the brightness of that amber color.

"You're up. Grab your plate. You'll need the nourishment for our adventures today," Hunter said with a full-blown, contagious smile.

Alyssa looked at him with adoring eyes and scanned him over from head to toe. She couldn't blame her friend. The guy was tall and handsome. Muscular, but not too bulky. He had great hair, too. Not too long and not too short. Thick, wavy, and dark, almost black. And his sun-kissed skin looked inviting to touch. If he was truly a nice person, he'd have the whole package going on.

Hannah slipped out of the tent and walked toward the picnic table. Alyssa handed her one of those blue enamel plates used for camping. With her plate in hand, she stepped over to the fire pit where Hunter waited for her with a pile of eggs on a spatula. He plopped them onto her plate, then scooped up a few strips of bacon for her.

"This looks delicious, thanks," she said.

His smile reached his eyes, and his white teeth gleamed.

"Got coffee, too," he said as he pointed at the metal coffee pot, with a tempered glass top, sitting on the cooking rack over the flames, but off to the side.

It looked just like the coffee pot she had in her camping supplies. Almost everybody who camped had that model.

She inhaled, catching just a hint of the eye-opening coffee scent among the mouthwatering bacon aroma. Her stomach growled.

With the spatula, Hunter pointed at her stomach. "You'd better get to it before you starve."

They shared a laugh.

"I guess so."

Hannah set her plate down and snagged a coffee cup from the table, and allowed Hunter to fill it. The liquid looked dark—strong, and that was fine by her.

Hannah sat next to Alyssa, who sat across the picnic table from Bianca. Here they'd just spent the night, crammed in a small tent, and Bianca still rolled out of the sack looking like a beauty queen. Her icy blue eyes were outlined with eyeliner, long lashes thickened with mascara, powder perfect nose, and her long, blonde hair was pulled into a tidy bun. When and how had she done all of that, and if she had made herself up in the small tent, how had Hannah not awakened? So, Bianca. Hannah was sure that if she looked in a mirror right now, the results would be quite the opposite of her friend's. She'd probably find dark circles under her eyes, and hair run amok. Yeah, that was more her speed.

Hunter took a seat across the table from her, stabbed a fork full of eggs, and emptied it into his mouth. He closed his eyes and chewed. His moan of delight almost made her laugh. They were just eggs, but he acted like he was eating the finest steak.

"Like those, do you?" she asked.

He opened his eyes, and the amber hues mixed in with the dark chestnut color danced with delight.

"Nothing like good farm-fresh eggs in the morning," he reached forward and snagged his cup of coffee, took a swig, "and a strong, dark brew."

Like her, he was a morning person.

Following suit, she took a bite of her fluffy eggs, then a bite of that delicious-smelling bacon. Meat was her thing. Yeah, the eggs were tasty, but the bacon was delicious. It was thick, yet crisp, but not burned. Done to perfection.

Glancing across the table, she caught Hunter's stare.

His smile widened. "Like my cooking, do you?"

She imagined the deeply satisfied look on her face had given her away, and she couldn't lie to the man who clearly wanted a compliment from her.

"Not bad," she said with a nod.

"I'll take that. Just wait until you see what I have in store for dinner tonight."

Bianca said something that she couldn't quite make out because her attention was solely focused on those chestnut irises holding her attention.

She took another bite of her bacon. Perhaps she should chew more slowly. Prolong breakfast for as long as possible so she could keep staring into those warm eyes of his.

The clink of Alyssa's fork against her empty plate pulled her attention away from Hunter.

"So, what's the plan?" Alyssa asked.

"Well, we'll pack up and canoe to the next campsite, then hike to Pine Loop Falls. It's a fun falls to see because the water circles around a big rock that juts out, and the falls surround nearly the entire rock. There's a bridge we can cross to get ourselves in the center of the rock."

"That sounds like quite the sight to see," Alyssa replied.

"That it is. It's unique. Not that the falls drop too far, but it is fun to see."

Hannah savored her last bite of bacon as long as she could, then drank the rest of the strong coffee in her mug.

Following suit with Hunter, she rose, fully intending to help him clean up the breakfast mess.

"I can do this while you ladies pack up your tent."

With a glance over her shoulder, she realized he'd already packed up.

"Okay."

It didn't take long to roll up their sleeping bags, reassemble their backpacks, and pack up the small tent.

They loaded their gear into the canoe, as he'd shown them yesterday, and she and Alyssa climbed into it. Hunter was about to push them off when the bright morning sun caused Hannah to realize she wasn't wearing her sunglasses.

"Wait!" she exclaimed as she turned her head to look at Hunter.

He stilled. "What's wrong?"

"I need my sunglasses."

"Where are they?"

She didn't recall seeing them in the outside, zippered section of her backpack when she dug through it a few minutes ago. She had worn them yesterday. When did she last see them? Maybe they were on the picnic table or the bench.

"I don't know for sure. Let me check the table," she said as she hopped out of the canoe and ran back to the picnic table.

No sunglasses.

She looked at the benches.

No sunglasses.

Hunter looked too. Even by the pit toilet.

"Are you sure they aren't in your backpack?" he asked.

"I'll check again, but I went through it when I packed up, and I didn't see them."

Back at the canoe, she rifled through her backpack.

No sunglasses.

"When do you last remember having them?" Alyssa asked.

"I may have set them on the table after we got back yesterday."

"Hmm, maybe a raccoon walked off with them," Hunter said with a chuckle.

Though he was just joking, Hannah didn't laugh. She felt demeaned.

"Hey, I'm just kidding."

"I know. But it's not like me to lose things. Though I

will say that I thought I heard a bit of commotion outside the tent last night when I first climbed in."

Was it possible one of those little masked bandits scurried off with her sunglasses?

"Yeah, I heard stuff, too. That's not uncommon," Hunter said in a comforting tone.

She assumed he was trying to put her at ease about the wilderness creatures that roamed during the night.

"Well, I guess I've no choice but to go on without them," Hannah said as she zipped up her backpack and stowed it back in the canoe.

She pulled the brim of her ball cap down a little to shield her eyes more from the bright sun rays.

They paddled at a comfortable pace in the slow-moving water. The clear water made it easy to see fish swimming under and around the canoe.

Bianca turned her head and glanced over her shoulder to look at Hunter, who did all the paddling work for their canoe.

"What kind of fish am I seeing?" Bianca asked.

"Brown trout, walleye, perch, among others."

"Looks like there are some minnows down there, too," Hannah added.

"Yes. I forgot to mention those. Lots of those."

After about an hour of leisurely paddling, their guide paddled up close to her canoe and pointed ahead to a small opening in the trees lining the river.

"There's our next camp. There's a small sand beach at this one."

"Nice."

Though she hadn't planned on swimming on this trip, having read in the informational packet, she knew there was at least one campsite with a swimmable beach, so she'd packed her swimsuit.

"There'll be plenty of time for a swim after we set up camp and hike to the Pine Loop Falls."

Bianca clapped her hands. "Yay!"

Hannah was sure it delighted her friend to show off her perfect body in a skimpy bikini to their good-looking guide.

After reaching the campsite, Hannah hopped out of the canoe and dragged it up onto the tiny sand shore. Hunter did the same with his canoe. It only took a few minutes to unload their gear and just a few more minutes to set up their minimalistic camp. She supposed Alyssa and Bianca moved at lightning speed to make sure they left enough time in the day to lie on the beach and soak up some of that fabulously warm sun in the sky. They were in Michigan. It certainly wasn't Florida hot, but it was warm. No doubt, though, it would cool down quickly in the early evening, so sunbathing time was of the essence.

"Chop, chop, ladies. We've got a waterfall to see," Hunter teased.

"I'm ready!" Alyssa replied with her camera in hand.

In that respect, Alyssa was in paradise. The natural beauty of the Upper Peninsula of Michigan was a photographer's dream.

They started down a narrow dirt path lined with bright green, soft-looking ferns; the forest floor was covered with them. Those, along with hearty white pines and tall, thin red pines, hence the trail and falls names, she supposed— Pine Loop Falls. It made complete sense. She paused, lifted her face to the sky, and drew in a long inhalation, basking in the calm, outdoorsy, pine scent.

When she opened her eyes and glanced to her left, then her right, she caught movement of the ferns about thirty feet away. Odd, since there wasn't a breeze to speak of. Her gaze fixed on that spot. Two beady little eyes came into focus.

"A red fox," she whispered.

Out of the corner of her eye, she saw Alyssa spin. She supposed her friend would want a photo, but if she moved, she'd surely scare the beautiful creature away.

"Don't move. Just look," Hunter said in a hushed tone.

The animal stayed statue still. Didn't even blink. Gaze glued to her. Orangish-red colored eyes, the same color as his fur, studied her. All at once, the animal bolted. She'd glimpsed the full body of the tiny animal, and then he was gone.

"How cool was that?" Alyssa asked.

Then she frowned. "But he was so quick, I didn't get a picture."

"You gotta be on the ready," Hunter replied with a teasing tone.

Alyssa arched a brow. "A good guide would have told me the fox was there. Instead, you just walked on by," she teased back.

Bianca threw her hands in the air. "Yeah, we paid good money for this service. I might file a complaint."

"She's right," Hannah added as she placed her hands firmly on her hips.

Hunter lifted his hands into the air submissively. Smart guy. He would not win against the three of them.

His stunning smile stretched. "You're right, ladies. I'll try to be more on my game for the rest of the trip. Please don't tell my uncle, or he'll put me on latrine duty or something."

They shared a laugh.

Hunter gestured for them to follow.

Snap!

Hannah halted on a dime and looked in the direction the noise had come from. There was no way that little fox made that noise—that branch break, or whatever it was.

She glanced at the guide. He faced in the direction of the noise as well. Like Bianca and Alyssa, Hannah returned her gaze to where the noise had come from.

Silence.

"Probably nothing," Hunter said as he began moving down the trail.

The pit of her stomach knotted. She had a bad feeling about this. Bear? Deer? Moose?

Returning her gaze forward, she caught Hunter peering back toward the noise. He looked worried, too. Not good.

Chapter Five

Hunter shot another glance over his shoulder. That crack wasn't an animal. It was too clumsy. Unless there was something wrong with the creature. Unfortunately, an injured animal was a dangerous animal, so he hoped that wasn't the case. He'd spent enough time in the woods to know that sound wasn't normal.

Judging from the fear in Hannah's darkening emerald irises, she was of like mind. He'd had to look away from her, as if to hide his uneasiness. She was already gun-shy about something, and he didn't want to make it worse.

Continuing down the trail in silence, he kept his eyes and ears peeled for anything out of the ordinary. Nothing.

Tension tightened in his spine with each step he took. The song of the woods was normal. The sight of the woods was normal. Had he imagined the strangeness of the sound? He supposed he could have.

Rushing water echoed in his ears as he drew closer to the Pine Loop Falls. The gradual ascension upward would turn steep in a few minutes.

He turned to look at his followers. "Almost there. Get ready to climb."

Bianca arched a brow. "Climb?"

"It's not that bad. No worse than yesterday, but this time we won't have the luxury of rocky steps. It's more of a dirt path with a steep climb, but no worries. There are trees that line the path. You can use them for balance, as handrails, so to speak."

Bianca looked back at her friends.

Alyssa wore a concerned expression. Hannah shrugged.

"It'll be fine. I take people up here all the time," he assured.

Hunter took a long stride, then a short one to begin the ascent. Since he'd climbed this hill hundreds of times, he knew to be on the ready for loose dirt. For him, using the trees for support wasn't all that necessary, but he gripped the trunk of a small pine tree between the sparse branches so the ladies could see how it was done.

"Ouch!"

Hunter stilled and turned to find Bianca rubbing her left palm with fingers from her right hand.

"What happened?"

"The needles poked me. "

He chuckled. "Next time, try to grab the trunk, not the branches with the sharp, sticky needles."

She scowled at him.

"Sorry, I should have warned you. When you can, try to plan and place your grip in a bare spot, but if you slip, grab what you can to steady yourself. Either way, your hands are going to get a little sticky from the pitch."

Bianca's pert nose wrinkled.

"It'll be fine. I have some hand sanitizer that will break down the sap."

He looked beyond Bianca.

"Are we all good to continue?"

Alyssa nodded.

"Onward, captain," Hannah replied.

He fixed his gaze on Hannah. "Captain is my brother."

"What?" she asked.

"Cap is my brother. He owns a charter fishing boat. My sister is his first mate."

"Really. Where?"

"Door County, where we're from."

The clap of Bianca's hands drew his attention.

"I love Door County. My grandparents have a cottage there. On the lake."

She closed her eyes and placed her hands over her heart. "The shops, food, wineries."

Her eyelids fluttered open and her icy blue irises fixed on him. "No offense, but that is my kind of weekend getaway."

He'd already figured as much.

He ran his gaze over the three ladies staring at him. "Well, if you ever want to hike there, I can help you out. I'm from there and I've hiked all five state parks, the county and city parks, and the land trusts. If there's a trail, I've hiked it."

Bianca pulled her lips into a pout. "The only hiking I'm doing in Door County is to a winery or shop."

"You're on your own with those. Maybe not the wineries, but definitely the shops," he replied with a chuckle.

He spun back around and gestured for the crew to follow him.

It took only a few minutes to reach the top of the hill, then just another couple of minutes to reach the Pine Loop Falls. The echo of the rushing water led the way. The heavy spring rainfall, coupled with the large snow melt in March, ensured the falls would be spectacular for most of the summer and into the fall. It wasn't always that way. A low snowfall winter and dry spring could lead to a disappointing trickle of a fall.

As he and his crew poked out of the cover of the pines, the large rock jutting out over the falls came into view.

He stopped, and when the three ladies stepped up to his side, he pointed at the narrow bridge he and his uncle had built to give their guests a spectacular view of the falls, just like they'd done for some of the other falls. The bridge led to a large rock that jutted out next to the falls. Water circled the rock, then fed into where the falls swept over the edge of the cliff. With as much water as there was rushing over the edge, they were sure to feel some cool, refreshing spray.

"We'll cross that and you'll get a better view."

"What I see already is gorgeous," Hannah said.

The gold flecks in her bright emerald eyes sparkled and his gaze was glued to hers. She lit up during the brief moments in which she seemed to allow herself to be happy. Even the worry lines around her almond-shaped eyes disappeared, making him want to stay in this moment forever. He wanted her to be happy and felt the need to fix whatever ailed her. Whatever it was that laced her gaze with sadness.

When she pulled her gaze from him, he felt empty. He willed her eyes back to him, but instead, she headed away from him, toward the bridge.

With her friends in tow, Hannah crossed the narrow wooden bridge first. He followed.

Standing at the center of the rock, he watched as Hannah slowly circled for the full effect of the three hundred sixty-degree view of the water rushing around the dome-shaped boulder. She stopped and stared at the spot where the two streams of water came together and became one, then flowed over the edge. The drop was only about sixteen feet, but the water made quite the splash when it hit the pool below.

Alyssa snapped photo after photo. Bianca leaned against the circular cedar railing and posed as she asked Alyssa to take a few shots of her. As much as the woman loved getting photos of herself, he couldn't imagine how much cloud storage her portfolio took up. He chuckled to himself.

He stepped toward Alyssa. "You want me to take a few photos of the three of you?"

"That'd be great," she said as she stretched her arm to hand him the expensive-looking camera.

The camera looked expensive, so snapping a nice photo didn't worry him any since it probably auto-focused.

"Just point it in the right direction and press this button," Alyssa said.

"Got it."

The ladies lined up at the rail. Bianca was between the two others with her long, slim arms draped over their shoulders. Alyssa turned slightly toward her and placed a hand on her hip. Hannah stood stick straight on the opposite side of Bianca. Almost like a third grader's rigid stance during a class photo. She looked uncomfortable, and he didn't understand that because she was the most beautiful of the three.

"Okay. On three. One, two, three," he counted as he snapped.

He handed the camera back to Alyssa, then stood silently and soaked up the sunshine and warm breeze. Inhaling deeply, he took in the earthy scent. Nothing beat this. Nothing. Sadness crept through him as he realized he'd have to give this up soon. Leave for his new job. Put his degree to use. God, he was going to miss this wilderness.

Shaking the depressing thoughts from his head, he looked at the ladies who oohed and aahed over the spectacular views. Bianca moved toward the railing, leaned back against it, and crossed her arms over her well-endowed chest. Yep, she was done. Alyssa still snapped photos. Hannah lifted her chin into the air, elongating her throat, exposing that milky white skin of hers to the sun. His fingers itched to touch her. His lips tingled at the thought of kissing her tempting reddish-maroon lips, then easing his mouth to her jawline, then to that earlobe of hers to nibble on it before running light kisses down the side of that long, slim neck of hers. No doubt his lips would enjoy touching her. His hands, too.

"Ahem," Bianca sounded.

His gaze sprang from Hannah's beautiful profile to Bianca.

The smirk on her face, coupled with her arched brow, let him know he'd been busted. Bianca knew he had developed a thing for her friend. So what? Yet, her knowledge of his romantic feelings for Hannah made him uncomfortable. Bianca's full lips turned into a thin, straight line, and she shrugged slightly. He interpreted that message to be pity. Either the woman thought her friend didn't feel the same for him, or she wouldn't allow herself to feel the same for him or any other man. From what little he knew of her, he still suspected she wouldn't allow herself to feel for any man, and it wasn't just him. He didn't like that such a beautiful creature had been harmed in some way that she'd not allow herself the pleasure of love.

"What's next?" Bianca asked.

"I thought we'd go back down the hill and view the falls

from underneath. There's a narrow trail that snakes behind it, and a small cave."

"Awesome!" Hannah exclaimed.

Her face lit up again. This environment was her thing. He could feed her this type of stuff all day to make her happy.

He led the way back down the steep hill, moving slowly and stepping with a slight side angle to keep his footing solid. With a glance over his shoulder, he observed the ladies doing the same as he'd suggested. He refocused ahead before taking another step. Only another couple of steps and they'd be at the bottom.

"Whoa!" Bianca screamed.

Her body crashed into his, and with flailing hands, he fell forward. Every stabilizing branch, just beyond his reach. Landing hard on the ground knocked the wind out of him. He gasped, then realized the woman on his back was doing the same, only worse, even though she'd been lucky he'd cushioned her fall.

He slid out from under her and pulled her up with him, but she doubled over with her hands planted on her knees and worked to catch her breath.

Alyssa and Hannah flanked Bianca.

"Are you going to be okay?" Hannah asked.

Bianca gasped and shook her head. "I..." gasp, "don't..." gasp, "know."

"You'll be fine. You just knocked the wind out of yourself," Hannah assured.

Hunter's racing heart stilled, and his gaze landed on the woman's designer tennis shoes. He should never have let her hike in those. Well, it was her own damn fault for not adhering to the packing list.

"I told you to pack hiking boots," Hannah scolded.

Bianca straightened her spine. "Don't scold me. We're on this trip for you. If it had been up to me, we'd be on a sandy beach somewhere."

Hannah's nostrils flared. "I didn't force you here."

Oh, God, this was all he needed. Clients fighting halfway into their trip.

Alyssa edged her way between her two friends. "It's all fine. Everyone is fine. Please, let's not argue and make the best of this. Okay?"

Not everyone was fine. His ribs and forearms hurt like hell. He'd taken the brunt of the fall, and yet nobody cared to ask him if he was okay.

Hannah and Bianca glared at each other.

"Please," Alyssa pleaded.

"Fine," Hannah conceded.

All gazes turned to him.

Hannah's emerald irises softened when she looked at him. "Are you okay?"

"All good. Thanks for asking," he replied as he brushed the mud and debris off his forearms and clothes.

After a few cleansing breaths, he gestured to the left. "Right this way, ladies."

Hopefully, the refreshing mist from the falls would cool his clientele down so they could get back to enjoying the hike.

In silence, the group followed him over the wet, narrow rock ledge behind the falls. They scooted along the ledge with their backs pressed against the stone wall. Being that the sheet of the falls was less than ten feet wide, it didn't take but a few side steps to get to the tiny cave. The mouth was barely wide enough for them to stand shoulder to shoulder to watch the mesmerizing flow of water. Though there was an inch or so to spare to the right of him, he slid over a smidge to touch Hannah's warm shoulder. Exhilaration shot through him.

The skin where she touched protested when he turned his body. He pulled a small flashlight from his pocket, flipped it on, and pointed the dim beam downward to a small entrance of a secondary cave within the cave.

"Any takers?" he asked.

They'd have to drop to their hands and knees to enter that part.

"No," Bianca immediately replied.

Alyssa shook her head.

He turned to look at Hannah and arched a brow in challenge.

"How big is it?" she asked.

"We only have to crawl a couple of feet before it opens into a room just large enough for me to stand in. If I spread my arms, I can touch both sides."

"What's in it?"

"Nothing really. Some pools of water and some mossy plants."

He put the penlight in his mouth and dropped to all fours. The rock beneath his palms and knees was damp and cool. The scent was mildewy, but he didn't mind.

Hannah was on his heels. Within seconds, they'd both popped up in the tiny space that would have been black as night without the light. He flashed the light along the walls to show Hannah. It really wasn't much to look at. Climbing into the cave was just something fun to do. He and his brother and sister spent hours in this tiny cave when they were kids.

Hannah quivered when he showed her the bats in the corner. He probably should have warned her about that. After the initial shock, she smiled.

"This is so cool. You played in here when you were a kid, didn't you?"

"Guilty."

"I would have, too."

Exactly what he wanted to hear. He liked her even more with each passing moment.

"You guys, okay?" Alyssa's voice echoed through the tunnel.

Hannah giggled. "I should yell back, no, and see if she does anything about it. She'll never climb in here. She's claustrophobic."

He nodded in acknowledgement. "Yeah, your friends aren't as adventurous as you are, that is for sure."

"Oh, I don't know about that. Bianca can tip that scale sometimes."

"I meant in an outdoorsy kind of way."

The corners of her mouth tilted upward into a full smile. She liked his compliment.

"That part's true. I like nature. The sight of it, the smell of it, the feel of it... all of it. And you're a great tour guide."

His heart hitched. She was definitely his kind of woman. He wanted to kiss her, but he hesitated, wondering if she wanted to be kissed by him. Recalling her standoffish behavior toward him the day before when he'd reached out to help her up the gigantic step to the top of the hill to see the Wild Canyon Falls. He thought he'd better hold off and see how today went.

Lifting his gaze from Hannah's kissable lips, he caught her staring at him. Even in the dim light, he saw the desire in her eyes answering his question. She wanted him to kiss her. He leaned forward and pressed his lips lightly to hers. Heat soared through him. His heart raced. He'd shared many first kisses before and experienced the thrill of that first shared kiss. This time, the exhilaration he felt kissing Hannah rocked his limbs so hard that he almost fell.

Hannah leaned against him and wrapped her arms around him—stabilizing him. The initial shock of her touch eased a smidge, allowing him to think more coherently. Their lips moved together in some sort of well-choreographed manner, as if they'd kissed many times before. His mouth hummed with delight.

"Hello?" Alyssa's voice reverberated in the small cave.

Hannah pulled away from him. The smile on her face let him know she was as pleased as he was with the kiss they'd shared.

He gestured toward the small tunnel. "I suppose we'd better get back out there before they think something bad happened to us."

She sighed. "I suppose. Or maybe we should keep them wondering."

He winked at her. He'd like that.

Chapter Six

HANNAH DROPPED to all fours to climb back out of the tiny cave she and Hunter had occupied. More than likely, she fell to all fours because of that mind-boggling kiss they'd shared. Her knees had filled with jelly. If he hadn't wrapped his long, muscular arms around her, she would have melted to the ground for sure. Exhilaration still hummed through her. She'd had no intention of kissing him, but when those amber flecks sparked in his eyes while he looked at her, she was a goner.

After having sworn off men, she'd never expected to want to be kissed again. Sebastián had done a number on her, and her instant attraction to Hunter scared her. Heat rose in her face at the thought of kissing him again. If they flamed any more, she was sure the tiny cave's temperature would increase a solid ten degrees.

She popped out of the short tunnel behind the veil of the waterfall to find Alyssa and Bianca exactly where she'd left them. She stood and stepped out of the way to make room for Hunter.

He popped up alongside her. Tall, lean, and handsome,

his sexy smile made her want to kiss him again. She had to stop looking at him, or she would. Her eyes practically scolded her when she pulled her gaze away from him.

"It was neat. Are you sure you don't want to go in?" Hannah asked her friends.

The eagerness in her tone as a result of kissing Hunter was unnatural. It was evident, even to her own ears.

Bianca's gaze bore into her. It went from Hunter, then returned to her. The smirk on her friend's face let her know, she knew.

"Well, you kids were in there a while. Exactly how big is that cave you explored?"

"It's small, but there was plenty to see," Hannah replied to justify the time they'd spent in there.

Her friend arched a brow. "Plenty to do as well, I suppose."

Hunter cleared his throat and gestured in the direction in which they'd come. "Shall we?"

Bianca arched her perfectly shaped blonde brow. "Sure." She made a move to lead the way back out from under the falls.

Alyssa fell into line, and then Hannah and Hunter followed.

Once out from behind the waterfall, Hunter took the lead down the path heading back to camp. He took his time walking at a mediocre pace and then stopping now and then to educate them about the trees, plants, and even animals. Other than the fox they'd seen earlier, they hadn't stumbled upon any other four-legged creatures. She would have liked to see some deer or other mild-mannered animals, but there were none. She'd almost given up hope when out of the corner of her eye she glimpsed a long, but tiny and slim brown creature scurrying up a tree. The animal spun around to the backside of the tree, then peeked around it and stared at her from about ten feet up in a pine tree.

It stared, she stared, neither of them moving. Those beady little eyes of his stayed on her with a look of intensity. His furry face was mostly reddish brown over his forehead and to the tip of his snout. His cheeks were lined with more of an off-white color that led up to his pert, rounded ears. He was adorable.

He disappeared, then poked his head out from the other side of the tree. Almost as if playing peekaboo.

"What do you see?" Hunter asked.

Wanting to bask in the enjoyment of seeing this beautiful, tiny creature, she didn't answer so as not to scare it away.

The shutter of Alyssa's camera sounded. The animal's head snapped in that direction. Alyssa snapped another photo before the animal disappeared higher up the tree and into the thicker branches loaded with pine needles.

"A pine marten," Hunter said as he stepped up to her side. "Nice find. They're pretty elusive."

"I thought that's what it was, but wasn't sure. I've never seen one before," Hannah replied.

"They were once extinct from the Upper Peninsula of Michigan," Hunter said.

"Really?" Alyssa asked.

"Yeah. Around the 1930s, between the unregulated trapping and logging of evergreen pine forests, they disappeared. They were reintroduced in the mid-50s."

"That's great, they were brought back. They're adorable," Alyssa commented.

"It is great, but don't be fooled. They're aggressive little buggers. They eat chipmunks, red squirrels, rabbits, just to name a few. So don't let their small size fool you."

Hunter reached out and placed his large hand on her shoulder. Her skin was sensitized by his touch.

"Good find," he praised.

She smiled at his compliment.

His hand lingered and his touch felt warm and comforting. She hadn't expected that from him. From any man. Not after what she'd endured from Sebastián.

When he pulled back, she felt sad.

"Alright. Let's keep moving. Keep your eyes peeled. As we've just learned, you never know what you'll see in the forest."

"Bigfoot?" Hannah teased.

Hunter's deep chuckle was pleasant to her ears.

"Be on the ready. You never know."

Hunter continued to lead them through the woods, still stopping occasionally to educate them about wild animals common to the Upper Peninsula. It was enjoyable. Almost as enjoyable as their stolen glances.

By the time they arrived back at camp, her stomach screamed for nutrition. It was nearly two o'clock.

"How about a snack or a sandwich?" Hunter asked as he pulled the cooler from the metal locker used to protect the food from being stolen by bears or other creatures of the forest.

"We have ham or salami, or venison stick sausage and cheese," Hunter offered.

Hannah grabbed the loaf of bread from the cooler and took the lunchmeat from him.

He followed her the few short steps from the locker to the picnic table with cheese, mustard, and mayo in hand.

She snagged a couple of venison sausage slices from the bag. It was delicious. She was used to venison and liked it. When she handed the bag to Bianca, her friend wrinkled her nose and held her hand in the air. Alyssa did the same, but wasn't as dramatic about it as Bianca had been.

"You don't know what you are missing," Hannah informed them.

She caught Hunter's smile.

Her friends split a ham sandwich and she ate her salami sandwich. Hunter consumed one of each.

"Now what?" Bianca asked.

"You are free to do whatever you want for the rest of the afternoon and evening. We can hike some more. Take the canoe out. Play camping games. Swim. Whatever you want."

With her long, slim fingers, Bianca pointed to the tiny sandy beach area. "I see me lying on a beach towel over there."

"Me, too," Alyssa chimed in.

"Have at it. Hannah, what are you up for?" he asked.

"Let's take the canoe out for a spin."

Hunter's handsome smile widened. "Let's do it."

She climbed into the front of the canoe, and he sat in the back.

They paddled out to the center of the narrow river and then made their way along with the current. Her eyes were peeled for wildlife.

After a few minutes, she stopped paddling, closed her eyes, and tilted her face toward the sun. The warmth of the rays seeped into her cheeks. The slight breeze kept her from overheating.

God, this feels good.

At that moment, she felt relaxed. More than she'd been in the past year. With all that had gone on with Sebastián, she'd never imagined she could feel as peaceful as she did right now. Maybe she should stay up here in the North-woods forever.

"Feels nice, doesn't it?" Hunter asked.

Hannah opened her eyes and glanced over her shoulder, back at her canoeing partner.

"It sure does."

"The temperature couldn't be more perfect."

"For sure."

A lazy grin lifted onto Hunter's face. His dark, wavy hair accented that tan of his. She could only ever dream of a golden tan like that. Her pale skin seemed to act as a sun reflector, not an absorber. Well, at least she didn't burn. Not too often, anyway.

Hannah resumed paddling. Slow strokes. Floating on this river for the rest of the day would suit her just fine. It relaxed her. Quick glances at the handsome man in the back of the canoe suited her just as well.

"There's a little inlet up ahead with a trail about a half-mile long along the shore. Do you want to stop and check it out? It's just a little loop."

She glanced over her shoulder. "Sure."

Lifting that long, muscular arm of his, he pointed to a spot on the shoreline.

"Got it," she replied as she helped maneuver the canoe in that direction.

They paddled right up to a grassy ledge where Hunter effortlessly landed when he jumped out of the canoe. He tied the vessel to a tree, then reached out to her.

Apprehension cracked through her like a whip as she stared at his hand. Remembering his touch and kiss earlier in the day had her wanting to grab hold of him, then thoughts of her past and Sebastián's harsh touch, sent her reeling. Sebastián was a total dick and sadly, she now judged every man based on his actions. She didn't want to, but couldn't help herself. She'd been so wronged by him and didn't know if she could ever find her way back to trust another guy. However, the one looking at her right now with those dark, dreamy irises had her reconsidering.

The amber hues in Hunter's eyes softened.

"I just want to help you out of the canoe. That's all," he assured.

The calming tone he used caused her to push her fear aside and reach out to him.

His grip was soft, yet firm enough to guide her out of the tippy canoe without falling. The second she gained her footing, he released her, taking the security of his hold with him. She felt disappointed.

"This way," he said with the gesture of his hand toward the evident trail.

She nodded and followed closely, within two steps. So close that she could smell his rich, earthy scent with a hint of chocolate. Though she had to wonder if the woodsy scent was him, or the woods itself. Either way, it was a relaxing scent, and her senses couldn't get enough of it. She raked her gaze over his backside. Broad shoulders, slim waist, muscular legs. There was no doubt this guy worked out in addition to getting cardio exercise during his guiding trips. Inhaling deeply, she took in the aroma that followed him. That fabulous fragrance she enjoyed had to be from him. They were among cedar trees along this shoreline, yet there was a hint of pine in the air. It was definitely his scent. He was one with the woods.

Hunter stopped, turned to look at her, and grinned.

"Isn't this great?" he asked as he whisked his hand through the air.

"Yes."

"I knew you'd like it here."

"It's beautiful and peaceful. Just what I needed."

His gaze held hers for a few moments before he cut her loose.

"It's none of my business, but whatever it is that's causing so much tension in your shoulders...well, I just hope it eases soon."

Her gaze landed on the ground. She was uncomfortable talking about her situation with Sebastián, especially with a man she hardly knew.

"Sorry. Like I said, it's none of my business and I wasn't asking to pry. I was just making a statement."

Believing him, she nodded and returned her gaze to him. She reached back and rubbed the base of her neck and left shoulder as far as her right hand would reach. If only the tension would disappear, she would be thrilled.

"Come here. Let me work that out for you."

"What?"

"Let me massage that for you."

She flinched as if physically struck by his words. Yes, she'd kissed him earlier and thoroughly enjoyed it, but the split-second thought of being touched by him caused her to recoil. She hated this involuntary reaction.

Hunter lifted his hand in the air, holding them submissively. Concern laced his gaze. "I just want to help. It's all good."

After a couple of seconds, he lowered his hands and then pointed ahead. "The trail just circles back now."

He turned away from her as if to lead her down the trail again.

"Wait!"

He spun around.

She stepped up to him and then turned her back to him.

The warmth of his large hands seeped into her skin as he placed his hands on her shoulders and used his thumbs to work out the knots in her shoulder blades. His magic touch was nothing short of amazing.

She closed her eyes and soaked in the feel of his exquisite touch. The pads of his thumbs firmly, yet soothingly, rubbed her shoulders in a circular motion, slowly easing the tension from her. With as good as his touch felt through the barrier of her clothing, she wondered how good it would feel for his hands to touch her skin directly. No doubt, she'd probably melt with direct contact from his fingertips, like she'd nearly done earlier in the day when their lips met. She eased her head back just a smidge, and the pads of his thumbs crept up to the base of her neck. Skin on skin. Excitement shot through her.

"I want to kiss your neck. Can I?" he asked softly.

She was shocked he asked, but then recalled he knew how jumpy she was around him and was doing her a courtesy to make sure she wanted that. He was so aware and kind.

"Yes."

She tilted her head to the side to give him better access.

Her heart rate jolted up another notch when his lips pressed to the side of her neck. His mouth skimmed lightly toward the sensitive point behind her earlobe. She leaned back and melted into him.

Large hands massaged her shoulder blades as soft lips massaged her neck. The enjoyment of it was almost too overwhelming, but not so much that she didn't let him continue. Good heavens. Her knees grew almost too weak to hold her up. As if he'd read her mind, he spun her to face him and wrapped his muscular arms around her lower back and pulled her toward him. It was easy to forget her earlier reluctance.

Their lips met in a light and feathery manner. The slow pace was delightful. This pace was about all she could handle right now, considering all that had gone on with Sebastián in the recent past. She hadn't thought she'd ever kiss again, but her fast-beating heart and humming lips urged her on.

Hunter kept the pace consistent. He'd obviously figured out that this was all she could handle right now.

His large hands loosened from around the small of her back, skimmed up her sides, not stopping until they cupped her cheeks. When his mouth stopped moving and he pulled away, she opened her eyes. Those beautiful, warm chestnut irises of his soothed her soul and had her wanting more from him.

"That was nice," he said.

His sensual, husky voice caused her to quiver.

She inhaled deeply to calm herself. That was a mistake. That outdoorsy scent of his enhanced her desire for him, but was she really ready for more? No.

"It was nice, really nice," she replied.

The amber hues in his irises brightened as he leaned forward and gave her a sweet peck on her forehead.

"We should probably get back to the others," he said as he pulled his hands from her face and took a step back.

Her cheeks cooled.

"I suppose," she replied with reluctance.

Though she didn't want to leave this moment, getting back to her friends was the right thing to do. They'd come on this trip to spend time together before going their separate ways onto the next phase of adulthood. She hoped this phase would be better than the last one. College started out great, but went downhill fast at the beginning of her senior year.

Hunter snatched up her left hand, and she flinched and reeled back as a sharp pain stabbed through it. Her heart pounded.

Concern and fear were emitted from his gaze.

Embarrassment and shame caused her to look away from him.

"Sorry. Are you okay?"

She stared at her hand as she rubbed the phantom pain away.

"Hannah?"

Slowly, she lifted her gaze, returning it to him.

"I'm okay," she whispered as she fought the tears stinging her eyes.

Hunter's gaze lowered to her hand that she'd practically rubbed raw. The top of it was red except for the one-inch scar, which remained bone white.

That scar would stay with her for life as an ugly reminder of what Sebastián had done to her.

"Did you get stung by something?"

"No. It's an old wound."

She had intended on leaving it at that, but words escaped her mouth.

"Somehow, pain flares up in it still."

"Can I see it?" he asked in such a soft and caring tone she couldn't resist his wish.

She lifted her hand.

Moving slowly, he reached out and took it in his hand, and held it gently as he moved it closer to his eyes. With his pointer finger from his other hand, he traced over the scar lightly with the pad of his fingertip. Then, he leaned forward and pressed his lips ever so gently to it. It felt exhilarating. Her heart swelled, and she leaned forward and kissed him. Hard. Pouring everything she had into it.

His warm tongue swept through her mouth. They kissed and kissed and kissed. She enjoyed the hell out of it. Hunter's arms held her tightly to his body. She liked it and firmed up her own grip.

After a few more moments of mind-boggling bliss, Hunter loosened his hold and edged back. He stared at her. Those amber specks in his brown eyes looked fiery. Her insides sizzled with delight. She didn't want to stop kissing him.

"We'd better get back and check on the others," Hunter said.

He was probably right. Bianca and Alyssa didn't fare well by themselves in the wilderness. She considered dismissing the thought, as they were probably still just sunbathing on the small sandy beach area.

They hopped back into the canoe and made their way back upriver to the campsite. When they got there, they found Alyssa and Bianca sitting on opposite sides of the picnic table wearing frightened expressions.

"Are you okay? What happened?" Hunter asked.

Alyssa stood with her camera in her hand. "We were just lying on the beach and I looked across the river to find this...a bear," she said as she handed the camera to Hunter to view the screen.

He studied the screen and smiled. "It's just a black bear. What awesome luck for you to see this."

"Are you kidding?" Bianca chimed in. "We could have been attacked."

Dread saturated every cell of her being. Her friend was right. Here she and Hunter had been off gallivanting around and kissing while her friends were in danger with no guide to protect them.

The concern and look of failure emanating from Hunter let her know he felt the same. He had a duty to protect them on this trip.

"I'm sorry. Yes. But the bear was across the water..." Hunter said before Bianca cut him off.

"What, they can't swim? And furthermore, if there's a bear over there, what says there isn't a bear over here? What if it had come over here?" Bianca's nostrils flared as she spoke.

"I wasn't all that frightened until we heard some thrashing around over there," Alyssa said as she pointed toward the trail they had hiked earlier.

"We didn't know what it was," she added.

"It's all okay now. Everything is fine. Nothing will happen to you. Animals are skittish. Unless you stumble upon a wild animal with babies, or a wounded animal, you've probably nothing to fear," Hunter tried to assure.

Bianca's nostrils still flared.

"Alyssa, look at that great photo you got. You can't get that in the city, now, can you?" Hunter asked.

Hannah supposed he was attempting to use the awesome photo as a distraction for Alyssa to get her mind off the potential danger she'd been in.

Alyssa took the camera from him and filtered through the not one but six photos she snapped of the bear, showing everybody her work. Yep, she was okay now.

The relief on Hunter's face was clear. She supposed the last thing he needed was unhappy customers and the last thing she needed was unhappy friends. Especially since they were kind enough to take this type of trip with her to help get her mind off things.

"Shall we get going on dinner? We're having pizza tonight" Hunter said, as he headed over to the cooler stashed in the metal box.

"Pizza?" Alyssa questioned.

"Yep, pizza made in the pudgy pie makers. Then we can have cherry or blueberry pies for dessert."

Hannah's mouth watered. She hadn't used a pudgy pie maker in years and looked forward to it.

Hunter pulled the cooler from the animal-proofed box. "Feels heavy. That's a good sign."

"What?" Hannah asked.

"It means the guys were here and stocked our cooler with dinner and tomorrow's breakfast and lunch," Hunter replied, then fixed his gaze on Bianca and Alyssa. "Take it you saw them?"

"Yeah, it was two guys in a motorized boat."

Hunter set the cooler on the picnic table and pulled out sausage, green peppers, onion, black olives, and cheese.

"I'll fry up the Italian sausage. We'll each make our own pizzas, so you can put on yours whatever you wish," he said.

From the cooler, Hannah pulled out the loaf of bread and butter, then retrieved the two pudgy pie makers from the supply box and explained to her friends how to make the pizzas.

"It's easy peasy."

The girls nodded.

"First things first, though," Hannah said as she headed toward the pit toilet.

First, she inspected the seat for spiders. She didn't really mind using an outdoor toilet, but didn't want any surprises, either. All clear. She sat and quickly took care of business. As she rose and pulled up her shorts, she looked ahead to see her missing sunglasses attached to a tree, staring back at her. She yanked them off the tree.

"Hilarious ladies," she yelled to her friends as she headed toward them.

"What?" Bianca asked.

"My sunglasses. Where did you find them?"

"I don't know what you are talking about."

"Right. Then who put them on the tree facing the toilet?"

"It wasn't me," Bianca replied.

"Me either," said Alyssa.

Hannah turned her gaze to Hunter and arched a brow.

"It wasn't me. I was with you," he replied defensively.

She bounced her gaze between the three of them. "You're all serious?"

They all answered with nods.

"Where did you find them?" Hunter asked. "Show me."

With the group in tow, she marched back to the pit toilet and then up to the small tree that had worn her sunglasses and pointed to the spot.

Hunter's gaze dropped from the tree to the ground and pointed. "The vegetation is disturbed."

He pinned his gaze on her. "Where did you stand when you retrieved them?"

She pointed, "Right there. I walked over from the toilet to here, then spun around and walked the same few steps back."

Hunter circled the tree and studied the ground. Then he stopped and looked at Alyssa and Bianca. "So, neither of you did this?"

"No," they replied in unison.

"Did the staff from the boat come back here at all?"

The two shook their heads.

"They just stocked the cooler and the woodpile, then left," Bianca said. "Maybe the campers from the site we were on yesterday found them and brought them here," Bianca added.

Hunter rubbed his chin with his hand. Simultaneously, his brows knit.

"Maybe, but likely they wouldn't. Their guide would have had to bring them here, and then why wouldn't they just put them on the table, and better yet, why wouldn't they just send them with the staff on the motorized boat? It just doesn't make sense."

"Unless they just thought they were being funny," Alyssa added.

That old familiar sensation of dread coiled in the pit of Hannah's stomach, and the skeptical look in Hunter's eyes let her know there was something more to this. Something was not right. Not right at all. This trip wasn't going to end well for any of them.

A branch snapped, and Hannah's gaze darted in that direction.

Chapter Seven

Hunter's stomach churned so much as he ate his pizza that he passed on the blueberry pudgy pie. He never turned down a pie before, but something wasn't sitting right with him. Yeah, it appeared it was only a pair of sunglasses that was out of order, and sure, someone may have put them on the tree by the pit toilet, thinking they were simply being funny. But, between that and a few out-of-the-ordinary noises he'd heard, he was on high alert. The feeling of being watched didn't help and stayed at the forefront.

He glanced at Hannah, who sat quietly on the bench, staring at the fire, picking at her cherry pudgy pie. The concerned expression she wore matched how he felt.

Darkness had settled in. The woods were quiet. His senses were in tune.

He could call base camp and have someone pick them up quickly. Get the ladies out of this potential danger. Or, at least, find out if anyone else had experienced any oddities. He shook his head. Was he just being paranoid?

Bianca rose to her feet. "I'm turning in."

"Me, too," Alyssa replied.

His gaze landed on Hannah. He hoped she wasn't of like mind because he wanted some alone time with her, wishing to resume what they'd started earlier in the day. She met his gaze, and a slight smile curved on her face.

She pulled her gaze from him and looked at her friends. "I'll be along shortly."

His pulse ratcheted up a notch.

The ladies disappeared into their tent.

He and Hannah sat in silence for a few beats before he rose from his spot, walked around the fire pit to where she sat on the bench and sat next to her. Close enough to her so that the side of his left arm and leg pressed against hers.

"I enjoyed the day," she said as she craned her neck to look at him.

"Me, too," he replied.

He slung his arm over her shoulders and scooted closer to her.

She felt nice to the touch, and it felt even nicer when she leaned toward him.

"Tomorrow's going to be great. We'll be hiking to Lover's Leap Falls. It's not huge, but it is the biggest one on the property."

"Sounds nice."

"The hike to this one is four miles round trip. Think your friends will be up for it?"

Hannah's pleasant, soft laughter wafted into his ear canals.

"I think the wilderness has already taken its toll on Bianca, for sure. I still can't believe she agreed to this kind of trip. Alyssa may be up for it, but I'm sure she would have preferred a trip to Nashville or somewhere of the like. I appreciate they did this for me. I told them they didn't have to, but they insisted. They're good friends, despite our sparring sometimes."

"You ladies seem so different. Your tastes, I mean."

"We are, but we were roommates throughout college. We got along well, but we didn't do everything together all the time. That's part of what was nice about our friendship."

"Nice."

"What was your college life and roommates like?" she asked.

"I was in the dorms for the first two years, then I moved into an apartment with three other guys whom I hadn't roomed with before. We all stayed together for two years. When they graduated with their bachelor's degrees, they left. I stayed on for another year to get my MBA degree, so I ended up with three new roommates. I hung out with all my roommates while we lived together. We keep in touch a bit. Mostly on social media."

She offered a slight nod.

"I wonder about the three of us. We're all headed in different directions. Bianca and Alyssa will return to their hometowns close to the Twin Cities. I'm not sure where I'll end up. Maybe I'll stay close to home, but it will depend on where I get a job. I have some interviews scheduled."

Hunter tilted his head to the sky. "If I had it my way, I'd never leave this place."

She chuckled again. "You've mentioned that a couple of times. Perhaps you should just stay here."

He lowered his head to meet her gaze. "All my best memories are here. Including this one right now."

Her gaze intensified, and she leaned in and kissed him.

Exactly the response he hoped for.

The kiss was soft and lingered. When she parted her

lips, his tongue met hers in a delightful, slow-moving dance. He wanted more. Needed more, but he let her set the pace so as not to scare her off.

She pulled away from him and pivoted in her seat. Then, she plopped herself onto his lap, wrapped her arms around his neck, and leaned into him.

In response, he enveloped her in his arms and pulled her in for a kiss. His lips, hands, and torso liked the feel of her. Hell, his entire body loved the feel of her. His pulse pounded, and he dove his tongue deeper into her warm mouth. The kiss turned hotter. Her small hands gripped his shoulders, and she pressed herself harder against him. The sensations of her touch were nearly too much, but he wanted more. He wanted to be with her, in her. He'd never moved this fast with a woman before, but if she gave any indication that she wanted to make love, he'd easily oblige.

Good heavens, Hunter could kiss. His kiss had been soft and controlled until she urged him on. Wanting more of him, she opened her mouth wider and ground against him. It was almost as if she couldn't control herself. His flavor was delicious.

Since the horrible betrayal by Sebastián, she'd never thought she'd allow this to happen again. Let her heart feel, but the way Hunter looked at her with those warm, chestnut eyes of his, and those sexy amber flecks that sparked, she couldn't help herself. And his touch nothing short of amazing. Those large hands that he splayed over her back and held her firmly were irresistible.

Her lips felt like they were on fire, but in the most delightful way. She poured everything she had into this kiss. Her body begged for more than a kiss, but she was still lucid enough to know this hot, mind-boggling kiss would be it for now. For now. Would she ever see him again after this trip? She hoped so.

His hand slid under her shirt and up her back. The sensation of his touch without the barrier of her clothing felt incredible. She missed human touch.

She lowered her hands from his shoulders, slid them under his T-shirt, and skimmed them up his sides. He squirmed. She laughed into the warm depths of his mouth and pulled back slightly.

"A little ticklish, are you?"

"Not really. It's just your touch is shockingly fabulous."

Her heart hammered at his words and the sincerity in his tone and eyes.

Moving her hands from his sides to his front, she enjoyed the feel of his rippled stomach. Hot and hard muscle felt incredible under her fingertips. She leaned back in and kissed him hard while her hands explored his chest.

When he cupped her breast, a spark of thrill shot through her. Her experience with men should have her running, but his touch felt too good.

Hunter released her breast and pulled back. "Are you okay?"

She closed her eyes for a couple of beats, then opened them and focused on his concerned gaze.

"Yes. It's just...I probably shouldn't have let things get this far. I'm..." She lowered her gaze.

Hunter pulled his hands out from under her shirt. Her skin cooled from the loss of his touch. He placed a finger under her chin and lifted until their gazes met.

"We can stop if you want and just sit here and enjoy the fire."

Even though she wanted to lean forward and kiss him

again, she thought better of it. She needed to slow this down. Think about what she was doing. She hardly knew this man, yet she just kissed and groped him and let him caress her. What was she thinking?

"Let's do that," she whispered.

As she pulled herself from her straddling posture, he assisted her but guided her to sit crossways on his lap. He placed one of his muscular arms around her back and the other in front of her, locking his hands at the upper part of her arm, cradling her. She leaned her head to the side and snuggled into the crook of his neck. Inhaling deeply, she took in that fabulous, earthy scent of his. The pine notes and hint of chocolate relaxed her.

There they sat, enjoying the warmth of the fire and each other's hold in the quiet confines of the night forest. It's funny how quiet the woods got shortly after sundown. A hoot of an owl here and there was the only sound.

"Hannah, Hannah."

Her eyes fluttered open.

"Yes."

"Let's go to bed."

"Huh?"

"Let's climb into our tents. It's almost midnight."

Good heavens, she'd trusted him so much that she'd relaxed and fallen asleep in his arms. Wow!

He loosened his grip, and she weakly slid off his lap, though he'd kept one of his hands fastened to her arm to help steady her as she stood. That was probably a good thing with the way she wobbled.

Hunter stood along with her, then freed her and stretched his arms over his head, and yawned. When he lowered his arms, he gestured toward her tent.

"I had a nice time tonight," she said, gluing her gaze to his, hoping to draw him in for a goodnight kiss.

He leaned toward her and gave her a sweet peck on the lips.

"See you in the morning."

He winked at her. Her heart fluttered.

"You're going to like Lover's Leap Falls. I can't wait to show it to you. The day will be epic," he advised.

"I can't wait. Promise?"

His smile stretched wide.

"I promise. Epic. You'll love it."

Chapter Eight

"Wakey, wakey ladies."

Hunter's deep voice rang through Hannah's ear canals. How was it morning already? She placed her fingers to her tingling lips. Those kisses she'd shared with Hunter were fabulous. Sitting by the fire, wrapped in his arms, had been comforting. A repeat of that tonight, the last night of their trip, would be absolutely wonderful. She frowned at that thought...the last night of their trip. The last night she'd see him. She finally took a chance on someone and likely this would be it. Just one more night, then they'd both be off living their new lives as college graduates.

The scent of taco meat wafted in the air. Had she slept so well it was dinnertime?

"Hey, the breakfast burritos are almost finished!" Hunter yelled. "Chop, chop. We have an awesome day ahead of us, and we need to get going."

The man sounded cheerful.

Bianca rolled over with an annoyed groan. "What time is it?" she asked. Frustration laced her tone.

"Almost nine," Hunter replied.

Holy shit. Nine. She hadn't slept this long or this well for quite some time. Her nightmares had been subsiding, but a good night's rest was still a rarity since her incident with Sebastián.

Hannah flipped back the top of her sleeping bag and snagged a fresh set of clothes from her backpack. She was more than ready to hit this day running.

Her stomach growled almost as loudly as Bianca, at the thought of getting out of the sack. Alyssa moved sluggishly, but with no verbal complaint.

The spicy aroma practically pulled Hannah out of the tent. As she slipped out, she caught Hunter's upbeat gaze.

"Good morning," he said as a smile stretched his sun-kissed, chiseled face.

The amber flecks in his warm chestnut irises sparkled with the help of a sunray, beaming through the trees onto him.

"Morning."

She pointed to the cast-iron fry pan on the camp stove. "That smells delicious."

"Breakfast burritos, just one of my many specialties," he bragged.

Now his full-blown smile bared his straight white teeth.

Hunter snagged a plate off the table and handed it to her. "I'm not waiting anymore. I'm starving. Let's eat. They can eat when they get up."

She piled scrambled eggs with peppers and onions, taco meat, and cheese onto a flour tortilla, wrapped it up and took a seat at the picnic table. He did the same, except he made two for himself, and then he sat opposite her at the table.

Gazing ensued over breakfast burritos. She enjoyed both and couldn't have asked for a better morning.

Hunter pointed to her tent. "Do you think they are ever going to get up? The hike into Lover's Leap Falls is farther than the other hikes we've taken. Not to mention that we need to break camp and canoe to that location. We're going to need a bit more time. Or..." he paused and winked at her. "Will it just be you and me today?"

The rapid flutter of her heart kept her words at bay for a moment, and that sexy as hell wink of his had her wanting him for herself today. She could probably make that happen. Letting her friends off the hook from hiking today would probably be easy. Except for being alone with that bear yesterday scared them, and they'd probably want to be near Hunter.

Alyssa slipped out of the tent and moseyed over to the picnic table, grabbed a plate, then made her burrito, and sat.

"Is Bianca moving?" Hannah asked.

"I don't think she's getting up today. We'll have to pack her with the tent. She's checked out," Alyssa said with a giggle.

"I'm coming," Bianca yelled.

She slipped out of the tent. Even with as annoyed as she was, she still looked like a million bucks. Hannah was sure she couldn't look more opposite.

Bianca wrinkled her nose at the burrito makings, then glanced over her shoulder at Hunter. "I'd like a spinach quiche and a dish of strawberries," she said as she batted her eyes.

"I'll get right on that," he joked in reply.

The only problem was that Bianca was probably serious and suspected he'd swim back to the main camp store and get the supplies to accommodate her wish. That's what she was used to. She arched her brow.

"There's a great family diner you can hit on your way

out of here tomorrow that can probably whip that up for you, but until then, it's breakfast burritos for you, sweet pea."

Sweet pea. Hannah laughed at the nickname he'd just coined Bianca with. She loved how Hunter didn't fall prey to or cater to Bianca like most men did.

The scowl on her friend's face let them all know she didn't appreciate it.

Sweetheart, gorgeous, or princess would be more to Bianca's liking.

With some reluctance, Bianca assembled her burrito.

After breakfast, they broke down camp, loaded the canoes, and headed to the next site.

A pair of eagles soared above them. Hannah stopped paddling and leaned her head back to watch the magnificent birds. Large and beautiful, the royalty of the sky, floating through the air with ease, with hardly a flap of their wings.

"Majestic, aren't they?" Hunter asked, drawing her attention from the birds.

She looked at him. He wore a soft smile. His and Bianca's canoe was only a couple of feet from hers. It crossed her mind to lean over and kiss him, but she wasn't ready for her friends to know that she liked Hunter. Not yet.

"They sure are," she replied.

Hunter tilted his face to the sky.

"I never tire of watching them."

"I don't doubt that."

"Hey, some help here would be nice," Bianca said as she shot a glare at Hunter.

He jokingly cringed and paddled again.

"You were the one in such a hurry to pack up camp and scoot along this morning," Bianca added.

After her tongue-lashing, Bianca faced forward again.

She shared a glance with Hunter.

Bianca hadn't taken her happy pill this morning. It still puzzled Hannah a bit that Bianca had agreed to this kind of trip, but sometimes friends just do the right thing, and she had to appreciate that Bianca would do this for her, even though her friend was cranky today. This was a long time for Bianca to go without modern conveniences like a flush toilet, a hot shower, and a latte. Only twenty-four hours or so and Bianca's life would be restored. Tomorrow they'd pack up, head back to the base camp, and then head home.

Home, back to the horrible life that loomed over her. The trial. But once that was over, she could move on. A slight shiver raked through her. What if Sebastián wasn't found guilty? What if he didn't get sentenced to prison? What would this mean for her with him on the loose? Her body tensed. She'd live her life in fear of what he might do to her.

"Hey, you okay?" Hunter's voice sounded.

She turned her head to face him. No, she wasn't, but he didn't need to know that.

"I'm fine, just sad we're on the last day of this fabulous vacation."

Those words drew a big smile from the handsome man in the canoe next to hers.

Bianca huffed.

"This has been great. I got some awesome photos," Alyssa said.

Within the hour, they'd paddled up to the next campsite, which resembled the others. A small sandy beach area and a campsite equipped with a picnic table, fire pit, tent pads, and a pit toilet tucked back into the woods a bit. Lovely.

Even with very little help from her friends, their tent was set up and their gear was unloaded from the canoe within thirty minutes. She hustled, wanting to get on the trail to Lover's Leap Falls. Their guide's vivid description of it had a heavenly image already planted in her head.

"We'll pack some sandwiches and picnic on top of the falls," Hunter said as he pulled lunchmeat, cheese, and bread from the cooler.

She walked over to the picnic table to help him.

"Ham or turkey?" he yelled out.

"Turkey," Alyssa responded.

"I'll do the same," Hannah added.

"Bianca?" Hunter asked.

Either she ignored him or didn't hear him because she stood with her back to them over by the water.

"Bianca?" Hannah yelled out.

Her friend spun to face them. "Huh?"

"Do you want a ham or turkey sandwich for our picnic lunch today?"

"I'm not going," she replied in not much more than a whisper.

She wore a strange expression. Not one of frustration with the trip. Oddly, more like one of concern.

Hannah walked toward her. "What's the matter? Are you concerned about the length of the hike?"

"It's not all that much farther than the ones we've already taken," Hunter added.

"No," Bianca said and dropped her gaze to the ground.

Now that Hannah was closer to her, she could see the deepened worry lines on her friend's face. What was that about?

Bianca's skin turned pasty white, and she wrapped her

arms around herself as if trying to contain her visible shivering.

"Are you sick?" Hannah asked.

Bianca lifted her gaze from the dirt but didn't meet Hannah's eyes. Something was not right.

"I do feel...I don't know. Just not right. Tired, I guess. I didn't sleep that well."

"Do you need a quick nap before we go?" Hunter asked.

She shook her head. "Why don't you guys go without me today? I'll just hang here on the beach and rest."

Hannah watched as Hunter studied Bianca. Probably debating if that was a good idea. Leaving one of his guests unattended in the wilderness after the bear incident yesterday.

"I suppose that would be okay. But, know that we'll be gone for the better part of the day. The staff will pop in while we are out to stock the food and ice, and firewood, so if you need anything, they can help you out."

"Okay," she responded, then turned and looked out over the water.

Unease coiled in the pit of Hannah's stomach. She could totally understand that Bianca was done with this trip, but her behavior seemed off, too off. She'd started the trip off on the right foot—accepting even though camping and hiking weren't her thing, but as the days came and went, she was less able to hide her displeasure, but still tolerated it. Now, it wasn't as much displeasure as it was despair, maybe. Hannah couldn't quite read it, and it concerned her.

"Bianca!" Hannah called out to her.

Without turning to face her, Bianca raised a sluggish hand in the air, waving her off.

Her stomach coiled into a tight knot. She had an eerie feeling this day would not end well. It started great. But...

Chapter Nine

HUNTER STOWED THE SANDWICHES, water, and Gatorade into his backpack and flung it over his shoulders.

"Ready?"

Hannah and Alyssa nodded. Then, he shot a glance at Bianca, who stood in the small sandy beach area facing the water. She hadn't moved at all since Hannah had walked away from her a couple of minutes ago. Not an inch. He understood she was a drama queen; even so, she'd tolerated this trip thus far and now she acted as if she couldn't tolerate another second of it.

"Last chance!" he called out to her.

No reaction from Bianca.

Hannah and Alyssa shrugged.

Whatever. He convinced himself she'd be fine. Wouldn't get eaten by a bear or something while they were gone. Yet, he felt an obligation to watch over her. After all, that is what they paid him to do. He was stuck. Either cancel the hike and stay at camp, depriving the other two of the adventure they paid for, or leave her behind and make the other two happy. Two out of three being happy wasn't bad. He'd go with that.

He led Hannah and Alyssa down the trail toward Lover's Leap Falls.

It was an easy and quiet walk for the first mile. He liked the quiet. It gave him time with his thoughts. As he walked, he mentally prepared for his upcoming job interviews. With as much as he wanted to land one of those jobs, he wanted to stay here even more. But it was time to move on.

He paused and looked around. A serene forest surrounded them. Inhaling, he expanded his lungs as much as possible. The earthy scent unleashed so many wonderful memories. As a kid, he hiked this trail with his dad, uncle, brother, and sister more times than he could count. They loved nature as much as he did. Uncle Lee had proposed to his wife atop Lover's Leap Falls. Why couldn't he? It was the most beautiful spot on his property.

Hunter glanced over his shoulder. Hannah's sexy as sin, kissable mouth turned up into a soft smile. His heartbeat stuttered. That's it. He planned to kiss her atop Lover's Leap Falls. He didn't care if Alyssa saw or not. The gold flecks in her emerald irises sparked. Had she read his last thought? He hoped so, and he wished for her to be agreeable.

His gaze floated down to her toned shoulders. Today she wore a sky-blue tank top under a lightweight, long-sleeved tan shirt. It had been cool out earlier when they'd left last night's campsite, but she removed the long-sleeved shirt during the canoe ride, exposing those milky white shoulders of hers. His fingers itched to touch her soft-looking skin and that tank top hugged her in all the right places. Admittedly, he was a breast guy, and it looked as though she had the perfect pair. Everything about her was perfect. Beautiful emerald eyes, milky white skin, long brown hair, toned muscles, yet shapely—curvy. Best of all, outdoorsy and nice. She was perfect.

"Here we go, ladies. Our gradual climb up."

"I can't wait to see it," Hannah said.

"Me, too," Alyssa added.

"You're in for a real treat. The falls are about a forty-foot drop from the very top. It's only about ten feet wide but has a profound gully allowing for some major water to flow into a deep pond. I would have shown it to you from the bottom first, but the forest is thick around the bottom with a lot of thorny vegetation. We can view it from that angle later if you want."

"I'd like to," Hannah said.

Of course, she would, and he'd be happy to show her.

The trail transitioned from mostly soil and tree roots to rock. It wouldn't be long before they'd reach the top.

He paused and looked back at the ladies. "Careful, the rocks are loose and they'll get larger as we near the top. Just make sure you have good footing before taking your next step."

"Okay," they responded in unison.

The scraping of rocks behind him caused him to halt on a dime and twist at the trunk to see what happened. Hannah and Alyssa looked back, too. So, it wasn't one of them who'd lost their footing. For another few seconds, they all just stood there staring in the direction from which they'd come. Then, both ladies turned their heads and fixed their gazes on him.

"Neither of you slipped?" he asked.

They both shook their heads.

"I suppose one of us could have loosened a stone or two on our way through. No biggy. This is why we have to be careful with our footing, not to slide down the hill with the rocks," he said.

He spun and resumed climbing.

His mind wandered back to the sunglasses incident and the feeling of being watched. Over the past couple of days, there'd been some strange noises he couldn't identify, and he'd been in these woods enough to know the sounds that animals make. These sounds were different—off—likely human. Was someone spying on them? He didn't like that thought at all. Why would someone be following them? It certainly wouldn't be any of their hikers and campers because the guides wouldn't allow it. They'd stick to the plans in place and not deviate from them for both the enjoyment and safety of the clients. State land surrounded his uncle's property, so he supposed hikers other than those signed up at Yooper Adventures could be milling around. Every now and then, he'd come across a lost hiker and help them back to civilization.

Hunter stepped up onto the bald top of the waterfall. Water flowed full force from the deep gully in the rocks, over the edge, and into the pool below. From this vantage point, he could see miles and miles of the lush green forest.

Hannah stepped next to him. She lifted her hand to further shield her eyes from the bright sun, even though she wore sunglasses. The sunglasses that had mysteriously disappeared and reappeared. Her long brown ponytail flung around in the shifting wind. It was always windy on top of the falls.

"This is lovely," she said.

"You should see it in the fall when the colors are at peak."

"I bet it's gorgeous."

"If you come back, I'll show you."

She fixed her gaze on him. "Maybe I will."

"What about me?" Alyssa asked in a playful tone.

"You are more than welcome, too," Hunter replied.

Alyssa swung her gaze between him and Hannah. "And be the third wheel. No, thank you," she replied with a wink.

His gaze quickly landed on Hannah, whose flush floated up from her neck to her cheeks.

"Let me get a photo of you two to capture this moment," Alyssa ordered as she pulled her camera from her backpack.

Hannah's cheeks flamed red. Why was she so embarrassed that Alyssa figured them out?

Hunter slung his arm over Hannah's shoulders and snuggled her close to his side. She didn't resist.

Alyssa snapped several photos.

"Why don't you move closer to the water's edge and I'll take a couple more with a bit of a different background. God, this place is gorgeous. A photographer's dream."

"So, Lover's Leap. What's the scoop? Who leaped?" Hannah asked as they moved to a new spot.

"The legend is like many others. A Native American woman, daughter of a chief, fell in love with a trapper, a white man. The chief would not allow his daughter to marry a white man, so she jumped off the ledge, and her lover did the same, so they would be joined in the afterlife."

"How awful," Alyssa replied.

"That's not the worst part."

"How could it get worse?" Hannah asked.

"She died and he survived."

Hannah flung her hand over her mouth.

"Once the chief figured out what had happened, he hunted down the trapper and sent him to the afterlife. So, I guess in the end, the young lovers got what they'd wanted. They say when the wind blows right, you can hear the two profess their love for one another, then silence, then the distinct splash of the two hitting the water, then the normal flow of the waterfall again."

"What were their names?" Hannah asked.

"Binishii and Luke."

Hannah lowered her hand. "Have you heard it?"

"No. But Uncle Lee and Aunt Heidi say they heard it the day Uncle Lee proposed to her up here. I believe them. They are the most honest and down-to-earth people you'll ever meet."

They edged closer to the gulley of fast-flowing water and posed.

Alyssa lifted her camera to her eye.

He snuggled Hannah closer to his side and posed for the photo.

The wind shifted. "Binishii, I love you. Now and forever," a man's voice sounded in the breeze.

Hunter's heart slammed in his chest. He turned his head and looked at Hannah.

The shock in her gaze let him know she'd heard it, too.

"I love you, too, Luke. It's time." The woman's tone was filled with sadness.

He glanced at Alyssa, who still held her camera to her eye. No look of surprise on her face. Had she not heard the profession of love from the two souls in the afterlife?

The wind stilled. The atmosphere went dead silent. Hunter's heart raced. Good God, he was about to hear the splash he'd learned about from the folktale.

BANG!

Shock shook his extremities as Alyssa fell forward, landing hard on the solid rock formation they stood on. Blood stained her shirt. There was no cry of agony. She didn't move.

There was no shelter on this massive bald rock.

Instinctively, he flung himself in front of Hannah.

"Hold on," he ordered as he wrapped her in his arms the best he could.

A second shot rang out. His shoulder burned, but he held Hannah tightly as he jumped over the edge of the waterfall, twisting his body to shield her from the protruding points of the rocks as they plummeted to the pool of water at the bottom of the falls. Pain shot through his hip as it hit an unforgiving, cement-solid, jutting prong. The impact shifted his body. They were now going to hit the pool on his side rather than feet first. Not good. Hannah's hands dug into his sides. Another blow to his side felt like a knife ripping through his ribcage.

A low splashing sound echoed in his ears as his back crushed against the surface of the water, knocking the wind out of him, and his mouth opened. Pain ripped through his spine. He gulped in water. His lungs burned. A vision of an angel appeared before him. His angel. Bright emerald eyes with gold flecks latched onto him and, as if magnetized, pulled him forward. Suddenly, he felt the firm grip of hands pulling him. His face broke through the surface of the cool water. He choked and gasped as she quickly pulled him along the surface of the water.

"Hunter. We have to get out of here. You have to help me."

He heard Hannah's nervous pleas among his choking and gasping, but he couldn't seem to gather his wits mentally or physically. Yet, the pain registered. His entire body throbbed and stung.

"Please, Hunter. You must get up!"

At the water's edge, he rolled over and tried to use his hands to push himself up. Agony ripped through his shoulder and back. Hannah grabbed him at the bicep and pulled him until he stood, but her hands stayed firmly on him. He wobbled. It was as if his right leg couldn't support him. Her grip tightened.

"We have to hide. At least get into the woods."

By memory, he knew the forest was only a few yards away from the water's edge, yet his blurred vision prevented him from seeing anything other than a mass of green that seemed so far away. Yet, moments earlier, while in the water, Hannah's angelic face was clear as could be.

His head throbbed.

Hannah lifted his arm and slung it over her shoulder. He leaned into her small frame and did the best he could to follow her lead.

He blinked rapidly to see if that would clear his vision. Not so much.

Between the scent of cedar and the tree roots, his sluggish feet nearly tripped over, he knew they'd reached the cover of the forest.

Hannah lifted his arm from around her shoulder, grabbed his hand, and set it on a branch.

"Hold that."

Then she placed her hand on his chest and pushed slightly until his back touched the tree trunk.

"Are you going to be okay if I let go of you?"

Would he? Jelly filled his knees. Everything hurt like hell and he could barely see.

"Hunter, can you hear me?"

Hannah's warm breath washed over his cheeks with her question. His cheeks. That might be the only part of him that didn't hurt right now.

His angel's hands gripped him at his sides.

"Can you speak?"

He closed his eyes and his head spun. He leaned it against the tree.

"God, Hunter. We have to get out of here. I don't know where the shooter is."

Shooter. Yes. A rush of adrenaline surged through him.

His eyes popped open. He let go of the tree and straightened his spine. Shear pain shot from head to toe.

"Yes. We need to move."

She released him. "Okay. Which way. I don't think we can go back the way we came, but I'm worried about Bianca. She's at the campsite alone."

Hannah paused and swallowed audibly. She swiped a tear from her cheek. "And, Alyssa..." she choked as she said her friend's name.

"I know. But I didn't hear any other shots. So, Bianca's probably okay for now. Who in the hell would shoot at us?"

Just speaking exhausted him.

"I don't know," Hannah replied.

Hunter lifted his arm and placed his fingers to the side of his head. It was moist. Water or blood, he wondered as he moved his hand to the front of his eyes. Blood.

"You're bleeding pretty badly. There and your shoulder. Your shirt is soaked with blood," Hannah said.

He felt lightheaded.

"I have some medical supplies in my backpack," she said as she made a move to pull it off.

"Wait, let's move farther away from here before we worry about this. It won't take him long to catch up to us if we stay still."

"Him?" she questioned.

"I don't know. Him, her, I don't want to hang around to find out."

"Come on," he said.

He'd only taken a couple of steps before he stumbled again.

Hannah grabbed his upper arm. "Are you alright?"

"No, but we've got to move. Problem is, I can't see very well right now. I know exactly where we are and how to get out of here without going back the way we came, but..."

"But what?" she asked, unable to hide the concern in her tone.

"It's not a simple walk, especially since we'll need to go off-trail, which is our fastest way out of here. Plus, I can't see well right now. God, my head hurts," he said as he swayed, barely able to catch himself.

She grabbed him by his upper arm.

"You're going to have to guide my steps, which will slow us down. Maybe you should just go ahead. Get yourself back to the river and follow it. Conceal yourself inside the tree line. It won't bring you back to the main camp that way, but within a mile or so, you'll come upon a small town called Iron City. You can find help there."

"I'm not leaving you."

"To stay safe. You have to. It's okay. I'll tuck myself in here and wait for you to send help."

This would be for the best. Sure, he told her he couldn't see, but what she didn't know was that it took everything he had to hold himself together right now and stand before her. The pain he endured had him on the verge of passing out, and he didn't want her to know that. He needed her to run to safety and not worry about him or have him slow her down. It was best for her if she'd just go.

"No. I'm not going without you," her conviction let him know she wouldn't.

He closed his eyes and drew in a deep breath. The pain

in his torso nearly sent him into shock, not to mention the bullet wound to his shoulder.

She placed her warm hand on his cheek. "I can't do this without you. I'm scared. I just can't," her voice shook.

He opened his eyes and tilted his head forward. The throbbing in his temples was unbearable. Lightly, he touched his lips to her forehead. "Okay, we got this. Let's move."

After drawing in a shallow breath, he snatched up her hand and headed south. He'd snake them back to the river and then to Iron City. The nearest city to his uncle's business with a police force.

Hunter willed his feet to move quicker, but he still feared he moved too slowly. His heart raced and his pulse pounded, but he thanked God that adrenaline took over the pain. Still though, he was cautious to make sure he picked up his heavy legs so as not to trip on the uneven earth below his feet. Hannah was a tremendous help, letting him know about exposed tree roots and rocky areas. He could see the trees and foliage, but it blurred together and the quicker he moved, the faster his pulse pounded, making his vision blur even more.

Heat scorched his skin. The increased pain and stinging throughout his body further distracted him from being able to pay attention to his footing. He fell, landing hard on his hands and knees. His right arm gave out, and he rocked back on his heels and cradled his right arm with his left. It felt like a knife stabbed him in the hip where he'd hit the protruding rocks as they tumbled over the edge of the waterfall. He pulled in a breath, hoping to soothe the pain, but all that did was sting his lungs and make his torso burn. He was a freaking mess. The right side of his body was useless.

"Are you okay? Can you get up?"

"You need to describe to me where we are."

"What?"

A shot rang out. His body tensed.

"Oh, God," Hannah exclaimed.

"Hannah, that's close, but not too close."

"How do you know?"

"I hunt and target shoot. I know. But if he heads this direction, it won't take long for him to catch up. You need to tell me right now what you see. For the most part, I know where we are, but I need our exact location. Describe it in detail."

He needed this detail from her because he was certain he would pass out any minute now and needed to give her good directions to save herself.

Hannah's breaths came quicker.

"Hannah, just take a second. Calm down. Everything will be okay. Just tell me what you see."

She drew in a long breath and squatted next to him. "There are fewer cedar trees now and more mixed hardwood, white pines, and hemlock."

"That's good. Any other distinct features?"

"To your right, ten yards away is a huge white pine stump full of woodpecker holes. Just beyond that is a hill with a drastic slope, and to the left of that is a low rock ledge that Ts into the hill. If we keep moving in the direction we're going, we'd hit the end of the ledge where it slopes down to the height of the ground level we're on. It's fairly level to our left. Right next to us is a large downed clump of trees with a huge exposed root ball and a large hole in the ground."

"Perfect. We aren't that far from the river, which is pretty narrow at this section. It may look as if the woods don't end, because you'll see the woods on the other side of the river from this vantage point, but know the river is there. It cuts between two rocky ledges standing about five feet or so above the surface of the water. We would have canoed that way tomorrow to get to the branch of the river we'd use to return to base camp. Still, I don't want you to go that way. Keep going south along the river to get to Iron City."

"What? By myself?"

"The best thing for you is to keep moving. My job is to keep you safe, and to do that, you need to go."

Hunter fell to his side.

"No, no, no. You have to open your eyes. Wake up. Please," Hannah pleaded.

He wanted to open his eyes, but he couldn't. He wanted to spring up and lead her out of the woods, but he couldn't move. Something tightened around his shoulder. Whatever it was suppressed the throbbing there. Then his temples pounded less. Was he dying? Nope, his lungs still burned, and his torso ached with every breath he took. Suddenly, he felt as if he was moving, but he knew it wasn't under his own power.

"Sorry, this might hurt," Hannah whispered.

She pushed him, rolling him to his stomach, then she pushed him again, and he fell, hitting the ground with a thud, landing on his back. Fell? What? Hadn't he already been sprawled out on the ground? A knife stabbed at his spine and hip. Something made a crinkling noise. Warmth washed over him.

He willed his eyes open to find Hannah's face only inches from his. He wished he could see her clearly. He wished he could save her.

"Stay quiet. You need to be silent. I'll send help."

Then, she leaned forward and pressed her lips to his, lingering only for a moment before his eyes fell shut.

Chapter Ten

HANNAH STOOD and stared down at Hunter's body, covered lightly with branches, leaves, and dirt. Just enough to hide the silver color of the survival blanket she pulled from her backpack to cover him with. It had worked great to drag him to this spot, and it should keep him warm in the event she didn't get back to him until after dark. Not that it got that cool during the past couple of nights, but if his injuries sent him into shock, the blanket would help. Only his face was exposed from the blanket and soil, but a leafy branch she'd found camouflaged it.

She hated leaving him, but his only chance of survival was for her to get help. Her only chance of survival was to get as far away from the shooter as possible.

"I'm coming for you!" a voice echoed in the distance.

Her heart beat wildly. It sounded like Sebastián. She felt sick. She caused all of this. When the man yelled again, she decided it wasn't him. The tone wasn't right. Her mind had played a trick on her.

She spun and ran in the direction Hunter had told her

to, leaping over downed trees, uneven soil, and low rocky ledges. The brightening light beyond the tree line let her know she was almost to the river. She kept her eyes focused ahead, glancing down regularly so as not to trip. She knew the person who'd killed Alyssa was on her tail. *Alyssa. Poor Alyssa.* Was Bianca okay? They had heard no shots other than the ones directed at them. That had to be a good sign, for Bianca's sake.

Alyssa, her friend, was dead. Tears blurred her vision. She swiped them away with her hand, but they kept coming. She needed to stop crying to mitigate the risk of tripping, but she couldn't. Her foot caught under a small downed tree and she tumbled forward. Hands flailing uselessly. She hit the ground hard. Pain shot through her right forearm when she pushed herself up and glanced at her arm. A few scrapes and a good-sized gash bled. She swiped the blood with her left hand, but it just kept coming. She pulled off her headband and quickly wrapped it around her arm over the gash. That was all she had time for now.

With her first step, she realized she'd banged her knee pretty good, too. *Walk it off.*

At a brisk, painful walk, she reached the river, but kept herself tucked just inside the tree line to avoid being seen. Only a mile or so to Iron City—to help.

A shot rang out. She flinched. It sounded close. Could he see her?

Her heart sank, and she swallowed hard. Had the shooter found Hunter? She'd done her best to hide him in the hole created by the root ball of the fallen tree.

She moved quicker. Even if the shooter hadn't found Hunter, he was in tough shape and still needed help.

Her feet scrambled for good footing. Her knee and arm

hurt like hell, and her breaths came harder. How far had she gone? Iron City had to be close. Help had to be close.

She blinked rapidly to relieve the pain from the sweat in her eyes and to clear her vision. It worked for a moment when she glimpsed a stone bridge ahead. Her heart raced. A bridge. If there's a bridge, there's a road. Adrenaline rushed into her, and her strides lengthened.

When she got to the bridge, she climbed the low, rocky bank and hoisted herself onto the road. Relief washed through her when the city came into view. She ran like her life depended on it, as it did. Hunter's life depended on her. Bianca's life depended on her. Choking back a sob, it was too late for Alyssa.

Hannah ran past businesses and people on the sidewalk. The folks eyed her strangely. Why wouldn't they? She probably looked like a hot mess, but she didn't care.

A young man, mid-twenties or so, appeared beside her, keeping pace.

"Are you okay? What are you looking for?"

"Police station," she blew out.

"Follow me," he said as he pulled ahead of her by a couple of strides.

Up ahead to the right, she spotted the fire station. Easy to notice with a large, bright red truck getting washed on the apron.

The man in front of her stopped at the end of that block and pointed. "Here's the cop shop."

He stepped forward and opened the glass door of the old stone building for her.

The receptionist's eyes widened when she noticed her. "Are you okay?"

"Yes, but I need to see the chief right away. I was shot

at. My friend was killed. Our guide is in the woods. Hurt bad," she blurted, and then gasped as if all her oxygen had been used up with those quick statements.

"Chief!" the thin, pretty woman with long blonde hair yelled with a bit of franticness in her tone.

A tall man with dark hair stepped through the door behind the receptionist's desk. He wore a blue police officer's uniform. His intense gaze latched onto hers. Within two steps, he stood before her at the counter.

His gaze fell to her arm. The blood had soaked through the headband wrapped around her wound.

He looked at the receptionist. "Mandi, call for medical."

"No, no. I'm okay. It's my friend and guide who needs help."

The man calmly nodded and then directed Mandi to make the call.

"I'm Chief Ricco. Can you tell me what happened?"

"My friends and I were on one of those guided hiking and camping trips through Yooper Adventures and my friend was shot..."

A sob choked off her words.

The chief's facial muscles tightened and his gaze turned black as coal.

"Mandi, get Dewey in here," the chief directed.

The woman immediately snatched a handheld radio from her desk and talked into it.

"On it," she replied.

"Is your friend..."

Quickly, Hannah shook her head, not wanting the chief to say the word.

Tears flowed from her, and Mandi handed her a box of tissues.

"Tell me what happened."

"We have to get to my friend Bianca and our guide, Hunter, right away. Hunter's been shot and Bianca. I don't know if she's okay."

"I thought you said your friend had been shot?"

"I was with two friends, and Hunter is our guide."

"Hunter Samuelson?" the chief asked.

"Yes, I guess. I don't know his last name."

The bells on the glass door clinked, and an officer stepped through. His salt and pepper hair and lines around his eyes indicated he was older than the chief, who looked to be in his early thirties. He stepped up to the counter, joining their conversation.

"Where did this happen?" Chief asked.

"Lover's Leap Falls. We were on top of the falls. They shot Alyssa, then Hunter. He grabbed me and we jumped over the falls. He shielded me from the shooter, and he got banged up as we went over the falls and landed in the water. Bianca stayed at the campsite. She didn't want to hike today."

"Where's Hunter?"

Her mind spun. "I don't know exactly. Near the pool of the falls. He's unconscious now. I hid him in a hole of an uprooted tree and ran here for help."

The chief looked at the other officer. "Get Hunter's Uncle Lee in here. We're going to need his help to find Hunter and the other woman."

So, they knew Hunter and his uncle.

The bells on the glass door clinked again, and a firefighter carrying a red medical bag walked through. He was a small man who looked to be about the police chief's age. Short dark hair with a few gray strands that matched those in his mustache.

"Matt," the chief said.

"Jack. What do we have here?"

"I'm guessing she's got a pretty nasty gash under that bandage," the chief replied.

Matt pulled up a waiting area chair and motioned for her to sit. His brown irises emitted warmth and concern.

"Go ahead and sit. We'll keep talking and get your friends some help," the chief said calmly.

She slipped out of her backpack and sat, and the firefighter undid her blood-soaked bandage with gentle hands.

"Yeah, that's going to need some stitches for sure. I'll put a new bandage on, but she'll need to get to the hospital pretty quickly."

She didn't have time for the hospital. They needed to find Bianca and Hunter.

"Dammit," Dewey said, drawing all gazes to him.

"What?" Chief asked.

"Lee's out of town. In Illinois for his friend's son's wedding. Seven hours away. He's leaving now."

"What about Hunter's sister and brother? Other than Lee and Hunter, they know these woods the best."

"I asked Lee that. They're both home in Door County, Wisconsin. That's only three hours away. But they may already be on their way up here. They're filling in while Lee and Heidi are gone."

"Call them. Let them know what's going on. We need them. Also, have Lee reach out to the other guides in the field to see if they're okay. Without alarming them."

"Okay."

Chief turned his attention back to her. "Tell me exactly what happened."

Hannah blew her nose and swiped her moist cheeks with a tissue.

"Me, Alyssa, and Bianca are on the last night of our

three-night trip. Hunter is our guide. Bianca stayed at the campsite today because she didn't want to hike. Me, Alyssa, and Hunter hiked to the top of Lover's Leap Falls. Alyssa was taking pictures. A shot sounded and Alyssa fell forward..." She paused to choke down the golf ball-sized lump in her throat that cut off her words.

"It's okay. Just take a breath," the chief advised.

She nodded. "Hunter threw himself in front of me and was hit in the shoulder. Then he wrapped around me and launched us over the falls. He hit his head on a rock, busted up his ribs and who knows what else. He was able to walk for a while, but it was just too much. He insisted I come here for help without him because he'd slow me down too much. After pointing me in the right direction, he passed out. I wasn't sure what to do. I just couldn't leave him for the shooter to find, so I dragged him over to a hole in the ground caused by a fallen clump of trees, shoved him into it, and covered him up with my survival blanket. Then, I covered him with some dirt and branches and ran here for help. Please. You have to find him," she pleaded.

"Do you have any idea who the shooter is and why he's after you, your friends, or Hunter?"

"No."

"Was he following you?"

"Yes."

"How do you know?"

She shuddered as she recalled the man's words. "He yelled that he was coming for us. He sounded close. I ran as fast as I could to get here."

"Did anything else happen before today to make you think someone was after one of you?"

Her breath hitched as she remembered the sunglasses incident. "Yes. My sunglasses disappeared from one campsite and then reappeared at another. I know it sounds dumb, and I thought one of my friends was just messing with me, but they said they didn't do it."

"What exactly happened to them?"

"I thought they were on the picnic table, but when I went to get them, they weren't. I looked everywhere for them and couldn't find them. At the next campsite, I found them in a tree."

The chief nodded. "Anything else?"

"I do recall that Hunter made a comment during one of our hikes that a noise we heard was unusual and he looked puzzled for a moment."

"Hunter would know. He's spent his life in these woods."

"You know Hunter?"

"Yes. It's a small town. Everyone knows everyone."

"Good news, Chief," the officer said from behind the reception desk.

"Cap and Cici are already on their way up here. They're already in Florence. Only thirty minutes out."

"Cap and Cici?" Hannah asked.

"Yes. Hunter's brother and sister. They've guided up here. They know the woods almost as well as Hunter and their Uncle Lee."

Hope filled her that with Cap and Cici, they'd find Hunter before it was too late.

"So, you have no idea who may have done this? Do you or your friends have anyone who's threatened you in the past? Any enemies?"

Hannah's heart sank. She closed her eyes and drew in a deep breath. She lifted her eyelids and zoned in on Chief Ricco. "Maybe."

He arched a brow.

"I have an ex. There's a trial in two weeks."

"Trial?"

"Yes. We broke up. He stalked, kidnapped...and beat me."

Her heart sank as she said the words. It still stung to know a man she dated would do this to her.

"Is he in jail right now?"

Her body shook.

"No. His parents are rich. He's out on bail."

"I'll need his information."

She nodded and then answered his questions about Sebastián.

"Let's get you to the hospital before Hunter's siblings get here," the chief said as he gestured for her to rise.

Pain ripped through her knee, and she wobbled. Chief wrapped his large hand around the upper part of her arm.

"I fell and hurt my knee."

"We'll get that looked at, too."

The chief looked at the officer. "You follow up about Sebastián and call in Officers Hansen and Collins so we can do a briefing. I'll take Hannah to the hospital. I'd like to think this shooting incident is..." The chief paused and looked back at the firefighter, "Matt, can you put your fire-fighters on alert to keep an eye out? Spread them out through town. Obviously, don't say anything to alarm the citizens."

"You got it," Matt replied.

His firefighters?

She glanced at the man's shirt. *Chief Ganea.*

Police Chief Ricco escorted her down a long, narrow hall and out the back door of City Hall. He opened the passenger door to an SUV squad detailed with the Iron City Logo and marked 'Chief.'

alerie J. Clarizio

She slid into the vehicle and then he did the same on the driver's side.

"The hospital is only a few minutes away."

She nodded.

The chief pulled up to the emergency entrance of the small hospital and escorted her into the building. Only one person occupied the waiting room. The older man looked up from the magazine he'd been reading.

"Hey, Chief," he said, then inclined his head, "Miss."

"Hi, Will," the chief said.

"Hi," Hannah replied.

She and the chief walked up to the reception desk.

"Hi, Gloria, can we get Hannah checked out? She hurt her arm and knee."

"Sure thing. Come on back."

The older woman wore pink scrubs with little clouds on them. Almost looked like pajamas.

The chief followed along but stopped at the doorway, not entering the examination room.

"I'll be right outside the door if you need anything."

She entered the room with Gloria.

"Alright. Let's see what we have going on here," Gloria said.

At Hannah's hesitation, the woman smiled and spoke again. "I'm an RN. I was just covering the desk for a moment. Jackie should be back there already. She just needed to step away for a moment. She'll get your information when we're done here."

The nurse looked at her knee and felt around it a bit while asking questions. It still hurt, but was already feeling better. Probably just scraped and bruised.

"I think it's just bruised. Good mobility. Let's look at your arm."

12

She pulled the butterfly bandage off that Chief Ganea had put on her.

"Oh yeah. We're going to need to clean and stitch it up."

She grabbed a thick gauze square from a drawer and held it to the wound with one hand as she picked up the phone receiver with the other.

"Hey, Jackie, can you send Dr. Fields to the ER? I have a patient who requires stitches on her arm."

Gloria hung up the receiver and peeked under the bloody gauze. Then she disinfected the area.

Within minutes, Dr. Fields entered the room. The old man smiled warmly.

"Good afternoon, Miss?"

"Hannah Rice."

"Hannah, we'll have you fixed up in no time."

She didn't doubt that. He looked like he'd been around the block a few times.

He pushed his glasses up on his nose and edged closer to her.

"Oh yeah. Four stitches should do it."

Gloria handed him a syringe.

"Okay, Hannah, I'm going to numb up the area."

Hannah closed her eyes and tried to relax to prepare for the sting of the needle, but relaxation didn't come. All she could see on the back of her lids was Alyssa's lifeless body. Lifeless, possibly because of her. She opened her eyes wide to rid herself of that horrible image. Tears flooded her eyes, and she sobbed. Her friend was dead because of her. Sebastián. It had to be him. He was probably aiming for her and hit Alyssa instead.

Gloria grabbed Hannah's hand. "It's okay, sweetie," the older woman assured her.

She probably thought Hannah was upset about the

needle, and that wasn't it at all, but the woman wouldn't know that. The next thing she knew, Gloria had wrapped her arms around her, holding her tight as she whispered everything would be okay, but Hannah knew it wouldn't. They needed to find Bianca and Hunter and get them out of harm's way.

After a few beats, Gloria released her. It was then she realized Chief Ricco had entered the room and stood next to the nurse.

"Hannah, you've got to let Doc get you stitched up so we can get out of here and focus on Hunter and your friend," the chief said with both firmness and empathy.

He was right. She swallowed back the next sob and nodded.

Gloria reached out and took her hand, holding it while Doc stitched her up. It didn't take but a few minutes, and she and the chief were on their way to meet Cap and Cici so she could describe to them where she'd hid their brother.

She and the chief arrived at Yooper Adventures. He drove past her car and parked next to the entrance of the office. Following his lead, she slid out of the vehicle and then walked to the back of the squad where he stood. He swung his gaze around. Looking deep into the woods.

A man resembling Hunter hurriedly walked toward them. A woman with similar features kept pace at his side. Both wore concerned expressions. Must be Hunter's siblings.

"Jack. What's going on?" the Hunter look-a-like asked.

He didn't call him chief, so they must know each other well.

"Is Hunter okay?" the woman asked.

Her dark brown eyes and hair matched Hunter's. The

man's did, too. The three of them looked so much alike they could be triplets.

The chief gestured toward her. "Cap, Cici, this is Hannah Rice. She and two of her friends were on a guided trip with Hunter. We have an active shooter situation."

"Oh, God," Cici said as her hand flew over her mouth.

The woman's eyes watered.

Cap swallowed audibly. "Is Hunter okay?"

"I'm going to give it to you straight. We don't know. When Hannah last saw him, he was alive but badly injured. We need to find him, and the shooter is still out there. We need to proceed with extreme caution to find Hunter, and we need to track the shooter. My staff is calling in the appropriate resources, but it will take a while to assemble them. We're going to look in the meantime."

Cici swiped a tear from her cheek.

The chief focused on her. "Cici, we've got this. Nobody knows this property better than you two. We'll find him."

She nodded and then looked at Hannah. "Where did you last see him?"

Hannah quickly explained what had happened and did her best to describe the path she and Hunter had taken.

"I've got a boat ready for us," Cap said.

The four of them climbed into a small boat like the one she'd seen servicing the campsites earlier in their trip. The boat provided little cover for them.

Cici reached down and pulled a handgun from a duffle bag and handed it to her brother, along with a holster. She strapped one on as well. Next to the bag lay two rifles similar to the one the chief had pulled out of the squad car. The chief didn't say a word about the sibling's guns. If he was good with it, she was good with it. In fact, she wished she had one, too. She had her conceal carry permit, but

Bianca threw such a fit about her taking a handgun on the trip, she'd left it back. With all that had gone on with Sebastián, she should have never caved on the issue.

Though they were well armed, her teeth still chattered with fear as they made their way down the river. Who knew where the shooter was? Who was the shooter? Sebastián? Was he watching them?

Chapter Eleven

CAP MOTORED them up to the small beach area of their campsite where Bianca lay on a towel in the small patch of sand. She lifted her head and shielded her eyes from the beaming sun.

She pulled a frown, cocked her head to the side, and fixed her gaze on Hannah. "I thought you were hiking?"

Her friend was clueless as to what had happened. Good, Hannah supposed, but she'd have to tell her about Alyssa.

"I was, but..." A sob clogged Hannah's throat.

"Bianca?" Chief asked.

Bianca stood and walked toward the four of them as they jumped out of the boat.

"Yes."

"I'm Chief Ricco of the Iron City Police."

He gestured toward Hunter's brother and sister. "This is Cap and Cici. They work for Yooper Adventures, and they're Hunter's siblings."

"What's wrong? What happened?" Bianca asked, then focused her attention back on Hannah.

"Alyssa and Hunter have been...shot. Didn't you hear any gunfire?"

"What? How?" Bianca squeaked out before her hand flew over her mouth.

No tears like the ones running down Hannah's face. Just the surprised hand-to-mouth gesture.

After a couple of beats, Bianca lowered her hand. "How is it you're okay? I don't understand."

The tone she used seemed as if she were surprised that she hadn't been shot, but the other two had been. If Hannah were in Bianca's shoes, she would have asked how Alyssa and Hunter were doing rather than comment about why Hannah hadn't been hurt. Odd.

"Alyssa was hit first, then Hunter shielded me from the gunfire."

"Oh."

Oh, that was it? That was her reaction to that news?

Bianca's eyes watered as if the information was finally sinking in.

"Did you hear any gunfire?" the chief asked Bianca.

"No."

Seriously, how could she not have heard the shots? The falls weren't that far from the campsite.

"None?" Chief persisted with furrowed brows.

"No. I fell asleep after everyone left for the hike."

"Did you see anyone else today other than your group?"

Bianca shook her head.

She still hadn't asked about the status of Alyssa. Was she afraid to ask?

Hannah closed her eyes, and a vision of Alyssa's lifeless body haunted her. She lifted her lids to rid herself of that sight, then she drew in a long breath and let it out.

"Bianca, Alyssa...didn't make it."

"What?"

Hannah shook her head, stepped toward her friend, and embraced her. They took a moment to comfort each other.

"Ladies," the chief said, "we need to find Hunter."

Bianca pulled from the embrace first.

Hannah focused on the chief, then glanced at Cap and Cici. Cici wore a large red medical backpack. The large white plus sign on it was the giveaway. Cap sported an orange, oblong bag, hooked over his left shoulder. She figured it to be a stretcher. This group was prepared. Thank God, for Hunter's sake.

"I'll lead us to the pool of the falls, Hannah, then you'll have to lead us from there," Cap said with urgency in his tone.

Hunter needed medical attention. She knew that and needed to focus. Silently, she prayed she'd be able to find him again. The woods were large, and she'd been so preoccupied with worry for Hunter and running from the shooter, she hadn't observed her surroundings as well as she should have.

Cap's long legs led them quickly. He moved effortlessly over the terrain. Cici did, too. It was obvious that hiking and this trail weren't new to them. Bianca's labored breaths behind her weren't a surprise either. She glanced from side to side, and then over her shoulder to the chief, who followed. Worry lines sculpted his face. She suspected, like her, he wondered where the shooter was.

When they arrived at the base of the incline to the top of the falls, Cap stopped and spun to face her. His chestnut irises focused on her. The color matched Hunter's. Her heart seized for a moment. *Hunter.*

"Where from here?" he asked.

Hannah's gaze rose to the top of the falls. A horrible

Valerie J. Clarizio

vision of her friend lying atop the falls made her want to cry again.

"Hannah?" Cap said, pulling her attention back to him.

She pointed to the left. "We landed in the pool and then went that way. We went through that clump of cedars."

"Okay," he replied as she backtracked a few steps and led them around the pool.

They followed along a stream flowing out of the pool for a bit until he found a narrow area with stepping stones to cross.

It was as if he and Cici didn't even have to look down to cross. She, on the other hand, placed each step carefully, and when she teetered on the last stone, Cap reached out and grabbed her upper arm, then pulled her toward him. His touch reminded her of Hunter's.

Once on the other side, she spun to see how Bianca fared. Chief Ricco had her by the arm and kind of pulled her across with him. Bianca was tall, about five foot nine. Still, the chief towered over her.

When they reached shore, he released her arm, then he took a moment to study their surroundings.

He focused on Cap. "I haven't seen or heard anything unusual."

"Me either."

Both men blew out a sigh of relief.

She followed suit, relying on the chief's skills as a trained observer.

Cap gestured to the area she'd pointed out earlier.

Wanting to put herself in the exact spot she and Hunter exited the water, she walked back to the pool of water, then up to the cedar trees she remembered walking through.

"We went through here," she said.

Cici nodded and pointed at the ground. "Yep, we can see the disturbed soil."

Hannah's pulse ratcheted up a notch. Would Hunter's siblings be able to track where she and Hunter had walked to?

Hannah led them through the small, thick patch of cedars and then stepped into the hardwoods.

Ten feet into that section of the woods, the trees and vegetation closed in on her. All sense of direction was lost. They had moved quickly. Hunter had led. She just followed. She spun in a circle. Everything looked the same except for the cedar section she'd just come through.

A warm hand rested on her shoulder. "Just breathe and take a moment," Chief Ricco said.

His warm, dark eyes emitted warmth with a tinge of concern.

As he suggested, she drew in a long breath and let it out, then looked around again before dropping her gaze to the ground. Still, it all looked the same.

She looked at Cap. "Can't you track where we went?"

"Depends on the signs you left behind. It was easy to see your footprints in the moist soil close to the falls, but it's more difficult in the hardwoods. From where you came out onto the street and what you said Hunter told you, you went south," he said as he lifted his arm and pointed.

"Can you recall any landmarks you saw? Any unique trees or terrain?" Cici asked.

The memory of the direction Hunter had given her suddenly flashed clear in her brain.

"Yes! When Hunter knew he couldn't go any farther, he collapsed and was on the brink of passing out when he told me to describe where we were."

"He couldn't see?" Cap asked worriedly.

The fear in the man's eyes matched that in his tone. He probably worried it was already too late.

"He could, but I think at that point it was blurry from the pain. I don't know."

"What did you see...tell him?" Cap asked.

"There was a huge white pine stump full of woodpecker holes. Just past that was a steep hill with a rock ledge that teed into it. The ledge sloped to the left as it leveled off with the ground. Where we were was beside the clump of downed trees. I put Hunter into the hole made by the uprooted root ball. He said we weren't far from the river. He said I should follow the river. We would have canoed there tomorrow. There is a spot we would have portaged, but he told me to keep going south to get to Iron City," the words rushed out of her mouth.

"I know where you mean!" Cici exclaimed. "The general area, anyway."

"Me too," Cap said as he spun away from her and bounded through the woods as if he were a creature of the woods.

His long legs carried him swiftly. Cici trailed behind him. She wasn't quite as quick, but she too moved swiftly, just like her brother, and just like Hunter had.

She followed Cici. With a glance over her shoulder, she looked at Bianca, who seemed to move sluggishly, like she had no interest in getting to Hunter quickly. Chief Ricco prodded her along. What was her deal?

"There, there," Hannah yelled as she pointed to the clump of downed trees.

Cap and Cici stopped and looked over their shoulders.

"He's over there."

Cap nodded and then moved even quicker than he had been, but now, in her excitement, she kept up.

When they reached the hiding spot, Cap bent over and pulled away the leafy branch she'd camouflaged Hunter's existence with, then he and Cici peeled back the survival blanket along with the light layer of soil used to conceal Hunter.

Hunter lay motionless. His sun-kissed skin was pasty white. His lips held a bluish-purple hue. Her gaze flew to his chest, hoping to see it rise and fall.

Chief slipped between Cap and Cici and placed his fingers to the side of Hunter's throat.

"His pulse is weak."

A rush of relief surged through her. They weren't too late.

Cap and Chief went to work, slipping a cervical collar onto Hunter, then they slipped the field gurney under him and lifted him out of the large hole. Hunter didn't move or make a sound the entire time.

They set him on the level ground and quickly assessed his other injuries. The wrapping she'd fastened around him to put pressure on the gunshot wound to his shoulder was saturated with blood but didn't look glossy, so it must have slowed, or even stopped. That had to be a good sign.

Chief studied the wrap. "It looks like it's working. We'll leave that for now and get him to the ambulance."

"Ambulance?" Hannah questioned.

"Yes, there should be one waiting for us where you came up onto the street, by the bridge," he replied.

Cici knelt next to Hunter's head. "Stay with us. We got you."

There was no response from Hunter.

Cici fought away tears.

The chief took a moment to study their surroundings. She presumed he looked to see if they'd been followed.

Cap and Chief each grabbed a handle of the stretcher near Hunter's shoulders, and she and Cici grabbed the handles by his legs. He was heavy, but come hell or high water, she'd hold her own and get Hunter to safety as quickly as possible.

Bianca followed them, carrying the backpack that Cici had been wearing earlier.

Hannah's breathing labored as she stepped on the uneven terrain and over downed trees. There was no simple path in sight, so she did the best she could.

When they got to the river, the chief looked over his shoulder and bounced his gaze between her and Cici. "Should we take five?"

"I'm good," Cici immediately responded.

If Cici could continue, she could as well. She didn't want to be the one to let everyone down, and she knew Hunter needed medical attention long before now.

"Me, too."

"Okay, but you have to say something if you need a rest. We don't need to be carrying two people out of here or hurt him any further if we..."

"We're good," Cici cut off his words.

"Okay."

Chief and Cap continued along the river, but just inside the woods for cover, like Hunter had instructed her to do, just in case someone was watching them.

Within minutes, the refreshing sight of that stone bridge she'd come across earlier came into view. Soon, Hunter would get the medical attention he needed.

Atop the bridge sat an ambulance.

Her feet moved quicker in response to the chief and Cap's increased pace. With the end of the trail in sight and help waiting for Hunter, it suddenly became easier to keep up with the long-legged men leading the way.

When they reached the low rocky bank, where she had to hurl herself up on earlier to reach the road, they paused and set Hunter on the ground.

The chief directed them to switch positions. He and Cap grasped the handles of the gurney, one at Hunter's head and one at his feet. He told her and Cici to lift from the side away from the bank to help guide him and Cap, as they lifted the gurney to the awaiting EMTs and two fire-fighters.

Once they handed Hunter off, the five of them climbed up the bank. She ran to Hunter's side. He'd been loaded onto the ambulance gurney, so when she leaned over to kiss him on the cheek, she didn't have to lean too far. His pasty white cheek was cool.

"Please be okay. Please," she whispered.

His eyes fluttered open for the briefest of moments, and in the split second before they closed again, those amber flecks in his chestnut irises flashed.

"We gotta go," one of the EMTs said.

Hannah stepped back.

They whisked him into the ambulance and took off.

Hannah focused on Cici. "He opened his eyes. Did you see that?"

"He did?" Cici asked as she blew out a relieved breath. "Thank God."

"Are you sure?" Bianca asked.

"Yes."

Bianca averted her gaze.

What in the hell was wrong with her friend? Everyone else looked relieved to know he'd opened his eyes, and she looked...she wasn't sure how her friend looked, but she knew it wasn't relieved. Why not?

Chapter Twelve

HANNAH, Bianca, Chief Ricco, Cici, and Cap climbed into the Iron City logoed minivan that Fire Chief Ganea picked them up in. For the first time, since...she swallowed hard...since Alyssa'd been shot, she felt safe. Still, who or where the shooter was, she hadn't a clue. She inhaled, catching Hunter's familiar woodsy scent. The pine and cedar notes brought back the pleasant memory of their shared kisses. She turned to look at Cap. Not only did he look like Hunter, he smelled like him, too. The man offered a crooked smile. She returned with one of her own.

Though he smiled, the worry lines did not erase from his face. He reached over and placed his large hand over hers that rested on the armrest of her bucket seat in the middle of the van.

"He'll be fine. He has to be," he said.

She nodded, then looked over her shoulder at Cici, who sat in the way back of the van. The woman's eyes watered. A quick glance at Bianca back there next to Cici offered no empathy or concern. She wore a blank expression, but looked a little pale.

Within ten minutes, Chief Ganea pulled up to the emergency entrance of the hospital.

Cap climbed out of the van and then motioned for his sister to do the same. "You go in and get things squared away here, and I'll go back to Yooper Adventures, and get everything and everyone back on track, then I'll come back here."

"Okay."

Cici slid out of the van and disappeared into the hospital.

Once Cap climbed back in, Chief Ganea drove off toward Yooper Adventures.

"What do you think, Chief? Justin texted and said the other two teams of hikers and campers have been pulled back to base and are fine. Luckily, two groups had finished their excursions this morning before this all happened, but we have a couple of additional groups waiting to go out. The ones Cici, and Hunter were going to guide."

"Until we figure out what is going on, we need to keep everyone out of the woods."

"What am I going to tell them?"

Chief Ricco thought for a moment. "A version of the truth. I'd be willing to bet by the time we get there, some variation of the truth will have beaten us there. I know this isn't great for your uncle and Yooper Adventures, but canceling will be best for everyone."

"I agree," Cap replied.

"What about Alyssa?" Hannah asked, choking on her friend's name. Hot tears burned her cheeks. She wanted to know that her friend had been taken care of and wasn't lying on the unforgiving rock atop Lover's Leap Falls.

Chief Ricco twisted in his seat to face her. His dark gaze emitted empathy. "She's been brought back to base camp."

She swiped the tears from her cheeks.

"How? Who?" was all she could muster.

"Dewey, the officer you met earlier, and three DNR officers took good care in bringing your friend back to camp. Dewey has called her parents, who she listed as her emergency contacts on the form she filled out for Yooper Adventures."

Hannah's heart felt like it exploded at the thought of Alyssa's poor parents getting this call from Dewey.

Chief Ganea turned into the parking lot of Yooper Adventures just as a hearse pulled out, followed by an Iron City squad. Hannah's chest tightened, and her eyes flooded with tears. Alyssa was in that hearse.

Chief Ganea parked near the front door of the office, and a tall, slim man who looked to be in his mid-thirties walked toward them. He sported athletic shorts and a Yooper Adventures logoed T-shirt.

Cap slid out of the vehicle. "Justin."

"Cap."

"The clients are waiting to hear from you," Justin swung his gaze to Chief Ricco, "or you, I guess, about what they are supposed to do."

The chief nodded. "I'll address the group. We're going to send them all home. We can't risk their safety, as we really don't know who's behind the shooting."

Justin nodded.

The chief looked at her and Bianca. "Give me a minute to talk with the campers, and I'll be right back."

She and Bianca waited quietly in the office with Chief Ganea as Chief Ricco and Cap addressed the crowd.

A few minutes later, Chief Ricco and Cap entered the office.

Cap looked at Justin. "I'm going to the hospital. Text me

129

once all the guests have cleared out. Uncle Lee is still a few hours out."

"You got it," Justin replied.

Cap spun to leave.

"Wait!" Hannah called out.

He looked at her.

"Please let me know how Hunter is doing?"

"You bet," he said and then left.

"I have all the gear sitting outside your SUV," Justin said to her and Bianca.

Their gear. Alyssa's gear. She hadn't really given that any thought, but now that he'd mentioned it, she was thankful she didn't have to go and get it. Chief Ricco probably wouldn't have let her anyhow. All she had was what was in her backpack, which was now in the minivan.

"Thank you," she responded.

"I need to get out of here," Bianca said as she wrapped her arms around herself. Those were the first words she'd spoken in a while.

"We'll get your stuff out of the van and I'll drive us back to town in your vehicle," Chief Ricco said.

Like her friend, Hannah wanted to be away from this place. Away from Iron City. Away from the Upper Peninsula of Michigan. She never wanted to lay eyes on this place again. She wanted to close her eyes and reopen them to find herself out of this nightmare.

The sensation of Chief Ricco's warm hand that came to rest on her shoulder reminded her that this whole thing was real. As far away from a dream as one could get.

Fire Chief Ganea disappeared with the minivan, and she, Bianca, and Chief Ricco loaded their gear into her SUV. Chief climbed into the driver's seat, she in the front passenger seat, and Bianca in the back. He drove them to the Iron City municipal building.

The chief led them into the building and partway down a long, narrow hall, where they took a left into a small conference room. A few eight-foot tables sat in the shape of a square. She and Bianca sat next to each other on one side of the square, and the chief sat opposite them. Dewey entered the room and sat next to Chief Ricco.

The pretty blonde woman who'd been working the front desk earlier in the day, when she first entered City Hall, entered the room.

"Can I get you anything to drink or eat? Soda? Coffee? Sandwich? We have a great deli down the street."

"Do you have any sparkling water?" Bianca asked.

"Yep."

"I'll take one, too," Hannah said.

She didn't really need sparkling water. Regular tap water would suit her just fine. But she'd go with the flow.

"Coming right up. Anything to eat?"

The thought of food made her stomach toss.

"No. Thank you," Hannah replied.

Bianca shook her head.

"I'm sorry, ladies. I know you're exhausted and emotionally drained, but I need to ask you some questions. We need to find out who..."

The chief paused for just a moment before saying the horrible words she knew he'd say.

"Who murdered your friend. Was it intentional? Random? Is there anyone who had issues with your friend? Anyone who didn't like her?"

"No. ..."

Suddenly, Hannah couldn't bring herself to say her friend's name. It was just too hard.

"Everyone loved her. She was so nice and thoughtful. She didn't even really want to take a trip like this. She did it for me. This is all my fault."

The chief held his hand up. "Stop right there. This is not your fault. You couldn't have known."

The man's dark eyes emitted sincerity, and she took a moment to soak that up. That was exactly what she needed to hear, yet she still had doubts and felt responsible for what had happened. Was this the infamous survivor's guilt she'd heard about?

He released her gaze, and then she craned her neck to look at Bianca. Her gaze was not warm or consoling at all. Did she blame her for Alyssa's death?

"Tell me again exactly what happened."

"We hiked up to the top of Lover's Leap Falls. Alyssa was taking a photo of me and Hunter. A shot rang out, and Alyssa fell forward, landing hard on the ground. At first, I didn't realize what was going on. Hunter must have though, because he threw himself in front of me and wrapped me in his arms. Then another shot rang out, and that one hit Hunter. It was then that he launched us over the falls. There really wasn't anywhere else to go because it's wide open up there. Hunter took the brunt of the fall. I pretty much came out of the fall scratch-free."

Hannah paused and took a breath. She felt anxious. Not because of how the chief and Dewey were looking at her, because truth be told, both men kept their gazes neutral with a bit of empathy. Their body language was the same. They actually made her feel more at ease, but the incident itself sent her into a state of fear and helplessness.

"Then?" the chief asked.

"We quickly got out of the pool of water and ducked into the woods. Hunter knew where to go to get away from the shooter, but his injuries slowed him down. We knew the guy was following us because he yelled at us. I stashed Hunter and kept moving in the direction he'd told me, then I came here. I don't know where I lost the shooter or when he stopped following. I'm just so relieved he didn't find Hunter. Maybe he thought we both kept moving."

The chief and Dewey nodded in unison.

The chief turned his attention to Bianca. "So, you stayed back at camp?"

"Yes."

"Why is that?"

"I don't really care for the outdoors. We're on this trip because of Hannah," Bianca replied.

The accusing tone her friend used stung.

The knowing look tossed her way from Chief Ricco let her know he felt the same about Bianca's accusing tone.

"What did you do while the others were gone?" the chief asked.

"I laid on the beach. Soaked up the sun. Took a nap."

"Did you see anyone or hear anything odd?"

"No."

"So, you came on this trip solely to support your friend Hannah?" Chief asked as he gestured toward her.

"Yes. That's what friends do. Support each other."

Right. It didn't sound at all like Bianca meant that statement.

"What about you, Bianca? Do you have any enemies? Anyone who'd want to do this to you? Maybe Alyssa was just in the wrong place at the wrong time."

"No. None. Why would you ask that? I wasn't even there," Bianca snapped.

Both the chief and Dewey leaned forward, resting their forearms on the table. Their gazes bore into Bianca.

"That's right. You weren't there. How lucky you are," the chief said as he tilted his head to the side a bit.

What was the man trying to imply? Did he think Bianca had something to do with this?

"I guess," Bianca replied.

Her gaze bore into the man, making it obvious she didn't appreciate his accusing stare.

"If I were you, I'd focus on the guy Hannah pissed off at the gas station," Bianca blurted, then shifted her gaze to Hannah.

"What? That guy. We don't even know him. He wouldn't know where we were. Why would he do this?" Hannah replied.

Bianca shrugged. "I don't know. You just made him so mad he practically had smoke billowing out of his ears."

"What guy? Gas station? What happened?" the chief asked.

Hannah shivered at the thought of the strange man at the station.

"It's dumb, really. We stopped at a gas station a little south of here, and I went in to get a cup of coffee. I drained the pot. I didn't know this guy was waiting behind me, and when he saw the pot was empty, he blew a gasket. Started yelling at me. Called me an entitled bitch. Cursed up a storm. I took a step back, and he stepped with me. I thought he might hit me, but then the attendant came over to make another pot. Maybe it was because the worker was a male that the guy stopped yelling at me. I don't know. But his death stare was horrifying. I swear his eyes glowed red. He was that angry over coffee. It was so bizarre."

"What happened then?"

"I paid for my coffee and we left."

"Did he follow you?"

"Not that I'm aware of."

"What gas station was this?"

"It was an Acer gas station. Near Rhinelander."

"What did the man look like? Any noticeable manner-isms? Anything uniquely identifying about him?"

Hannah leaned back in her chair and thought for a moment. "He seemed kind of average. Maybe five ten. A little on the chunky side. Forty-five or so. He had long, dark brown hair with some gray mixed in."

The chief nodded. "You're doing well. Anything else? Scars? Tattoos?"

Hannah leaned her head back and closed her eyes, trying hard to picture the man. "I don't know. He scared me. I just wanted to get out of there."

"Bianca, did you notice anything else about him?" the chief asked.

"No. Nothing to add, except he was dressed kind of sloppy."

Of course, her vain friend would pay attention to the man's clothing when she was getting yelled at and was prob-ably on the verge of being struck.

"Sloppy?"

"Dewey, call the gas station and see if they have video."

"Yes, sir," the officer replied as he rose and walked out of the room.

"What about a vehicle?"

Hannah perked up at the thought of the vehicle she saw parked near the front entrance.

"There was an old, rusty Ford Bronco parked by the entry. Maybe that was his."

"Did you see him get into that vehicle?" the chief asked.

"No, but it seems like a vehicle that kind of guy would drive. And there weren't many other people there. There was a lady with a couple of small kids, an older couple, and two guys getting breakfast sandwiches. They looked like construction workers. I suppose I could have missed seeing some other people. Honestly, I wasn't paying attention. I just wanted out of there," Hannah answered.

"Bianca?"

"I noticed the woman and kids and the mean guy, but nobody and nothing else. Sorry."

Hannah's breath hitched, and she felt taken aback by the lack of sincerity in the mechanical tone her friend used when she apologized.

"What exactly are you sorry for?" Chief Ricco asked. "Sorry you're unable to recall details to help us find the person who murdered your friend, or sorry that you've been inconvenienced by all of this. Which is it?"

Whoa! Hannah's pulse hitched at the attitude in the chief's tone, coupled with the expression he wore. It was one thing for her to question her friend's sincerity in all her confusion right now, but to have the chief imply the same justified her emotion, and that made her even sadder. Still, hearing him, a stranger, think bad thoughts about Bianca, made her want to defend her friend's genuineness. Did he honestly think Bianca knew more than she let on? Did he think she had something to do with Alyssa's murder?

Bianca's eyes narrowed and her facial muscles tightened. The chief had struck a nerve.

"How dare you imply I don't care about what happened to Alyssa. She was a dear friend. I loved her," Bianca replied through gritted teeth.

"I didn't imply anything. Just looking for clarification."

Dewey stepped back into the room, leaned over, and whispered to the chief.

The man sighed and nodded, then returned his attention to Hannah.

"The gas station has video cameras, but, unfortunately, the recording system has been down for weeks. They've been waiting for a technician to come out and install a new system. However, we're waiting for a call back from the employee who worked that day, hoping he can shed some light on who the guy is."

Hannah shifted nervously in her seat. Could this random person from the gas station have killed her friend over a cup of coffee?

Her body quivered. Was SHE really the target?

Chapter Thirteen

"I NEED TO CALL MY PARENTS," Hannah stated to Chief Ricco.

The chief nodded. "Okay. We're done here for the moment."

"My phone is dead. It got ruined when I landed in the water."

He pointed to the phone on the wall. "You can use that one. Dial nine first."

Hannah's knees wobbled when she stood. The last thing she wanted to do was upset her parents more than they already were over this whole Sebastián thing, but she needed to hear her mom's voice. She needed to tell her what had happened. She needed Mom to tell her everything would be okay, but would it?

With shaky fingers, she dialed her mom's cell number. No answer. She dialed her dad's number. No answer. Dread laced every cell of her being. They always answered. Of all days to not answer, why today, when she desperately needed to hear their voices?

She hung up and spun at the waist to look at the chief. "They aren't answering. I'm going to try my brother, Kane."

The chief nodded.

Her chest tightened. Something just didn't feel right.

She dialed her brother Kane's number, and he answered on the first ring.

"Hello."

"Hi, it's Hannah."

"The number came up as Iron County Police. Are you okay? I've been trying to call you," her brother replied.

The tension in her unexcitable older brother's voice let her know her heart was right. Something was wrong.

"What's wrong?" she asked hurriedly.

The dead air scared her, but it was her brother's audible swallow that horrified her.

"Are Mom and Dad okay? Is Lance okay?"

Kane cleared his throat. "Lance is fine, but Mom and Dad were in a car accident."

"Are they...okay?" her voice squeaked.

Chief Ricco appeared in front of her. His curious gaze glued to her.

"No," her normally confident brother's voice cracked.

She felt hot. Her knees grew weak.

The chief grabbed her upper arm and steadied her as he yanked a chair from beside the table with his other hand and then motioned for her to sit.

Until she heard the chief speak, she hadn't realized he'd taken the phone receiver from her.

"This is Chief Ricco from the Iron City Police Department. Who am I speaking with?"

Hannah heard her brother's voice over the phone's speaker.

"I'm Kane Rice, Hannah's brother. Is she okay?"

Hannah nodded at the chief as if giving him permission to speak.

"She was involved in an incident today. She's got a few scrapes and bruises, but physically she'll be fine."

"Incident?"

"We can get into that in a minute. I heard her ask you if they were okay. Who was she referring to, and what happened?"

"Our parents," Hannah whispered in unison with her brother.

"What happened?" the chief asked.

Hannah drew in a breath, waiting for Kane's response.

"They were...killed in an accident earlier today. From what I understand, they were run off the road. Their car rolled down a steep ditch, and the other driver sped away."

Hannah buried her face in her hands and wept.

Her brother's voice faded, and all she could hear were her uncontrollable gasps. Arms wrapped around her, and she clutched herself to the person.

"Shh. Oh my. I'm so sorry," an unfamiliar female voice comforted.

The surrounding arms tightened, and she rocked her slightly in a soothing manner, like one would a baby.

Hannah let this stranger hold her. *Stranger*. Hannah pulled back and used her hands to swipe the tears from her eyes. The woman kneeling in front of her eased back, but kept her hands on her shoulders. Sympathetic green eyes studied her.

"Can I get you anything? Water?" the woman asked softly.

Hannah shook her head.

"I'm Clare Ricco, the chief's wife."

Though the woman wore a navy business suit, she

stayed kneeling on the floor in front of her. Long, wavy red hair framed her pale face. Empathy emanated from her gaze. Where had this kind woman come from in this split second?

Hannah nodded, then turned her head to find Bianca, who still sat on the opposite side of the metal table. She stared into space, looking emotionless. Why hadn't her friend come to her side to console her? Yet this woman she didn't know, had seen fit to do so.

"Bianca," Hannah said.

Her friend snapped out of her trance and looked at her.

"I gotta get out of here," Bianca said, as she rose to her feet. "I need out of here now, and I need to call my dad."

Hannah's heart slammed in her chest. Her friend offered her nothing. No comforting words. No consoling hug. Nothing. She just wanted out. They'd lost their best friend today, and she lost her parents, and Bianca couldn't see fit to help her through this devastating moment.

Bianca looked at her cell phone. "It's dead."

The word triggered Hannah, and she sobbed.

"Use this one," she heard the chief say.

Clare rose, guiding Hannah up along with her.

"Let's go to my office. It's more comfortable."

Not knowing what to say or do, Hannah followed the kind woman without question. She couldn't think.

Clare held the upper part of her arm as they walked down the long, narrow corridor they'd been in earlier toward the back of the building. They stepped through a glass door etched with white lettering. The letters were just a blur to her through her watery eyes. After walking past a couple of waiting room chairs, the kind you see in a doctor's office, they passed through another doorway into an office.

Clare motioned for her to sit in an oversized leather

chair, then she walked over to a small counter area and filled a glass of water from a dispenser.

She handed the water to her, and she took a sip of the cool liquid before setting the glass down on the square cocktail table in front of her. Clare sat in an identical chair opposite the table.

Hannah looked around the office. A desk sat in the corner, along with a couple of file cabinets. The walls were painted a warm green color. Her gaze was fixed on the framed degree hanging by the desk. The woman held a Ph.D. in Psychology. This made sense. This is how she knew how to comfort her. Unlike Bianca. The thought of Bianca's icy heart made Hannah angry.

The anger quickly disappeared, pushed away by overwhelming grief. Her parents. She sobbed. Any more pressure on her heart and it would surely explode.

Clare tried to comfort her.

How could she live without them? What was she supposed to do? She needed to get home. Be with her brothers. Kane was home in Minnesota, but Lance would have to come home from Germany. Would the Army let him?

Hannah plucked a handful of tissues from the box Clare handed to her and dried her eyes and wiped her nose.

"I need to get home."

"I know, sweetie. When you're ready. Just please take a few minutes to process what's happened. Make yourself comfortable in here. I can sit with you, or leave you alone. There's a phone on my desk you can use to call your brother. Just let me know what you want to do."

"I don't know what I'm supposed to do."

"I know. Do you want to call your brother again?"

She nodded and rose. Good heavens, her knees felt so weak.

Her brother answered on the first ring. "I just finished speaking with Chief Ricco. Jeez, Hannah, I don't know what to say. This is all so unbelievable."

"I know."

"Between what happened to you and your friends today, and Mom and Dad, the chief thinks you are in real danger. Who would do this to you?"

"What do you mean about Mom and Dad? Someone intentionally did this to them?"

The question she asked made her head spin.

The longer the silence from her brother, the faster her pulse pounded.

"According to the witnesses, it appears the other vehicle intentionally ran Mom and Dad off the road. Who would do that to them? For heaven's sake, they are...were, just your normal, everyday people."

"What are we going to do?" she asked.

"I don't know. But what I do know is that we need to get you home. I need you here. I need to watch over you."

Kane was always the overprotective older brother, as was Lance, and as a teenager, it drove her insane, but now, she wanted nothing more than to be with them. Comforted and protected by them.

But did she really want to be home? Home would be different now. Forever changed.

Chapter Fourteen

Hunter shifted. Pain shot through his entire body. His temples throbbed. His eyes felt glued shut. He groaned.

"I think he's coming around again. Maybe this time he'll stay awake," his sister's voice sounded in a whisper.

Was she talking about him?

"Thank heavens," Mom said. Relief laced her tone.

Why relief?

"It's about time," his brother replied.

"Hunter. Can you hear me?" Dad asked.

"Dad," Hunter replied in a voice so raspy he hardly recognized it as his own.

He fought to open his eyes, and his dad came into focus. Mom stood at his side. Her eyes were watery.

"Yeah. I'm right here. Welcome back," Dad said.

"Back?"

Mom leaned forward and kissed him on the cheek. "You had us worried. You were in surgery for a long time."

"Surgery?"

"Don't you remember what happened?" she asked.

He thought for a moment. He recalled working—

guiding the three ladies. Today, they would hike to Lover's Leap Falls. Hannah. Sweet Hannah. He recalled her lovely emerald eyes and those luscious lips of hers. He planned to kiss her at the top of the falls today. That kiss they'd shared in the small cave and the hotter one they'd shared at the campsite had his juices flowing. Everything was fine. Wait! Why did he have surgery? Why did he feel like he got hit by a semi? His brain felt jumbled.

After refocusing on Mom for a beat or two, he glanced around the room. When he tried to sit up, pain shot throughout his body, and when he attempted to use his right hand to help lift himself, something restricted it.

Mom placed her hand lightly on his shoulder. Even that hurt.

"You need to lie still. Rest. I'll raise the bed a bit for you."

He eased back down, and she depressed a button on the bed, causing it to rise, lifting him into a more seated position.

The cast on his arm seemed a mystery to him, and he studied it for a few seconds before returning his attention to his family.

"You're going to be just fine. Do you remember what happened?" Mom asked.

He thought for a moment. His mind was blank. Yet here he lay in a hospital bed, so something surely happened, and it wasn't good.

Thankfully, she told him he'd be fine because between the throbbing headache and the pain in his shoulder, he wouldn't have drawn that conclusion.

He cleared his dry throat.

"Do you need some water?" his sister asked.

He nodded.

There were two bottles of water on the side table. She opened one and poured it into a glass.

When he lifted his left hand to take the glass from her, his arm felt heavy, as if a twenty-pound weight was strapped to it.

What in the hell?

Mom grabbed the glass from Cici and brought it to his lips as if he were a tiny child who couldn't do it himself.

The cool liquid soothed his scratchy throat.

"Hannah?" was all he could muster before his throat went desert dry again.

He took another sip of water.

"So, you do remember," Mom said.

"I was guiding three ladies. We were going to Lover's Leap today. Where are they?"

Mom pinned her bottom lip between her teeth and locked gazes with Dad. Cap and Cici stared at the floor. What in the hell happened?

Dad leaned toward him. "Hunter, you were shot today. In the shoulder."

Adrenaline coursed through his veins as his gaze flew to his shoulder. But his arm was in a cast.

"What? Why?" was all he could mutter.

Mom's eyes watered. There was more.

"We don't know why. Chief Ricco is hoping you can shed some light on this. It looks like it has to do with one of the women you were guiding."

Hannah. Dread coiled in the pit of his stomach, making him nauseous.

"Are they okay?"

Again, his parents shared a glance.

"One of the ladies was shot as well...she didn't make it," Dad said.

Hunter's nerves rattled, and a quiver rocked his body. He squeezed his eyes shut. A vision of Alyssa's face came into focus. Her big, dark eyes widened as her body fell forward, landing hard on the unforgiving rock formation. He flinched as he recalled the gunshots that rang out. His eyes popped open.

"We jumped over the falls."

"Yes. You remember," Dad affirmed.

"Where is Hannah? What about Bianca?"

"They are both with Chief Ricco."

"So, they're okay?"

"Yes."

Relief washed through him. Suddenly, question after question bombarded his weary brain.

"Who did this?"

Dad shook his head. "We don't know yet."

"How did I get here?"

Cap stepped forward. "Hannah saved you. She's one tough cookie, that one."

"Of course, you saved her first," Mom beamed proudly.

"Huh?"

"To get away, you leaped over the falls with Hannah tucked in your arms," Mom said.

Yes. He remembered now.

"That's how you wound up with a broken arm and four broken ribs. Not to mention all the cuts and bruises."

"Ya hit your head pretty good, too. But I'm sure with as hard as that is, there's no damage there," Cap joked.

Cici punched Cap in the arm.

"I remember jumping. It seemed like the only way to get away. To not be so exposed standing on top of the falls. But the last thing I recall is running with Hannah to get more distance between us and the shooter. I don't recall making it to the road."

Hunter closed his eyes. A vivid picture of him and Hannah climbing out of the pool of water below the falls came into view. Despite the pain from his body slamming against the rocky ledge of the falls, adrenaline carried him as he and Hannah ran through the woods. That's it. Running through the woods was the last thing he could recall before waking up in this hospital bed.

"Hannah stashed you. You lost too much blood and were in so much pain that you passed out. Hannah hid you and found the road you instructed her run to. She ran all the way to town and got Chief Ricco," Dad informed him.

He didn't recall giving her instructions, but obviously he had, or she probably never would have made her way out of the woods. Well, with as smart as she was, maybe she would have figured it out.

Hunter swung his gaze around the small hospital room.

"So, how did I get here?"

Cici and Cap both grinned.

"We saved your ass," Cap said as he pointed between him and Cici.

"Huh?"

"Hannah led us to where she stashed you. Well, us and Chief Ricco. Luckily, the shooter didn't find you again."

"We don't know who or why someone shot at you guys," Cici said.

"Yeah. About that. What in the hell? Who would do this?" Hunter asked.

"Chief Ricco is investigating this. The girls don't seem to have a clue as to who did this. It's rumored it could be Hannah's ex-boyfriend."

"Yeah, I guess he's a piece of work," Hunter replied.

Hunter shifted and pain ripped through his shoulder. His mother's eyes watered at his grimace.

"Do you need something for the pain? I can go get the nurse," Mom offered.

He drew in a long breath. "No, I'm fine."

He shifted on the bed, trying to sit up straighter. The pain was no less this time than it was a few seconds ago. The good news was that when he stopped moving, the pain subsided, except for the throbbing in his head. That stayed constant and hurt enough to be distracting.

"I want to see Hannah. Cap, can I use your phone?"

His brother pulled his phone from the holder on his hip. "I'll call City Hall for you and see what's going on and ask about Hannah. I'll be right back," his brother said as he quickly ducked out of the room.

Why wouldn't he just let him use the phone? Was there something more going on?

"Hannah's okay, right?" he asked Mom.

"She's fine, dear..."

"Then why..."

"Just let your brother do this for you. You need to rest. In fact, you should probably just lie back and close your eyes. With your concussion, your brain needs to rest."

Concussion. That would explain the pounding in his head. Mom hadn't mentioned a concussion before. Or, because of it, did he not recall all of what she said? Was there more wrong with him?

"Concussion?"

"Yes."

"Anything else I should know about besides the shoulder, ribs, and concussion?"

Mom and Dad shared a glance. A lump the size of a golf ball clogged his throat. It was the kind of glance where he knew something was wrong and they didn't want to tell him.

He choked down the lump. "What...what's wrong?"

"It's not that bad," Mom said as she reached forward and placed her hand softly on his forearm.

Oh God, that maneuver made him worry more.

"What is it?"

"Your hair. They had to shave your hair to stitch up two nasty cuts on your head. It'll be fine. It'll grow back."

His hand flew to his head. Bald. He was bald.

"I know how you feel about your hair. It's just a matter of time, and your full head of hair will be back."

Oh man, not his hair. He loved his hair. Women loved his hair.

"Oh, for God's sake, you're worried about your hair. You've been shot, your arm and ribs are broken, your head is stitched up, and your face is the color of an eggplant. Your hair will be fine," Cici said with a roll of her eyes.

"Eggplant?"

His sister pulled a small mirror from her purse and held it in front of his bloodshot eyes. She wasn't kidding. His skin couldn't be more purple. Why that surprised him, he didn't know, as he recalled tumbling and crashing into the rocky surface on his way down the falls.

"So, Hannah wasn't hurt at all?"

Mom smiled warmly. "A couple of bumps and scratches. She said you wrapped around her, shielding her from taking any brunt of the fall. You probably saved her life. The doctor said if you weren't in such great physical condition, your injuries would have been much worse."

"And if your head wasn't so hard," Cap roused.

His brother had stepped back into the room during this conversation. He didn't mind his brother's joking.

That was how he dealt with things. It meant he loved him.

"Hannah's fine. She's still at City Hall talking with the chief. That's all Mandi said," Cap informed them.

Hunter lifted his good arm. Well, he thought it was his good arm, but the deep muscle pain let him know he'd thought wrong. He stilled and then lifted it further to press the tip of his fingers to ease the hammering in his temple. It didn't work.

"Damn, the throbbing."

"That bad?" Mom asked.

He squeezed his eyes shut for a moment, then opened them. "It's okay," he whispered.

"I can see that. I'll go talk to the nurse to see if they can give you anything more for the pain," Dad said.

"Well, now that we know you aren't going to die on us, Cici and I need to get back to camp. We've got guests to reschedule. That is, if Chief Ricco gives the go-ahead," Cap said.

Hunter's pulse ratcheted up. "I don't know if that's a good idea. What if the shooter is still out there?"

"That's why we need to talk to Chief Ricco."

"Don't risk anything. Just cancel the trips. I'm sure Uncle Lee will be fine with that," Hunter urged.

The last thing he wanted was to put his brother and sister in danger.

"Uncle Lee has said to do what we think is best. He's on his way home."

"None of this makes any sense. Who would do this?" Hunter asked rhetorically.

Cici and Cap exited the room, leaving just him and Mom. The worry lines she wore were blatantly visible.

"I'm fine, Mom. No need to worry any longer."

She nodded as she lifted her hand and placed it lightly on his cheek. Her touch was loving.

"I know, but still."

"I want to get out of here. See Hannah. Make sure she's okay."

The corners of Mom's mouth lifted upward. "You like her?"

His face heated, and he wondered if she could see him blush through his eggplant-colored skin.

Mom's eyes probed for an answer.

"Yeah."

"The doctor will check on you during rounds. He thought maybe you'd be released tomorrow."

"Let's call City Hall again and see if Hannah can stop by here. I don't want her to leave town without talking to her first," Hunter said.

"I'll make that call in a minute. Right now, I think you need to close your eyes and rest until the doctor comes in to check on you," Mom mothered.

Where was Dad with word on a pain reliever?

Mom lowered his bed, and he shut his eyes.

His last thought before nodding off was of Hannah. Thinking of her bright emerald eyes with gold flecks comforted him. The thought of touching her milky white cheek with his fingertips warmed his hands. He needed to see her. Get to know her. His heart rate kicked up a notch. How could he like someone—feel so strongly about a woman he'd just met? He didn't know, but he did.

Chapter Fifteen

TWIN CITIES – Three weeks later

Hannah sat in the witness stand for over two hours answering questions as her ex-boyfriend sat behind the defendant's table with his attorney. Sebastián remained emotionless except for that slight eye tic. She'd seen it before and concluded it occurred when he was angry, which later in their relationship was frequent.

His dark brown gaze felt so heated she feared it would burn her skin. His lawyer worked to trip her up, but hers had coached her well. Numerous times, she'd told her to only answer what was asked. Offer nothing else. Think before you speak.

Sweat moistened her skin. She wasn't sure how much more she could take. Why did it feel as though she was the guilty party having to defend herself when she was who'd been beaten and left for dead? Yet, here she was under fire.

Beyond Sebastián and his slick-looking and poised attorney, sat Sebastián's parents. Lucia wore a flamboyant hat like one would wear to the Kentucky Derby. It matched her maroon dress with large polka dots. The woman was always well put together. Never a hair out of place. Makeup applied just right. She was thin but curvaceous. The perfect specimen for Sebastián's father, who was a bit older than her. Marco was a nice-looking man and always dressed in the best of suits or golf attire.

Sebastián was the spitting image of his father. Handsome and smooth-talking.

How did she ever get mixed up with these people? They had nothing in common. For starters, the Garcias were rich and walked in a completely different circle than her middle-class family did. She and Sebastián shared very few similar interests. She liked the outdoors. Him not so much. She liked quiet and surrounded herself with just a few good friends. He liked parties and being the center of attention. She never fit the mold of what he wanted in a girlfriend. She'd figured that out quickly, but he was insistent they give their relationship more time. Why he was so adamant about this, she wasn't sure. His family's money and power could garner him a chance with any woman. Why her? Now, here they sat, in a courtroom. Maybe he was so adamant they stay together because he wasn't used to being told no and not getting what he wanted. It had to be that, because they weren't together long enough for him to really fall in love with her.

Long enough to fall in love...that word made her think of Hunter. The man she'd thought about every waking moment since she'd met him. The man she'd cut loose three weeks ago. Her heart squeezed. It was for his own safety to not be near her. She swallowed hard. In her heart, she was one hundred percent sure that Alyssa had been murdered because of her. Her parents had been murdered because of her. If Hunter stayed near her, he surely would be in danger.

Rumors had surfaced recently that Sebastián's father was the head of a drug cartel. Recalling comments and actions by him and his family, she believed the rumors. She quivered and her throat closed. She felt anxious. If Sebastián's family was really from a drug cartel, and the outcome of this trial didn't suit them, would she and her brothers have to go into hiding...or witness protection? As discussed with her lawyer, they didn't qualify for formal witness protection. This trial was related to Sebastián having kidnapped and beaten her within an inch of her life. It had nothing to do with the Garcias allegedly being the head of a cartel. She supposed she and her brothers could do their own sort of hiding, change their names, and move. It wouldn't be too hard to disappear, since they had little family remaining. They wouldn't leave many inquiring relatives behind. Their grandparents had died some time ago. Tears burned her eyes at the thought of her parents' untimely death only three weeks ago. Maybe a fresh start was what she needed, but she'd be dragging her brothers along with her. They had a couple of aunts and uncles and a few cousins, but they'd certainly understand if she and her brothers simply walked away. She wanted to cry at the thought of starting over and leaving them and her friends behind.

"Hannah."

The sound of her name jerked her out of her horrible thoughts, and she turned her head to look at the judge.

"You need to answer the question," Judge Herman said.

Compassion laced the woman's dark eyes.

"Sorry. What was the question?"

Sebastián's attorney repeated his question.

The courtroom door slammed shut and all gazes flew to the back of the room. The old, bearded man with his arm in a sling took a seat in the back row as he'd done every day during this trial. Only today, he was late. The man's empathic gaze comforted her. Every day, they'd shared a glance. She didn't know the man, and she wondered why he showed up every day. He didn't wear a press badge, and he wasn't well-dressed like Sebastián's family members. Yet, he was in the courtroom every day.

Hannah took a breath and then focused on Sebastián's attorney and answered his questions. She took some relief in knowing this trial was almost over. Sebastián would likely not testify, so she should be the last person on the stand.

"No more questions, the defense rests," Sebastián's high-priced attorney stated.

Hannah felt relieved that it would soon be over, even if the verdict ended up being not guilty.

"Court is adjourned for lunch. We'll proceed with closing arguments at one," Judge Herman said as she tapped the gavel against the wooden puck.

Hannah sat with her brothers and the prosecutor at a long wooden table in the conference room near the prosecutor's office on the second floor of the courthouse. The prosecutor's administrative assistant entered the room with four Styrofoam boxes filled with pot roast, the daily special from the diner across the street. The prosecutor and her brothers dug in. She tried, but her swirling stomach played havoc with her ability to keep the food from threatening to come back up, so she closed the lid and pushed the box forward.

"Hannah, please eat something," Kane urged.

"I can't," she replied.

"Try. You can't lose any more weight. It's not healthy," her brother Lance added.

She knew that, but she couldn't help it. Maybe when the trial was over, she'd be able to eat again like she used to, without the threat of vomiting. Would she, though? The investigation into who murdered her parents and Alyssa was still ongoing. The district attorney had no one to charge. In her heart, she knew who to charge. She'd been staring at him for several days during this trial, but Sebastián had a rock-solid alibi. However, that didn't mean he or his dad hadn't contracted someone for the murders. That's what cartel people did, right? During the weeks between the horrible trip to the Upper Peninsula of Michigan and now, no further attempts on her or her brother's lives occurred. Lance would probably be safe when he returned to his Army base in Germany, but she and Kane would be here in Minnesota, in the wide open.

Thinking about the angry man from the gas station who'd chewed her out over coffee, she supposed there was still a chance he was the one who'd tried to kill her atop Lover's Leap Falls, but he certainly wouldn't have been the person to run her parents off the road. He'd no reason to. Plus, he would have had to hurry out of the woods and drive to Minnesota. That didn't seem likely. Who would go that far over coffee? Someone unhinged, she supposed. Nope, it was Sebastián, or someone his dad hired. Unless the gas station guy was who they hired.

Hannah closed her eyes and drew in a long breath. This whole thing was just exhausting.

When she opened her eyes, Kane slid her lunch closer to her and handed her a plastic fork.

"Eat."

She took the fork from her brother and picked at the pot roast.

"We're going to get a conviction," the prosecutor said.

Hannah looked at her. At this point, she wasn't sure if that was good or bad. For what Sebastián had done to her, she wanted him to spend years, if not the rest of his life, in prison. He'd kidnapped her and tried to kill her. He belonged in prison. On the other hand, how would his family retaliate if he was found guilty? A golf ball-sized lump formed in her throat. What would that mean for her and her brothers?

"From what was presented and the condemning evidence, how could he not be found guilty? The DNA doesn't lie," Kane replied.

"That's right," Lance added.

She pushed her food around on her plate again, then looked up. "That's what I'm afraid of. If he's found guilty, then what will he do, or his family do, to me...us? I feel like I should have just kept my mouth shut and moved on."

Kane's hand flew over hers. "No. You did the right thing. People like him need to be stopped. Would you want him doing what he did to you, to someone else?"

"No."

"Then this was the right thing to do. Now eat," Kane demanded.

She forked a few bites of pot roast into her mouth. That was all her rolling stomach could handle.

"It's time," the prosecutor said as she rose from her chair.

She and her brothers followed suit.

Once the people in the courtroom settled, closing arguments began, and after listening to both sides, the evidence was strong for a conviction, but who knew how it would go?

From what she had learned of the Garcias, she wouldn't be surprised if they threatened or paid off the jury.

At the conclusion of the closing arguments, the judge gave the jury instructions as to the expectations, including explaining the legal principles applicable to the case, and she informed them what they needed to consider to reach a verdict. The jury rose and exited the courtroom to begin their deliberations in the jury room. She tried to read the jurors' expressions as they exited the room, but not one of them made eye contact with her. However, one short, stout woman who looked to be in her early forties shared a long glance with Sebastián's father. The fear lacing the woman's gaze sent an eerie chill to snake up Hannah's spine. That was the juror the Garcias had gotten to. She'd stake her life on it. This would not end well.

Hannah spun around and watched the people exit the courtroom. There were so many people and press in the room. It had to be the Garcia family that drew the attention to this case, because it certainly wasn't her small family or limited circle of friends that filled a room that was bursting at the seams. Thinking of her friends made her think of Bianca, who'd seemed to fall off the face of the earth.

The old man with long gray hair and matching beard, who showed up every day, stepped into the aisle and headed toward the exit. He didn't so much as glance in her direction on his way out, but recalling his familiar eyes from their many shared glances had her racking her brain to figure out how she knew him. He had to be at least in his mid-sixties. Had he been a friend of her father? When the man stepped into the threshold, he glanced over his shoulder, meeting her gaze. He nodded and exited the courtroom.

"Still don't know who that is," Kane said to her.

Lance shook his head in unison with her.

"I'm going to see if I can catch him in the hall. Figure it out, so you know," Kane said as he made his way to the exit.

He returned a few minutes later and joined her and Lance in the hallway.

"I couldn't find him. I looked all over the hall, lobby, and even outside. It's like he vanished into thin air."

"I feel like he's here rooting for me, but why?" she said.

The jury deliberated for a couple of hours, then broke for the evening. They resumed deliberations at 8:00 a.m. the next morning. Hannah was sure she hadn't slept a wink and she felt as exhausted as she'd ever been.

At 9:30 a.m. court reconvened. Hannah's nerves were rattled, as the jurors returned to the jury box. Mistakenly, she risked a glance at Sebastián. If looks could kill, she'd be six feet under. That look from him meant he was worried. Good. He should be. But she was worried, too. If found innocent, would he—his family still retaliate? If found guilty, she was sure of it. How had it come to this? How had her life come to this? Since all this started, she felt like a pawn in a game she had no control over.

She glanced at her brothers, who sat to her left in the first row. Both offered reassuring looks. Needing a bit more reassurance, she looked for the old man. He wasn't in his usual spot. Every day he'd been in the courtroom, and today of all days, he wasn't. Of all days not to be here, the day she needed him most. What a strange thought, that she needed this stranger, but she did. The door creaked open, and he stepped through the threshold. He limped his way to the second row and squeezed himself into the aisle seat. Never had he sat this close to the front. Now that he was closer to her, she noticed that despite the gray hair and beard, he didn't look that old. His skin was not wrinkled. Not even around those warm, familiar eyes of his. The judge spoke, pulling her attention away from the stranger, and she focused on the front of the courtroom.

The jury foreperson rose. "On the charge of attempted murder, we find the defendant not guilty."

Sighs of relief sounded on the opposite side of the courtroom. Hannah's blood froze in her veins. Dread coiled in the pit of her stomach. Her pulse pounded, and she broke into a full-bodied sweat. Sebastián was going to walk. How could this be? The prosecutor glanced over her shoulder. The woman looked shocked, but not nearly as shocked as her brothers. What would this mean for her—them? Would they have to look over their shoulders for the rest of their lives? She couldn't breathe.

Kane placed his hand over hers.

"On the charges of kidnapping and assault, we find the defendant guilty."

A cry from Sebastián's mom rang out. Hannah snapped her head in that direction.

Out of the corner of her eye, she caught Sebastián's movement. He lunged toward her, knocking over his chair and his attorney. Hannah lurched to her feet to get away. The old man from the second row threw himself between her and Sebastián. Her brothers positioned themselves between the old man and her. Sebastián fought to get around the old man, only to be tossed aside like a rag doll, even with the sling on the man's arm. The court security officer pounced on Sebastián and pulled him to his feet. Still, Sebastián spewed comments of hatred toward her over his shoulder as the officer pulled him out of the courtroom. Sebastián's dad had stood and made a move toward her, but Kane and Lance stood in his way. He threw his hands in the air submissively, but the stone-cold look in his eyes let her know this wasn't over. The man's gaze bore the same hatred as Sebastián's.

Once the chaos settled, Hannah looked around for the old man who'd saved her from Sebastián's hands. There was no sign of him. Kane and Lance stepped away from Mr. Garcia and moved closer to her.

"Where is the old man?" Lance asked her.

"I don't know."

"You didn't see him leave?" Kane asked.

"No, I was focused on Sebastián and his mom and dad," she replied.

Kane quickly made his way to the exit. Dipped into the hall for a moment, then returned.

"I didn't see him in the hall. He was so quick to fly out of his seat and hurdle over the railing. I couldn't believe it. He moved like he's twenty years old," Kane said.

"Who is that guy, and why does he show up here day after day? It's like he comes in late and is the first to leave so that we can't find out who he is," Lance said.

"Maybe he'll be at the sentencing and we can find out more about him then," Kane said.

Though Hannah was more than curious to find out more about this mystery man, she was more interested in Sebastián's sentencing hearing. She'd hoped the judge would pass down the sentence right away, but with all the chaos just now, she suspected a delay, which was common practice anyway.

The judge slammed the gavel down. "Order!"

"We will take a thirty-minute recess and reconvene for the sentencing."

Hannah looked at the prosecutor. She looked as shocked as she felt regarding the immediate sentencing.

It was a long thirty minutes as she, the prosecutor, and her brothers discussed the verdicts. The prosecutor was in complete disbelief about the not guilty verdict on the attempted murder charge. She was convinced the Garcias got to the jurors, but if that were truly the case, he should have received not guilty verdicts on all the charges. The best she could hope for now was a long sentence for the kidnapping and assault convictions.

Hannah followed the prosecutor back into the courtroom. Her nerves rattled and her skin felt slick with sweat. They sat and waited. The room was eerily silent. The court security officer entered the room with Sebastián in his grip. She'd never seen such anger and disdain on a man's face as her ex displayed. Their gazes locked, and his heated gaze practically burned holes in her irises. No matter what happened with the sentencing, this would not be good for her and her brothers. The Garcias had already taken her parents and Alyssa from her. In her heart, she knew it, but there was no evidence to support that theory, so they would get away with it.

They rose when the judge entered the courtroom and then sat.

Hannah placed her entwined hands on her lap. Her grip was firm. She swallowed hard and braced herself for the outcome.

"The defendant shall rise," the judge ordered.

Sebastián stood.

"Having considered the overwhelming evidence in this case and the conduct displayed by Sebastián Garcia in the courtroom, it is the judgment of this court that you, Sebastián Garcia, are sentenced to ten years for the crimes of kidnapping and assault."

Sebastián's mom cried out. His dad looked stunned, and

his gaze flew to the jury box. The man's deadly glare was enough to scare the devil.

Hannah's hand flew over her mouth. This wasn't good for the jurors, or the juror Sebastián's father likely threatened to get the not guilty verdicts. Why wouldn't the jurors not go along with the not guilty on the kidnapping and assault, and only the attempted homicide charge? What price would they now pay? What price would she pay?

Chapter Sixteen

GREEN BAY WISCONSIN – *April 2025*

Orion's gaze stayed glued to the familiar woman as she wrapped up her marketing presentation. *Katrina Holmes.* That name was unrecognizable to him. But the portion of the tattoo she revealed a moment ago when she'd leaned slightly forward, had to belong to that beautiful butterfly tattoo he'd seen on Hannah Rice almost ten years ago. Just now, he'd only seen bright orange, outlined with black, but he'd put his life on the fact that what he saw were the tips of the wings of the butterfly. His heart raced. He had her within his reach. Finally.

To get out of this room, she'd have to get through him. He was tired of only dreaming of her. Nearly ten years had passed. Would she talk to him now? It was time. Her hiding —disappearance— was crazy. No, it actually wasn't. He fully understood why she'd done what she did. Her ex was part of a cartel. They'd killed her parents and her friend, so she made herself disappear. At least, that was how it appeared.

His heart sank, and dread coiled in his stomach at the thought she'd had to do this on her own. No help from the authorities. As he watched from afar, he knew she and the police could not prove the Garcias were responsible for Alyssa's murder and the accident that killed Hannah's parents. Though Sebastián Garcia was convicted of kidnapping and assaulting Hannah, the murders remained unsolved. Everyone knew the Garcias were behind the deaths, but they were never charged. So yes, it wasn't a surprise to him that Hannah made herself disappear. It was for the safety of all of them: hers, his, and her brothers.

Knowing what he knew, he should let her simply walk out of this room, but would he be able to? He loved her. She'd ruined him for all other women. There'd been a few in his life, but none that could measure up to her. Funny, though, he'd only spent one weekend with her. He kissed her twice, never had sex, but somehow knew she was the one for him.

He broke into a sweat. What if she'd met someone during the past ten years? A woman like her would surely have been scooped up by any man in his right mind. His gaze flew to her left hand. No ring. He sighed with relief. Then, in remembrance of her parting letter to him and the silent promise he'd made to her, sadness laced his next sigh.

"Thank you, Ms. Holmes, we'll be in touch," Aaron Carlson, his CFO, said, knocking him out of his reverie.

Shit. She was going to leave the room. He couldn't let that happen. Now that she'd practically been delivered to his front step, promise or not, this had to be a sign that it was meant to be, and he would not let her leave without at least talking to her.

After shaking Aaron's hand, she spun to leave without so much as a glance in his direction.

He stood.

"Ms. Holmes, may I have a minute?"

She stopped dead in her tracks for just a moment, then took another step away from him without looking back at him.

"Hannah."

She paused again, but this time she turned slowly toward him. His pulse ratcheted up a notch when she met his gaze.

His team's gaze was on him. They probably wondered why he'd just called Katrina, Hannah.

"I just need a moment with Ms. Holmes. You can all go," he said to his staff.

Aaron parted his lips as if he were going to speak, but then he simply exited the room with the rest of the crew, and shut the door behind him.

He would be content to stare into her bright emerald gaze forever, but he had questions for her. Lots of them.

When her eyes watered, he wanted to rush to her and wrap her in his arms, but his feet froze to the floor. What did she want him to do? Why were her eyes watering? Over the past ten years, had she thought about him at all? As much as he did her?

By the way she clutched her portfolio to her chest, he could only assume she was uncomfortable, maybe scared, but why would she fear him? They'd gotten along great in the short time they were together. He had abided by her wishes in the parting letter she'd left on his hospital bedside table almost ten years ago. She'd asked him not to contact her, thinking it was too dangerous for her, her brothers, and him. The last thing he wanted to do was put her and her few remaining family members in harm's way. She'd already suffered so much, losing her best friend and parents. He abided by her wishes. She believed the Garcias would harm him, her or anyone she was close to.

After the trial, she fell off the face of the earth. It was as if Hannah Rice disappeared. He'd tried to locate her several times over the years, not to see her in person, but hoping to see from afar that she was doing well. He'd even tried to find her brothers. They, too, were gone. Now that he saw the name Katrina Holmes, he realized, as he suspected, Hannah had intentionally disappeared. But she was delivered to him now, as if by fate.

Hannah cleared her throat. "What are you doing here? How did you find me?" she asked as her brows knit, "and why did those people listen to you?"

At her questions, it occurred to him that she didn't recognize his real name. Back then, when he'd first met her, he never used his given name. He went by Hunter, not Orion. Still, most times he used Hunter. He liked it better.

"Do you work here?" she followed up at his hesitation.

He grinned and nodded. "I own the stores," he beamed proudly.

He'd come a long way during the past ten years. His business had grown far beyond his expectations. To own five thriving sporting goods stores at the age of thirty-three made him proud.

Hannah cocked her head to the side, loosened her grip on her portfolio, and opened it.

"Orion Samuelson," she said.

"Yes. I'm Orion. My mother is a fan of Greek mythology and the stars, so she named me Orion, the God of hunting. Hence, Hunter."

She pulled her brows together as if confused by his statement.

"Imagine as a kid, being named Orion. Hunter seemed like a cooler name, so I adopted the nickname and it stuck."

Her almost scowl softened along with her gaze, but her stance remained stiff.

"You own all these stores?" she asked.

As if he couldn't even control it, his smile widened.

"I do."

"Wow."

The corners of her mouth lifted slightly.

"So, where did Katrina come from?"

"Katrina was my grandmother's name on my dad's side, and Holmes was my grandmother's maiden name on my mother's side. I didn't know how else to pick a new name."

"It's a nice name. How deep are you into hiding?" he asked, cutting to the chase.

Her facial features stiffened, and she pulled her portfolio tight to her chest again.

He cringed inside. Had he asked too much, too soon?

Her eyes shifted to the doorway, and he feared she'd bolt.

"I'm sorry. I shouldn't have asked," he stated.

"It's okay. I probably owe you an explanation for disappearing the way I did," she said in practically a whisper.

When he thought about it, she didn't really owe him anything. The Dear John letter she'd left behind almost ten years ago said it all. She cut him loose for his own good, as well as her well-being, and that of her brothers. They all knew in their hearts, the Garcias were responsible for three deaths, so for the safety of everyone, she disappeared. He got it.

"Share with me what you want. I don't want to pressure you."

She snagged her bottom lip with her teeth and hesitated, letting him know that at least a small part of her wanted to continue talking with him.

The door to the conference room opened, drawing his attention. Sally poked her head through the crack.

"Sorry to interrupt, but your four o'clock appointment is here. Do you want to meet with him in here or in your office?"

"My office. I'll be there in a minute."

She nodded and shut the door.

"Hannah, can I take you to dinner tonight so we can catch up?"

His heartbeat ratcheted up a notch when those familiar gold flecks sparked in her emerald eyes. She was going to accept his offer.

Silence.

When those sparks of gold faded, he knew he'd be disappointed at any moment now.

"I can't, and my name is Katrina."

Those words felt like a champion boxer's blow to his stomach. Her use of Katrina reaffirmed that Hannah no longer existed.

After all these years, they'd finally reconnected, only to have it end the same way—apart. He nearly doubled over in pain.

She spun and bolted out of the room.

He'd taken three long strides after her before he halted on a dime.

With as much as it pained him, he'd abide by her wishes. Pressing his palm to his chest did nothing to relieve the refreshed pain from the old wound.

. . .

Katrina practically ran out of the building, not allowing herself to glance back. She knew if she looked into Hunter's beautiful eyes one more time, she'd cave and leap into his arms. She had longed for the comfortable embrace of his arms countless times over the past ten years. Good heavens, she missed him. This hiding was bullshit, but had to be done. It was best for everyone.

Those damn Garcias. She loathed the day she met Sebastián and fell for his charms. Though it didn't take long for her to figure him out. She'd thought when he'd been sentenced to ten years, she'd freed herself from his and his family's control, but she was wrong. Every decision she'd made during the past ten years had been made with him in mind. What she called herself. Where she lived. Who she associated with. Her social media presence was nil because she didn't want to be found. Who in the hell at thirty-two didn't have a social media presence? She, that's who. Explain that to someone who wanted to connect.

She started her SUV and pulled out of the parking lot of the downtown headquarters of Stars Sporting Goods.

Stars Sporting Goods. Now that she thought about it, Hunter or Orion, was named after a constellation, so the *Star* name made complete sense.

How had they both ended up living in the same city and not run into each other? Wait, did he actually live in Green Bay? His five stores were located throughout Wisconsin and the Upper Peninsula of Michigan. Did he live in the U.P.? She recalled how much he loved it up there, working for his uncle as a guide. She sank into her seat. She'd never know. because she could never make contact with him again. So much for landing this account and the promotion it would likely garner her. Damn, Sebastián. Damn him for ruining her life.

Katrina pulled into her single-stall garage unit and immediately shut the door, as she always did. Most of the other apartment dwellers left the doors open during the day and into the evening, but not her. She wasn't that trusting. Her doors and windows were always locked. Though Sebastián was still in prison, she feared his and his family's reach.

She exited the garage using the utility door that led to the stairs to her small two-bedroom apartment above the garage. The smaller of the bedrooms she used as an office, since she could work remotely most days. She didn't enjoy the loneliness of rarely leaving her apartment, but she preferred the security of it. Not being seen was a good thing.

She set her portfolio on the desk and stared at it in disappointment. Not that the presentation went poorly. In fact, it went well. The disappointing part was that she couldn't accept the account, if offered. Especially since Sebastián would be released from prison in several months. Would he search for her? Would he search for Hunter to find her?

She logged into her computer to check her email. Then, she clicked on the pictures file and migrated to the pictures Alyssa had taken while on their trip to the U.P. Chief Ricco had retrieved Alyssa's camera from atop Lover's Leap Falls along with all of her, Bianca's, and Alyssa's other belongings they'd taken on their trip. The camera had broken when Alyssa fell—when she'd been shot. Luckily, her techie friend was able to retrieve the photos from the broken device. That hole of despair in Katrina's heart widened as she recalled the memories of that fateful day.

Unable to resist, she flipped through the photos. Admittedly, the trip started slowly because she was a little edgy. Her prickliness resulted from the pending trial, not the company she kept or the nature of the trip. She loved both. Hunter's smiling face lit up the screen. Alyssa had taken a lot of photos of him. Actually, she'd taken a lot of photos in general. That was her thing. Not many photos of herself though. She'd only set up the delay photo option a few times to capture all of them in pictures. Alyssa was very photogenic. Dark hair framed her creamy, flawless skin, and her big, dark eyes emitted warmth.

Tears blurred Katrina's vision. Her friend was beautiful inside and out and would forever be twenty-two. That was so sad. Alyssa had been full of life and was ready to hit the ground running after college. She'd planned to work with her mother in the interior design department of their family-owned furniture gallery. With her taste, she would have been great at that.

The next photo was of Bianca. Her icy blue eyes sparkled in every photo. No doubt Bianca was model-grade with her beautiful, long, blonde hair and slim physique. When the camera came out, Bianca practically threw herself in front of it. But she was not nearly the friend that Alyssa was to her. Katrina always knew that. Bianca was self-centered, but they were still friends through college. What was disappointing, though, was how Bianca seemed to fall off the face of the earth the second Alyssa had been murdered. She didn't even support her through the trial. Nothing. It was like she didn't exist, even before she became Katrina.

With a click of the mouse, a photo of the four of them centered on the computer monitor. Bianca on one side of Hunter, her on the other side, and then Alyssa at her side.

Bianca leaned into Hunter with a possessive hand placed on his chest. His right arm draped over Bianca's shoulders, but his body tilted toward her, and she recalled how he'd placed his other arm around her, sloping downward, pulling her to his side in a similar possessive way that Bianca seemed to hold him. His fingers wrapped around her waist as hers wrapped around his. Their slight turn toward each other, as shown in the photo, reaffirmed their feelings for one another. This probably pissed off Bianca. She wasn't used to a man liking anyone other than her.

Katrina stared at that photo for a long time. Mostly, she studied Hunter, recalling the kisses they'd shared during that trip. Her lips warmed at the thought. A couple of hours ago, she was within an inch of throwing herself into this man's arms again. Once he'd entered the room during her presentation, she could think of nothing else. His warm chestnut irises were like a magnet. That rich, earthy scent of his that held a blend of cedar and dark chocolate filled the conference room, unleashing warm memories of their stolen moments. He really hadn't changed much through the years. His thick, dark hair was cut shorter now, probably a result of the professional image he needed to keep. He was still muscular and lean. Sexy as sin.

Her heart fluttered. Why did she have to run into him after all this time? It wasn't fair to have to summon the strength to separate from him again. Damn Sebastián.

"Oh, Hunter, if only we'd met under other circumstances," she whispered to no one.

Katrina placed her fingertips to her lips and then to the computer screen like she'd done hundreds of times before. This was it for them. This was their final story—how it would end. They could never be together.

Chapter Seventeen

A KNOCK SOUNDED on Hunter's door. He looked up to find his right-hand man and CFO standing in the doorway. "Katrina Holmes with Jameson and Holt declined. Do you want me to make the offer to Bayland Marketing?" he asked with little emotion.

The man's lack of emotion didn't surprise him. Aaron was a no-nonsense guy, and any of the four marketing firms they interviewed could certainly do the job, but the executive team decided they liked Katrina's presentation best and offered the account to her firm. Bayland ranked second. He certainly supported his team's ranking. Especially since she came out on top, but he knew she'd decline the offer.

"Not yet. Give me her contact information."

"I'll email it."

"Okay."

"Did she give a reason?"

Aaron shrugged. "Something about not being a good fit, which makes no sense at all. It's a marketing firm. They market all different types of products. But whatever."

Aaron spun around and exited the room.

How in the hell was he going to leave her alone as she wished, and get her to accept the marketing contract offer at the same time? He could reach out to the owners of Jameson and Holt and make sure they knew of the offer which could force her into accepting it, but that would probably make him look like a controlling ass and might get her into trouble if they found out she declined the offer. No, that idea wasn't an option.

Dammit. He needed to accept that they would never be together, but he didn't want to, especially since he'd laid eyes on her again. She was all he thought about over the past three days.

He couldn't sleep. His stomach swirled with anxiety to the point he couldn't eat. He couldn't even think straight. As for his chest, for chrissake, he thought he was having a heart attack. These feelings hadn't been this strong since the initial weeks following her cutting him loose almost ten years ago. Why did she have to pop up in his life after all this time? Now that she had, he didn't know if he had the strength to walk away from her again.

Screw it. He opened his email to find one from Aaron with Katrina's contact info, then he yanked the handset off the phone and dialed her number. On the third ring, Hunter assumed she would avoid the call altogether since Stars Sporting Goods likely popped up on her phone display.

"Katrina Holmes, how may I help you?"

His heart instantly fluttered at the sound of her sweet voice.

"Hi. It's Hunter. My CEO just informed me you declined our offer."

After a couple of beats of silence, she replied, "That's true."

"I'm sorry to hear that. Your credentials and pitch were the best of all the competing firms, and we'd love to have you handle this account."

It was difficult to speak professionally and not beg her to take the job on a personal level. He hoped this approach would have her reconsider taking the job.

"It's very kind of you to call, but I just don't think it is a good idea."

The crack of her voice at the end of her sentence let him know that this happenstance meeting of theirs had put her in a tailspin of emotions as well.

"Will you at least think about it for a few days?"

"I can't." But there was enough hesitation before she answered that he knew she wanted to.

"Katrina..." he said and paused. It didn't sound right to call her Katrina rather than Hannah, but he'd do it to prove he could keep her secret. Maybe that way she'd reconsider taking the job and seeing him.

He cleared his throat. "Katrina Holmes, I'd like to take you to dinner tonight. How does six o'clock at Malone's Steak House sound? I can pick you up at five-thirty, or we could meet there if you'd prefer."

The silence was excruciating. He'd never felt so vulnerable. He wanted to see her so badly.

"I don't like to be seen in public much."

He blew out a relieved breath. It wasn't a hard no.

"I'm a master at grilling steaks. I can cook for you at my place, or bring takeout to yours."

Like a teenager, he crossed his fingers, waiting for her response.

"It's probably best and more discreet for me to come to your place. Text me your address. What can I bring?"

Adrenaline rushed through him so hard, his extremities shook.

He drew in a breath to calm himself.

"Just yourself. I'll text my address. See you at five-thirty."

"Okay. Bye."

Hunter hung up the phone receiver and leaped out of his chair. After pacing his large office a couple of times, he sat back down and mentally prepared his menu. He'd grill some ribeyes, potatoes, and asparagus. For dessert, some Dutch apple pie with ice cream. The steaks he'd pick up from Downtown Market. They had the best steaks and nothing but the best for Hannah. Katrina, he reminded himself. That part was going to be difficult. The rest of the items he'd get at the supermarket. This meal had to be perfect. This night had to be perfect.

Though the office closed at five o'clock, he left at four. He liked to lead by example, so he rarely left early, but today he practically ran out of the building an hour early. At Downtown Market, he picked out the two biggest ribeyes they had. At the supermarket, he grabbed the vegetables, pie, ice cream, and two bottles of red wine. He had beer at the house, but maybe she liked wine. He didn't know, and he wanted to be prepared.

Once home, he seasoned the steaks and busied himself with cleaning up his large house. It wasn't like it was a mess or anything; he lived alone, but he tidied up the papers on his desk in his home office. Then, he organized the sporting goods samples wholesalers had sent to him for review, hoping he'd stock them in his stores. He loved trying out new products.

He returned to the kitchen, grabbed the potatoes, and put them on the grill just outside the sliding patio doors.

Back inside, he dusted off the dining room table that he never used, but planned to use tonight. Then, he snagged the table settings from the cupboards.

Why was he so nervous? Why, because the stakes were high and he had everything to lose all over again.

Katrina wrapped her nervous fingers around her steering wheel so tightly her knuckles turned white.

Relax.

She shouldn't have agreed to this dinner, but couldn't help herself. She wanted to be with Hunter. Her desire for this man had always been strong, but until she saw him again three days ago, she'd done a good job of ignoring her desire to see him.

Seeing him in person, hearing his deep voice, staring into those warm chestnut eyes had her arguing with herself to let him back into her life. Still, the danger was real, and if the Garcias connected her to Hunter, it could mean trouble for both of them.

A lump rose in her throat. She'd put Hunter, her family, and friends in danger before, and it didn't end well for most of them. After she and her brothers changed their names and went into their own form of hiding, the fear of threats to their lives lessened. Her brother's fear as well, she assumed, because as far as she knew, her brothers had never actually been threatened. She wondered if their hiding stopped threats, or were there never any to begin with? Since Sebastián was in prison, that probably had something to do with it as well. Yet his family was still on the loose. Maybe the Garcias thought better of more deaths in her family and the negative attention it would bring them. How was it that nobody other than her and her brothers could see that the

Garcias were behind the murders of Alyssa and her parents? Would things change when Sebastián got out of prison? Would he come after her?

Katrina spun her car around and headed back to her apartment. Being with Hunter was too risky, and she needed to cut him off now, before she got in so deep that she couldn't.

Tears of anger burned her eyes. *Dammit.* She had a life to live and wanted so badly to live it.

She pulled a U-turn at the next intersection and drove toward Hunter's home located on Eagle Lake. Eagle Lake was in Door County, south of Sturgeon Bay. She'd seen the sign for it plenty of times when she frequented the state parks in Door County, but she'd never actually viewed the lake.

Once on the highway, it only took a few minutes to see the sign. She turned right onto the county road lined with woods. About a mile or so down the road, the woods cleared, and the large homes that lined the lake came into view. To live in this neighborhood was another sign that Hunter had done well for himself.

According to the GPS, she could see that Hunter's home was on the north side of the lake, settled on a point. Most of the homes looked new, and the newer ones were much larger than the few older ones, which seemed little more than cottages. The earlier settlers on the lake, she presumed.

A large, two-story log home came into view, and before verifying the house number on the mailbox, she knew that it was Hunter's. That style of home suited him. It looked lovely.

She pulled into the driveway and cut the engine. Before she even opened the door, Hunter stood next to her vehicle.

"I'm so glad you came," he said.

The well remembered amber hues of his eyes comforted her, wiping away some of the anxiety swirling in her brain.

"Me, too," she replied.

His smile widened.

"Welcome to my humble abode," he said as he gestured toward his home, which certainly did not qualify as humble.

"Thank you. It looks lovely."

"Let me give you the outside tour, then we'll go in."

She nodded as she flung her handbag over her shoulder and shut the SUV door.

"Well, here's the front," he said with a nervous chuckle that showed he was as nervous as she was.

"The back is where it's at, though," he said as he stepped onto a stamped concrete pathway leading downward as it wrapped around the home.

She hesitated for a moment before she fell into step with him. The black T-shirt he wore fit snugly around his shoulders and biceps. His muscles were thicker than what she'd remembered. Maybe years of working out had done that. He was slim at the waist. The jeans he wore snugged his thighs. He was a mouthwatering sight, no matter the angle she saw him from.

Once in the backyard, she understood his earlier comment about the back being where it was at.

"Oh my, this is beautiful," she said as she stared out over the small lake.

It was a sunny April evening, and the lake sparkled from the sunrays. Several docks and boats were already in the water for the season. A large dock jutted out from Hunter's property, but there was no boat tied up to it.

"Yeah, she's a great little lake. Good for a lot of activities. Swimming, paddle boarding, kayaking, even waterskiing."

"I bet you just love that," she replied.

His wide smile reached his eyes.

"I do. You know me."

That she did, or felt like she did, though they'd only spent a small amount of time together many years ago.

She spun to look at his house. The walkout basement led to a good-sized patio that housed an enormous stone fireplace, some outdoor furniture still covered up, and a grill emitting a mouthwatering scent. Lifting her gaze upward, she eyed the wall of windows on the first and second floors of the home. Windows stretched from the ground to the rooftop in the center of the home but tapered off toward the sides. The logs used for the home were large and a light brown color with red undertones, a perfect color for a home of this type.

"It's beautiful. I can't wait to see the inside," she said.

She walked alongside Hunter toward the patio, where he stopped to check on their meal.

"How do you like your steak?"

"Medium well to well."

"Great, me too," he said as he flipped the steaks.

They entered the house at the lowest level, which sported a wooden bar flanked with tall chainsaw eagle carvings. The room held a pool table, a dart game, and a large television with a few theater seats in front of it.

Hunter pointed to a doorway to the right. "That's just the basement full of stuff."

He pointed to the left. "Utility room and stairs leading up to the garage."

She nodded, then she followed him up the steps in the center of the room, which brought them into the grand living room. The floor-to-ceiling windows she'd seen from the outside were part of the open concept living room, kitchen, and dining room area.

Everything about his home was stunning.

"Would you like something to drink? Beer, wine, soda?" he asked.

"A glass of wine would be nice."

She needed that to take the edge off. She was happy to be here, but scared and nervous.

"Merlot?"

"Perfect."

He pulled a bottle from the freestanding canoe-shaped, metal wine rack next to the kitchen counter and poured them each a glass.

"Cheers," he said, and they clinked glasses.

"I'd better go grab those steaks and potatoes before they're extra crispy. I'll be right back. Make yourself at home," he said as he grabbed a tray from the kitchen island and disappeared back down the stairs they'd just come up.

She watched him out the window. He was a sight for sore eyes, for sure.

When he returned, he set the tray on the counter and then placed the steaks and potatoes onto plates and handed one to her. He led her to the dining room table, where he'd already placed the silverware and condiments.

The room was awkwardly quiet.

"The steak tastes wonderful."

He grinned.

"Thank you."

More silence and gaze avoidance.

Hunter's chest rose with the deep breath he took.

"I'm going to cut to the chase. I don't know why this seems so hard. I couldn't wait for you to get here, and I had so many questions I planned to ask you about how you are doing and what you've been up to, but I'm hesitant to ask," he blurted.

She stared into his caring eyes. He reached over and placed his large, warm hand over hers. The familiar comfort of his touch was overwhelming. She wanted to tell him everything. He was one of the few people who already knew some of the details, but the less he knew, the better. Other than her two brothers, she was close to no one. It was too hard. New friends wanted to know her past, like any friend would. The simplest of questions she couldn't answer. Where did you grow up? Where did you go to school? What are your parents like? Are you going home for Christmas? Her old life as Hannah was a past she couldn't share, and she hated telling the story of her made-up life. Sometimes, especially in the beginning, she'd slip up on the details of her alter-life, and that made her look like a liar. It became easier not to make friends. It was a lonely life. Her brothers felt the same.

"Han...Katrina, you don't need to tell me anything you don't want to."

He just slipped up, almost calling her Hannah. She shouldn't be here. She should jerk her hand back, but she couldn't. Didn't want to.

She nodded.

He pulled his hand back, forked a piece of meat, and popped it into his mouth. His gaze stayed on her.

She cleared her throat. "I never thought my life would turn out this way. It got so derailed."

He nodded.

"Every day, I think back to that hiking trip when I met you. Even before that, when I met Sebastián. If I had just made different decisions."

184

"Whoa," Hunter said as he held up his hand in the stop position. "You didn't do anything wrong."

She hung her head.

"Katrina, look at me."

Slowly, she lifted her head to meet his gaze.

"Obviously, I don't know everything that transpired leading up to what Sebastián did to you, but the version of Katrina Holmes that I know is a smart, kind, intelligent woman. He caused this. Not you. You can play the coulda, woulda, shoulda game all day long, but he did this, not you."

"I keep trying to tell myself that, but it's hard."

He covered her hand with his again.

"The guilty verdict and his prison sentence are proof that it was all him," Hunter said with conviction and a hint of anger in his tone.

"Yeah, but he got away with killing Alyssa and my parents. I know he did it. Or at least had something to do with their deaths, but nobody could prove it. And...we believe his family is in a cartel. I can't prove it, but I know it. I just do, which was the main reason for the change in identity."

It was still difficult for her to say that out loud, even though nearly ten years had passed.

He gripped her hand more firmly.

"And he's due to get out soon. On the one hand, I can't believe so much time has passed already. The memory of it all is still raw. I live it every day with my new identity."

"Makes sense. Well, with your new identity, he shouldn't be able to find you. I mean, the witness protection program should keep you safe, right?"

"Sadly, I didn't qualify for witness protection."

His brows knit.

"But your name."

"My brothers and I did this on our own. We had little family left, so we just made ourselves disappear. We took on new names, moved, and cut off all ties with family and friends. It was best for everyone. My brothers wouldn't let me do it alone, so they made the sacrifice as well."

The expression on Hunter's face was one of compassion.

"I'm so sorry for all of this. That must have been so hard."

"It was...is. But in any case, I hope our hiding pays off when Sebastián is released. I fear he'll look for me. I already feel like I'm always looking over my shoulder for his family or a hired hand. It will be worse when he's on the loose, too. And what if he tries to find me through old friends...you?"

She choked down the obstruction that clogged her throat.

"Which is why I shouldn't be here."

Her eyes watered. She'd thought about Hunter so many times and missed him. Though she hardly knew him—hadn't spent but a few days with him, the connection they shared was strong.

Hunter's shoulders rose and fell with his quick breaths. His hand perspired. Or was that hers? He flew off his chair and pulled her into a protective embrace.

She melted to him.

"I'm so sorry, Han...Katrina. So sorry you've had to live like this."

The sincerity in his voice brought more tears.

"You've been so brave. I wish I could have helped you."

If she hadn't cut him off, maybe he could have. The warm body she pressed herself to, reminded her of all she'd lost by making that decision. Inhaling, she took in that earthy scent of his. The cedar notes further reminded her of their time spent together, making her regret the decision to go into hiding.

He loosened his grip a smidge and ran one of his hands up and down her back comfortingly. Why did he have to do that? It was making her feel worse, yet better at the same time.

She should have never come here. She needed to cut this off now. If she didn't, she may never be able to.

Her body stiffened. His did the same.

"Please don't," he said.

Pushing away, she put two steps between them.

"I have to."

She spun and snagged her purse off the counter.

"One kiss then and I'll leave you alone," he said.

More than anything right now, she wanted that, and she risked a glance at him. The amber hues in his irises pleaded for her to agree. She had to stop looking into his eyes or she'd cave, so she lowered her gaze. It landed on his mouth. That mouth that had delivered kisses she'd thought about every day. Would one simple kiss hurt? Her betraying heart tried to rationalize with her brain.

Her lack of verbal response answered his question. He stepped forward and cupped her cheeks with his palms, and then, about as slowly as anyone could, he leaned forward and lightly pressed his mouth to hers.

Though it wasn't but a wisp of a feathery touch, her heart beat wildly. When he edged back, her lips protested, and she leaned toward him. The amber flecks in his eyes sparkled, and he pressed his lips to hers again.

Slow, soft kisses ensued. Unleashing the full force of the feelings she'd suppressed for him. She reached up and gripped his muscular shoulders, pulling him tightly to her.

His hands slid down from her cheeks and hooked at the small of her back, holding her firmly to his body.

When she parted her lips, his warm tongue dipped into her mouth. The pleasant hint of merlot on his tongue seeped into hers. The kiss turned deeper and hotter. She welcomed the intensity of it, encouraged it even. The feel of him in her mouth and against her body was even more fulfilling than she'd remembered from years ago. She'd longed for him more times than she could count. Now, here he was. She'd never imagined she'd get to kiss him again, but fate brought them together, and she loved every second. Perhaps she should pinch herself to make sure it was truly happening.

They kissed and kissed and kissed. It was sensational. She wanted to do this forever. Stay lost in the moment, but that wasn't realistic. None of this was realistic.

Hunter pulled back, but kept his arms loosely around her. The desperation in his dark gaze tugged at her heart.

"Are you sure we can't figure out a way to be with each other?"

"I wish we could, but the risk…"

"Shouldn't I get a say in that decision?" he asked.

She sighed.

"We don't even know for sure what or if Sebastián will do anything when he gets out. Hell, we don't even know if he had anything to do with…" he stopped mid-sentence.

"The murders," she finished for him.

He was right. She'd often wondered if she was too hasty in her decision to go into hiding. Who knew for sure? When doubt overshadowed her, she convinced herself she only questioned her decision out of selfishness and her desire to be with the man standing before her. She had to stay strong.

"Trust me when I say I'd love to give up hiding and live

my life without always looking over my shoulder, but the dread that is coiled deep in my gut tells me to stay on full alert."

He dropped his arms to his sides and stepped back.

"I understand."

Her chest squeezed. This was it. She swallowed hard. He was just going to accept this? Why did that upset her and make her sad? He only agreed to do what she'd asked.

She spun to leave.

"Just know one thing before you go."

She stilled in her tracks but didn't look back at him.

"I love you."

Her heart hitched, and tears flooded her eyes. That was the last thing she wanted to hear from him, yet the thing she needed to hear most. He wasn't playing fair.

Without so much as a glance back, she exited his home. Regret in every footstep.

Chapter Eighteen

THE SPRING SUN peeked through the window blinds, distracting Katrina from falling back to sleep. Who was she kidding? She hadn't slept for nearly a week since she'd had dinner with Hunter. Her heart sank. Hunter. If only she hadn't run into him. If she'd just put two and two together before accepting the interview at his company, she could have turned it down and avoided him. But no, and now she realized the man she longed for was within reach. Recalling his hold and kisses warmed her, yet saddened her. *Dammit.*

She flung back the covers, rolled out of bed and moseyed into the kitchen to start coffee. As part of her Sunday routine, she called up the online version of the Minnesota Press. Though she hadn't lived in Minnesota for almost ten years, she still liked to keep up on the news there, her small hometown news in particular. She missed the Northwoods. Not always the extreme winter cold, but missed it nonetheless.

The Minnesota Press had changed through the years, focusing less on the smaller communities and more on the

Twin Cities. She still got a few nuggets of information about her hometown and the people she'd left behind.

The coffee pot buzzed, and she rose from her chair to nab a cup of hot, strong black brew. Back at her laptop on the kitchen table, she scrolled, stopping on the crime report page. Twelve hundred and twenty-two assault offenses so far this year. Eighty-three sex offenses and two homicides. Wow, not much had changed in the past decade from when she first thought to check the numbers after she'd been assaulted.

She clicked on the headlines tab. The shock of the first headline nearly knocked her off her chair. Her breaths came quickly. Her heart raced. Extremities went numb. The computer screen faded to black. No, that was her vision. She placed her palms on the tabletop and squeezed her eyes shut, and rested her cheek on the edge of the table. It couldn't be. It just couldn't.

After choking down the lump in her throat, she sucked in a breath and let it out slowly, then she lifted her head and opened her eyes. Blinking rapidly, she cleared her vision. ***Hennepin County Assistant District Attorney Disappears***. The professional photo was of the assistant district attorney who prosecuted Sebastián's case. Katrina skimmed the article. The ADA didn't show up to work on Thursday. Neither family nor friends knew of her whereabouts.

Katrina sprang from her chair and double-checked her door to make sure it was locked. She shouldn't have to, because she had probably checked it three times before she'd gone to bed. She returned to her laptop to read the brief article again.

She supposed the list of suspects could be a long one, as the ADA charged a lot of criminals and prosecuted some as well. At least Sebastián shouldn't be on that list since he was still in prison, yet the anxiety swirling in the pit of her stomach told her it was a possibility. After reading the article a third time, she moved on to another story. Then another. Typical stuff. She moved on to the state news. ***Prison Overcrowding Causes Early Releases.*** What? She couldn't have read that title correctly, so she reread it. Overcrowding. What in the hell? Who cared if they were overcrowded? There was a reason they were sentenced to a specific period, and they should have to serve that time. She continued to read. No! Her hand flew over her mouth. It couldn't be. *No, no, no.*

She flew out of her chair again and checked the lock on her door, then she grabbed her cell phone and paced her tiny kitchen as if she were a caged animal.

"Hello," her brother, Kane, aka Kent Holmes, said.

"He's out. Sebastián is out of prison, and the ADA is missing!"

"What?"

"I just read it in the Minnesota Press. Because of over-crowding, there was an early release of prisoners. Anyone set for release in the next two years, who served over five years, was released. Sebastián was set for release later this year. He's out!"

"Are you sure?"

"Yes!"

"Okay. Okay. We prepared for this. Right? You're safe. You'll be fine. We have new identities and have made no contact with anyone from our past."

Silence.

"Katrina?"

Silence.

"Katrina?" he said louder, snapping her out of her reverie about Hunter.

"I need to tell you something. I ran into Hunter."

"Hunter?"

Her brother said that as if the name didn't click with him.

She inhaled slowly and let it out as slowly as she took it in.

"The guide from Yooper Adventures."

Now it was her brother's turn for silence.

"It was a total accident, but he recognized me and he knows we're in hiding, but not formal hiding."

"Does he know that the Garcias are a cartel?"

"Yes."

"Shit!"

"I know. It was purely an accident. I was pitching a new client, and he walked in. Turns out he owns the company."

"You didn't know that going in?" her brother asked accusingly.

"No. The name on the company material was different. It said his name was Orion, not Hunter."

"Jeez, you couldn't put that together?"

That comment made her feel stupid. Obviously, Kent connected the names immediately.

"I'm sorry. I didn't mean that the way it sounded. I'm just a bit on edge," Kent said before she could reply.

"What are we going to do?" she asked in desperation.

"Nothing. We have new identities. We'll be fine. I can try to reach Logan to let him know, but he's hard to reach when deployed."

"What if Sebastián tries to find us through people we once knew...like Hunter?"

"We've done a good job of disappearing. Living up to

our new identities. We'll be fine," her brother assured. "As for Hunter, he was just a guide. Sebastián would have no reason to think he could find you through him."

That was true, yet she was still worried.

"Did you get the job?"

"I got the offer, but turned it down. If my boss finds out, I'll probably get fired. It was a big account. Hopefully, he'll think we just didn't get the offer."

"That's probably good you turned it down."

So, her brother worried about the connection to Hunter, too.

"What now?" she asked.

"We go on as normal. You still carrying?" he asked.

"Yes."

She'd gotten her concealed carry permit immediately after Sebastián had tried to kill her. He'd been out on bail, and she felt she needed to protect herself, just in case he came after her again.

"I'm sorry, but I have to go. I'll call you later. You'll be fine. We'll all be fine," her brother assured.

"I know. Bye."

Goosebumps lined her arms. Though she'd told him she'd be fine, she wasn't sure.

Hunter stared at the cell phone in his hand, debating calling Katrina like he'd done at least one hundred times since last Tuesday. *Katrina.* Part of him couldn't get used to the new name. Not that he didn't like the name, but it was Hannah whom he'd first met and fallen in love with. To have her, though, he'd gladly comply.

His heart begged him to call her, but his brain rejected the idea. It was for her own safety. He understood her concern, but didn't like it at all. His pulse pounded as he selected her from the contact list on his cell phone, but his shaky thumb prevented him from pressing the call button.

He tossed the phone onto the kitchen countertop and put his back to it, as if not seeing the phone would help him fight the urge to call her. The illogical part of his brain took over, and he snatched the phone off the counter and hit the call button.

After the third ring, he debated hanging up. She wasn't going to answer. Ever. He knew it. She was scared, and withdrawal was the easiest and safest for everyone involved.

"Hello."

Stunned by the fact she answered, he was speechless.

"Hunter?"

"Yes. Han...Katrina," he stuttered.

At the rate he couldn't seem to remember to call her by her new name, it would take some work to convince her he could live with her new identity. He had to pull it together before he lost her again.

"Katrina, I know we have some things to deal with, but I need to see you again. I can't stop thinking about you."

There, he laid it on the line. He held his breath, waiting —preparing for a rejection.

"It's gotten worse, which is why I answered your call."

She sounded defeated.

He closed his eyes, leaned his head back, and let out his breath. Then, he opened his eyes and lifted his head into the normal position.

"What happened?"

"I just found out that Sebastián received an early release."

"What?" Hunter squeaked out.

"I guess the Minnesota prisons are overcrowded and the

state, in its infinite wisdom, released anyone with less than two years left on their sentence and who've already served five years. Sebastián was due for release in a few months."

"Are you sure he's out? And if so, when was he released?"

"I haven't verified it with anyone yet. I just saw the news article this morning. It's Sunday. I'll have to wait until tomorrow to call...I don't know who to call."

She sniffled.

Dammit. She was crying, and he wasn't there to comfort her.

"Let me come to you. We'll figure this out. What's your address?"

Her hesitation worried him. She was going to shut him down.

"There's more," she replied, ignoring his request for her address.

"What is it?" he dreaded asking.

She sniffled again.

His hand tightened around the phone.

"The assistant district attorney who prosecuted his case has gone missing."

Of all the things she could have said, he hadn't expected to hear that.

"You think he has something to do with that?"

"Well, the timing works. All these prisoners are being released, and now she goes missing."

"That doesn't mean it was Sebastián. It could be any of them, or even someone else," he tried to assure her.

A burning sensation and sharp pain shot through his right shoulder, and he pressed his left hand to it. It wasn't warm to the touch, yet his skin burned. What in the hell? Why did it hurt suddenly? Then he realized the exact spot of the pain. It was where the bullet had ripped through his flesh atop Lover's Leap Falls. Strange. The phantom pain in that spot had disappeared years ago, but now, at the mention of Sebastián's name and the disappearance of the assistant district attorney had caused it to return.

"I know it could be, but still, it's a possibility. We're talking about the cartel here."

"That's just it. The cartel. Certainly, if they wanted to do something to the assistant district attorney, they would have done it long ago."

"True. I thought that, too. I guess I just want everyone involved to be aware of the possible danger."

So, she thought of him as *Involved*.

Her quick breaths and sniffles broke his heart.

"Please let me come to you."

"I can't."

"Then come here."

"I can't. It's for your own safety."

"So, I don't even get a say?" That came out edgier than he'd hoped.

"No. Please take care of yourself."

She disconnected the call before he could reply.

His chest squeezed as if belted. That was it? Done? No. That was bullshit. He'd finally reconnected with her, and he would not let her go again.

God, his shoulder hurt almost as much as his rejected heart.

He went into the bathroom and yanked his T-shirt over his head, and studied the round, purplish, jagged-edged scar on his right shoulder. Surgery, followed by months of physical therapy, and he was able to regain ninety percent mobility. Every now and then, he was reminded it wasn't one hundred percent. It was usually when he did strenuous sporting activities. Right now, his shoulder burned as if the flesh had just been torn open. Since that wasn't the case, he pulled his shirt back on and ignored the phantom pain.

Weren't the scars he bore from that horrible day atop Lover's Leap a rite of passage to Katrina? Shouldn't she give him some decision-making authority? For chrissake, he'd been shot, had two nasty scars on his head that required his hair to be shaved off in order to stitch them up, and he had had more bumps and bruises than he could count on his arms, legs, and torso. And now, he didn't get any decision-making authority? This was bullshit.

He dialed her number again. No answer. Anger had him dialing again. Nothing.

Rethinking his actions, he blew out a sigh and tossed the phone back onto the counter, supposing the last thing she needed was another man in her life trying to control her. That didn't work out so well the last time for her. If he wanted a chance at staying in her life, he needed a better plan.

He sank into his oversized leather recliner and thought. What would be a better plan?

Hell, he didn't know. He just knew he needed one. Maybe his sister Cici could help, but calling her would involve another person in this mess and maybe put her in danger. For now, he'd have to come up with a plan on his own.

Chapter Nineteen

From the driveway, Katrina stared at Hunter's beautiful log home. She didn't remember driving here, but here she sat.

His pleas on the phone tugged at her heart. The hurt in his voice when she shot down his request for a say in the matter brought more tears. The man had done nothing wrong. In fact, he'd done everything right by risking himself to save her. He'd wrapped her in his protective hold and thrown them both over Lover's Leap Falls, even after getting shot. He never even hesitated. He just reacted.

Then, he abided by her wish to stay away. Until recently, when they happened upon each other by accident. Guilt consumed her after she ignored his calls earlier in the day. She couldn't stand herself. And now, here she was in his driveway. Still, she debated going in. She wanted to, but should she?

Before she cut the engine, she glanced around one more time to see if anyone had followed her. It didn't appear so.

She slid out of the car and hurried to his front door and

depressed the doorbell. When the door opened, she threw herself into his arms.

"I'm sorry."

"For what?"

"For all of it. Getting you shot. Putting you in danger. For ignoring your calls. For all of it."

She sobbed into his chest. He pulled her into the house, kicked the door shut, and held her firmly. She couldn't stop crying. Years of pent-up fear and anxiety had taken over as if she had no say about it.

"Shh. It'll be okay. It'll all be fine. I'm not going to let him hurt you again," Hunter whispered into her ear.

She wished that were true, but she honestly believed Sebastián was capable of anything. The fact that he was likely out of prison now provided a better opportunity for him to get even with her for what she'd put him through. The trial and almost ten years in prison. Without a doubt, she knew he'd come out of prison an angry man.

When her tears subsided, she edged away from Hunter's comforting hold, but he protested only by letting her slip back a few inches. His warm gaze held hers as he slid his hands from around her back, up to her shoulders, then farther until his palms rested on either side of her head. He used his thumbs to swipe the moisture from her cheeks.

His soul-searching stare bore into her, warming every cell of her being.

"I'm so glad you came here. Everything will be okay. I will protect you at any cost."

Tears rushed into her eyes again at his words and the conviction in his tone.

"That's just it. The last thing I want is for you to get hurt again."

"We can't live in fear of what this guy may or may not do."

"I know. I tell myself that every day, but it's hard to let my guard down."

"I understand, but now that I have you back in my life, he'll have to go through me to get to you."

She flung herself against him and pressed her mouth to his, pouring years of suppressed passion into the kiss. Digging her fingertips into his shoulders, she pulled him closer and kissed him harder, needing more from him. He plunged his tongue into her mouth, deepening this already mind-boggling kiss. His lips were hot, his tongue was hot. Good heavens, her nerve endings were on fire.

She released his shoulders and slid her hands down, then up under his shirt. His hard, rippled abs tightened under her touch. She needed his shirt off him, wanting the feel of his skin against hers.

His hands slid down from her cheeks, then over her sides, and landed at her hips, where he gripped the hem of her shirt and tugged it up. They pulled their mouths back from one another as they rid each other of their shirts. Then she edged back to allow his large hands to cup her breasts. The sensation of his touch, even through the thin material of her bra, was overwhelming.

In one swift movement of his thumb and forefinger, her bra floated to the floor, and he fastened his mouth to her right breast as his hand massaged her left breast. She tipped her head back, enjoying the sensation of it while holding his broad shoulders for support, fearing her weak knees would give out on her.

Desire throbbed between her legs.

He trailed his mouth down from her breasts to her belly button, then he undid the button and zipper of her jeans.

His warm lips left her skin, and he tilted his head upward to look at her from his kneeling position, his eyes pleading for permission to remove her pants. Upon her nod, his irises darkened, and he slowly pulled her pants over her hips, and they dropped to the floor. Then, he hooked his fingers over the waistband of her panties and pulled them off her, all the while boring into her with that mesmerizing stare of his.

There she stood, in front of him, fully exposed. It wasn't just the nudity, it was her soul, too. Everything she had was fully exposed to him. It was frightening, yet exhilarating beyond words. For so many years, she'd cut herself off from everyone, not allowing herself to get too close to new friends or get romantically involved with men. But she had needs, and now and then she'd allow herself to indulge in intimacy with the opposite sex. Though full-blown relationships were simply out of the question since keeping up with the lies associated with her new identity was too difficult. Now, here she stood as vulnerable as ever, and deep down, she knew it would be okay.

She reached down, offering her hand to him. He took it and led her to the bedroom.

A large log-framed bed sat in the middle of the room. The thick, inviting mattress called out to her. She wanted him and her on that mattress now. Why she felt so urgent about this, she wasn't sure. It had been a while for her, and she generally liked slow lovemaking, but today, with him, she felt impatient. Perhaps because she'd thought about Hunter so much in the past, she was eager to have him, and that hot, passionate kiss they'd just shared had her pretty revved up.

Hunter turned toward her, lifted her hand to his mouth, and pressed his lips lightly to it, lingering there for a moment before lowering it.

"I've thought about you so much over the years. I can't believe you're actually here."

"Me, too," she replied.

He leaned forward and kissed her softly. Slow, lingering kisses pursued. Much like the one they shared earlier. She liked it. Their mouths moved together as if they were experts at kissing each other. As if they'd done this a thousand times before. His reaction to her and her reaction to him couldn't have been choreographed any better.

Hunter pulled back, but the dark desire in his eyes let her know he wanted more and was ready. He took off his tennis shoes, then slid off his jeans, boxers, and socks. The man was a glorious sight.

Stepping toward her, he took her lips again. The soft, slow movements transitioned to hot, wet, and urgent. His large hands gripped her butt and when he lifted, she wrapped her legs around him and he moved them to the bed. He lay beside her, kissing her, stroking her body with his hands. His touch felt exhilarating.

She pressed her fingertips to his heated skin. Soft skin, with hard muscles beneath it.

His mouth fastened to her breast, and he circled his tongue around her nipple. Her need for him wound tighter. He moved his mouth to her other breast. Moisture pooled between her legs.

She reached down and circled her fingers around his erection and stroked, then ran her thumb over the tip. He pulled his mouth from her breast and it chilled in the air, causing her to reach up, place her palm to the back of his head, to pull him back to her breast. When he simply kissed her nipple, the sensation of it pulled a soft moan from her lips.

Hunter rolled away from her and snagged a condom

from the drawer in the nightstand. She stared at his erection as he kneeled on the bed and sheathed himself. The slight smile he flashed her sent her heart racing. They were really going to do this after all this time.

He nestled himself between her legs, kissed her lightly, and then slid into her. Long, slow strokes and tender kisses ensued. His gentleness moved her. The way he looked at her was endearing—both sincere and overwhelming.

Her hands explored him. His hard muscles and soft skin were delightful to her fingertips. With each stroke, he drove her closer to the edge. His eyes darkened, and he reached down between their bodies and circled her clit. Her back arched as he swallowed her groan in his mouth. He applied pressure to her sensitive, swollen bead, and she came apart, pulsating around him and quivering beneath him. Complete loss of control of her body. The force and pleasure of her orgasm were exhilarating. He stroked a couple of more times before his own groan of pleasure filled the room.

The weight of Hunter's muscular body atop hers felt soothing. His warm breath caressed her ear.

After a few beats, Hunter rolled off her, pulling her along with him. She curled into the curve of his arm and rested her hand on his chest. His heartbeat tapped against her palm.

"I'll be right back," Hunter said as he edged away from her and slid out of bed.

She stared in awe at his backside as he slipped into the bathroom to rid himself of the condom, she supposed.

He returned a moment later, leaned the pillows up against the headboard, and climbed back in beside her, propped up just a smidge. The quilt covered him up to his mid-torso.

She elbowed herself up and stuffed a pillow behind her

back to align herself with him. That's when she noticed it. The scar from the bullet. That incident would haunt them forever. They'd never escape it.

"What's wrong?" he asked.

"Nothing," she responded, not wanting to ruin the beautiful moment they'd just shared.

He arched a brow.

She reached up and lightly placed her fingertip to the round, jagged-edged scar on the front of his right shoulder.

"We'll always be reminded of that day. Those days, weeks, and years."

"It's okay. Just a scratch. All good."

It wasn't, though. He'd been shot.

With her fingers still touching his scar, he covered her hand with his.

"You didn't do this."

She hung her head.

He released her hand and placed his fingertips under her chin and lifted slightly, not stopping until their gazes met.

"I'm so glad you are here. You know that, right? I know we hardly knew each other, but I felt such a connection to you, and I missed you. I thought of you every day, hoping I'd see you again."

"I thought of you too."

He lifted his hand from hers, reached forward, and touched the small butterfly tattoo on her upper left breast. He traced the outline of it. She shivered.

"This is what finally gave you away, you know."

"What?"

"The day of your presentation. Your face, eyes, and the way you moved were all familiar to me, but I didn't believe it was really you because your name didn't match, so I thought you were Hannah's doppelganger. My mind worked to trick me that it wasn't really you. But when you leaned over the table to gather your things, I saw it. Actually, I only saw the tips of the bright orange wings, but that was when I realized it was really you. As if you dropped on my doorstep for a reason."

"I never showed you my tattoo back then."

Because of its location, she hadn't shown hardly anyone. The tattoo was personal to her. Not meant for just anyone to see.

He smiled softly.

"No, not intentionally, anyhow. One of my last memories of you was you dumping me into the hole created by the uprooted tree. You leaned over and kissed my forehead and apologized for leaving me covered in dirt and branches. I saw the tattoo when you hovered over me. It was the last thing I remembered of you."

Shock raked through her.

"I was certain you were unconscious when I did that."

"I nearly was. At that moment, everything cleared for me. I saw and heard you clearly through my slitted eyes. Then, the next thing I knew, I was surrounded by my family in a hospital room, and you were nowhere to be seen. Actually, I have to confess, the memory of that incident didn't come back to me right away. It took a while."

"I left a note," she said weakly, suddenly feeling like a heel for the Dear John letter she'd left him.

"I still have it. And if you recall, I abided by your wishes. Under protest, but I did."

"You kept it?"

"Yes. It's in the box on my dresser over there. I'm pretty sure I've read it a hundred times over the past few days. I'm a glutton for punishment."

"I'm sorry."

"I know."

Though she had told him to stay away years ago, a small part of her was disappointed he hadn't come after her. She could have used his support through the heartache following her parents' death, Alyssa's death, and the long, drawn-out trial. How could she be angry with him when all he did was accommodate her request? Then, she disappeared altogether, making it harder for anyone who once knew her to support her. Yet, anger laced her thoughts sometimes when she thought about him.

"Katrina?"

She flinched at the sound of her fake name.

"Yes," she replied, as she refocused on him.

"Where did I lose you to?"

"I'm just thinking back to the trial. Sometimes I felt so alone. My parents were gone. Alyssa was gone. My brothers were there, but Bianca bailed, and I'd pushed you away."

Hunter reeled his hand back from her tattoo and stiffened. Did he think she'd scolded him just now for not coming after her? That was the last thing she'd meant to do.

"I was there. Every day I sat in that courtroom supporting you the best I could. Wanting to reach out and hold you. Comfort you when you cried. It killed me to watch you go through the torment of the trial and not touch you. Hold you. Dry your tears. That hurt, but not nearly as much as when you seemed to fall off the face of the earth."

"What?"

Her heart raced and her pulse pounded.

"You were there? I never saw you."

He leaned toward her. That glint in his chestnut irises brought her right back to the moment the old man in the courtroom, the one with a casted arm, leaped over the railing between her and the spectators, protecting her from Sebastián.

"Oh, my God! That was you. The entire time you were there."

She threw her arms around his neck and pulled him to her, kissing him hard, leading to another round of heart-stopping lovemaking.

Chapter Twenty

THE ANNOYING SOUND of Katrina's phone alarm rang through her head. She yawned and stretched, pulling away from the warm body curled around her. Hunter pulled her back to him and nibbled on her earlobe. She giggled.

"I can't. I have to go home and get ready for work. I have an on-site meeting this morning."

A protesting sigh drifted into her ear.

"Stupid Mondays," he said.

"Agreed."

She'd love nothing more than to stay in this large, warm bed with this handsome man, but work called, and if she wanted to pay her bills, she'd better show up.

That man probably had no idea how hard it was for her to pull herself away from him and his comforting hold—his protective hold—his loving hold. With as long as she'd dreamed for this to come to fruition, it about killed her to roll out of his bed. She'd never expected this to happen. Ever.

She flung the covers back and padded off to the bathroom, first retrieving her clothes from the floor in the other room.

When she returned to the bedroom, she found Hunter dressed and ready for his day, but wearing a solemn look.

"What's the matter?" she asked.

"I guess I'm just worried about you."

"What do you mean?"

"Your concern about Sebastián being released and coming after you. I really hope that's not the case, but who knows? The disappearance of the assistant district attorney is alarming. Though there could be a number of criminals responsible for that, or maybe it's someone else altogether. But who knows? I'm sorry, I feel like I'm rambling and I don't want to scare you. I just...I don't know. I guess I just feel like we need to be aware of the possibility."

"I know," she whispered, as she stepped into his open arms.

Stepping out of his comforting hold was difficult, but had to be done.

"I need to go."

"I'm going with you."

The conviction in his gaze told her she wasn't getting out of this house alone, and with as much as she liked that thought, she had to. She couldn't rely on Hunter to be with her everywhere. That was too much to ask. He had his own job to attend to, and she'd decided long ago that she'd let Sebastián control her life too much, and this was where she drew the line. After all, she'd changed her identity. The person he knew had disappeared nearly a decade ago. She should be safe. Apprehension coiled in the pit of her stomach. She should be safe, but would she be?

Katrina held up her hand.

"You don't need to. I'll be fine."

His gaze intensified.

"Please don't push me away this time. I just want to make sure."

His enduring look and words pulled on the heartstrings of the heart he already owned.

At her hesitation to speak, he spoke again. "Okay, how about I just follow you to your place, and then to work? Then, I'll head on into my office. Make sure you get to both places safely. Then, home again. Please let me do this for a while anyway. At least until they find out what happened with the assistant district attorney."

How could she refuse that pleading look in his eyes? She couldn't. But if she let him follow her, he'd know where she lived. Not that she minded him knowing, but that could lead to Sebastián or his family knowing if they tried to reach her through him.

Her heart begged her brain to agree. "Okay."

His tense facial muscles relaxed.

Katrina watched in the rearview mirror as she drove back to her apartment. The wonderful man following her matched her speed and every turn. She also watched for any other vehicles that may be tailing her. Those freaking Garcias. She hated living this way. For about the millionth time, she regretted the day she met Sebastián. How on earth did she ever get mixed up with a cartel family? She was so plain and down-to-earth. What did he ever see in her? A conquest, maybe?

Hunter parked next to her and eased his truck window down. "Can I come in and wait?"

They'd gone this far, so she supposed that wouldn't hurt anything, so she offered a nod.

After keying herself in, she spun and locked the door behind Hunter. Growing up in her small town, her family rarely locked the door; now she locked doors and windows.

Hunter didn't comment; he just went with it. He followed her into the kitchen, where she started brewing a pot of coffee and then let him know she planned to shower quickly and they'd be on the road in forty-five minutes.

"Help yourself to some coffee and a muffin if you'd like. There are some hard-boiled eggs in the fridge and some bread if you want to make toast while you wait."

"I'm fine, thanks."

She smiled and tilted her head to the side. "That's not what your growling stomach is saying."

He laughed. "Maybe I will."

In the shower, she regretted scrubbing Hunter's outdoorsy scent from her body. All the while driving from his home to hers, the very scent brought her peace of mind and assured her everything would be okay. It reminded her of the hours of lovemaking they'd shared. Never in her life had she spent that much time in bed with a man. The hours just flew by. He gave her everything she needed last night. Comfort, love, and understanding. The nourishment she needed to face the next day.

The coffee pot beeped, and Hunter poured himself a cup of coffee. He popped some bread into the toaster and pulled two hard-boiled eggs from the six in the bowl in the fridge. The tiny kitchen was clean as a whistle and organized, making it easy for him to find what he needed. The plain-ness of everything didn't surprise him at all. Han—Katrina was no-nonsense. White plates, plain silverware, tan placemats on the table, smooth-edged salt and pepper shakers, one would find at a family diner.

The shower water shut off as he sat to eat. She wasn't kidding when she'd said they'd be out the door quickly. When he finished eating, he rinsed his dishes and placed them in the dishwasher, then he refilled his coffee cup and headed into the living room. A brown loveseat and matching recliner faced the television. To the side was a forest green and tan plaid side chair. The window shade blocked any sunlight from entering the room. He supposed she kept the shades pulled all the time. What a shame she had to live like this. It wasn't fair.

On the bookshelf in the corner, one shelf was reserved for photos. Curiosity drew him in to take a closer look. The largest photo seemed to be a family photo. Katrina looked to be about fourteen or so. Trees full of colorful fall leaves provided the backdrop. Katrina stood next to her mom, who she resembled, and her brothers stood at the ends, with her dad opposite her mom. They made a nice-looking family. He swallowed hard at Katrina's loss of her parents at such a young age. On either side of that framed photo were smaller photos of people that he assumed were her grandparents.

Behind the larger photo, a photobook lay flat. He reached around, grabbed it, and flipped it open. An electric shock zinged straight into his heart as he stared at a photo of him and Katrina standing atop Lover's Leap Falls. Her smile lit up the sky. He recalled that she hadn't smiled much at the start of the trip, but she did that day. Before all hell broke loose, anyway. Within seconds, the exhilarating shock of their photo turned dismal, as the reality of that day set in. Still, he flipped the pages to see the rest of the photos. There were so many. He remembered Alyssa constantly snapping photos. It was her thing. Obviously, Katrina had gotten hold of Alyssa's camera and printed everything.

There were single photos of Bianca, Katrina, and him. There were photos of combinations of all of them. But what he quickly realized was that the photos of him and Katrina outnumbered the other photos. They were smitten. Alyssa must have realized that and felt the need to document it for her friend. What he also realized was the way Bianca looked at him and Katrina. Sideways glances with her eyes slit and brows furrowed. Recalling the way Bianaca tended to touch him possessively, and now, seeing the look on her face when she watched him and Katrina, she was jealous.

"I see you found my treasure."

He flinched at the sound of Katrina's voice. So engrossed in the trip down memory lane, he hadn't heard her walk up to him.

"Sorry, I didn't mean to snoop. The picture of your family caught my attention, and then I saw this book behind it."

Katrina edged closer to him and placed her fingertips on a picture of Alyssa. The expression of sadness Katrina wore broke his heart.

"I miss her. She was such a good friend."

He slung his arm over her shoulders and pulled her to his side while still holding the photo album in his other hand.

"She was a talented photographer, and she captured so much of that trip."

"Yeah. I was happy to see that when I viewed her camera chip. I look at this book often, though it is bittersweet."

He nodded, imagining how it was for her.

He pulled his arm away from her, shut the book, and put it back on the shelf.

"And nothing from Bianca?" he asked.

"Nope. It's like she fell off the face of the earth. Well, and then I assumed a new identity. There is that."

She shrugged. "Maybe she tried to reach out to me at some point after I disappeared, but I doubt it."

Katrina was probably right about that.

Hunter looked at his watch. "Are you sure I can't bring you to work and then pick you up later? I'd feel better. At least until we learn more information about the disappearance of the assistant district attorney."

He liked that she at least appeared to consider his offer.

"No," she said as she shook her head.

"I vowed to never let him impact my life more than what he already has. I've been careful. There's no way he should know where I am."

He felt defeated, but he knew not to pressure her. The last thing he wanted was to show any signs of similarity to Sebastián, starting with being controlling or pressuring her.

"Okay, still, since I'm here, I'd like to follow you to work. Then, I'll be on my way. Can I see you tonight, though?"

The smile on her face gave him the answer.

"Yes," she confirmed.

He followed Katrina out of the apartment.

She looked professional in her navy suit, made-up face, and hair fastened high on the back of her head in a tightly wound bun. A much different look than the outdoorsy Han...Katrina, he'd first met.

He trailed her as she drove to work and even followed her into the parking lot. She slid out of the car and headed for the front doors of her office building. His heart skipped a beat when she glanced back, smiled, and nodded before slipping through the entrance.

He couldn't wait to see her again and wished it was tonight already.

After parking in his usual stall, he slipped out of the truck and practically skipped into the building.

He'd been in the office for a couple of hours before he succumbed to the urge to call Katrina. He didn't care if she thought of him as a love-crazed teenager. He needed to hear her voice.

Katrina smiled as she hung up the phone. It was nice to hear Hunter's voice, and she couldn't wait to see him again tonight.

"Katrina Holmes?" a voice rang out.

She pulled her gaze from her phone and focused on the guy standing in her office doorway. He held a vase full of daisies. Her favorites.

"Yes," she replied.

The tall, thin man grinned and stepped toward her and stretched out his arm, offering her the flowers.

"Special delivery."

"Thank you," she replied.

The man wasted no time exiting her office.

She pulled the small envelope from the plastic holder nestled among the cheerful daisies. Of course, she knew who the flowers were from, but how did Hunter know daisies were her favorite?

The card simply read, "Can't wait to see you again."

Hunter was amazing. He made her feel valued and warm and fuzzy on the inside. She couldn't wait to see him tonight, too.

Her gaze landed on the clock again. Would this Monday workday ever end? She wasn't normally a clock-watcher and had no reason to be. Not until today, that is. She glanced at the bouquet on her desk. The thought of seeing Hunter soon had her reeling with anticipation. She hadn't felt this invigorated since...she'd kissed Hunter a decade ago.

After her three o'clock meeting ended at five o'clock, she ran home, changed, and headed over to Hunter's place as he'd reluctantly agreed upon when they'd spoken on the phone earlier in the day. He'd insisted he should follow her home, but she threw cold water on that, ensuring him she'd be fine. The measures she'd put in place would keep her safe.

By six o'clock, she'd parked in Hunter's driveway. He waved her in through the garage door.

Once she was close enough to him, he reached out, cupped her cheeks with his large, warm hands, and then kissed her softly, before stepping back.

"I was just pulling down my old kayak from the rack because I got a new one," he said as he gestured toward a long, sleek red kayak on the floor next to one that was wider.

Glancing around his tidy garage, she studied all the sporting goods. Skis and snowshoes hung on the wall. Inner tubes, life vests, paddles, camping equipment. You name the sport activity, and there was something in this garage to help partake. It was his own mini sporting goods store. Made complete sense.

He abandoned the kayaks on the floor and motioned for her to follow him into the house. Once in the kitchen, a wonderful aroma hit her nostrils.

"I hope you like venison loin. I took a chance you did because of your outdoor nature, but I can whip up something else if you want," he said as he lifted the lid of the pan on the stove.

Lean meat and onions were browning in the sizzling butter, making her mouth water.

"It smells fantastic. I haven't had venison loin in years. Not since my brothers and I moved out of the Northwoods. They'd be so jealous if they knew about this. Every now and then, someone brings venison sausage to work, but that's it."

He spun, put the lid in the sink located in the island, and then turned around and lifted the lid off the pot on the stove.

"And here we have wild rice."

"Great."

"I still guide hunting trips occasionally for my Uncle Lee, and I get to do a little hunting for myself."

"Your Uncle Lee, how is he?"

"Good as ever, still living the dream in the Upper Peninsula of Michigan."

"And your brother and sister?"

"They're still in Door County doing fishing charters. And they still work for Uncle Lee, too."

Katrina hesitated before she asked the next question that popped into her head.

"Have you ever gone back to Lover's Leap Falls?"

"I have, and it was hard. Even of late, it is difficult to stand up there. But, that's part of the guided hike, so I still do it when my uncle needs me to."

Hunter's gaze hit the floor for a couple of beats before returning it to hers.

"Honestly, I go up there every summer...on the anniversary date. I'd hoped to see you there. Silly, I know, but I held hope."

Her heart slammed in her chest.

He stepped toward her. "Are you okay?"

"Yes. I missed you then."

His brows knit. "What?"

"I've been up there twice. Once on the first anniversary and once a couple of years ago. I snuck in from the back way...retraced the steps I'd taken when I went for help."

"Really?"

"Yeah, even though I was in hiding, a large part of me hoped to see you there."

He pulled her to him and kissed her tenderly, then released her.

"Life is strange sometimes."

"Don't I know it?" she replied.

They filled their plates with venison and rice and sat at the table across from one another. Gazing like love-crazed teenagers. It was nice.

"Thank you for the flowers. Daisies are my favorites."

Hunter cocked his head to the side. "Flowers?"

"The bouquet you sent to my work."

He studied her.

"I should have thought to do that, but I didn't."

"But the card said, 'can't wait to see you again,'" she said as she yanked her cell phone off the table and scrolled to the picture of the bouquet and the card.

She handed him the phone.

He looked at the photos and handed it back to her.

"I didn't send those."

"Well, who did then?"

"I don't know."

"Have you been seeing someone? I mean, that's okay if you were, but..."

"No!"

Her pulse pounded.

"Oh, no!" she exclaimed and threw her hand over her mouth.

"What?"

"Sebastián," her voice squeaked.

"That might be a stretch," he tried to assure.

She lowered her hand from her mouth and rested it on the table.

He reached across the table and took hold of her hand.

"He once sent me daisies knowing I liked them. Nobody else would send me flowers. Especially for no reason. It's not my birthday, work anniversary, nothing."

She sprang up, pulling her hands from his, and paced the kitchen.

"No, no, no."

"Stop. Please. Let's just think about this."

She stopped and collapsed into his open arms.

"It's him. I know it. I can feel it. He knows where I am and he's going to come for me."

"If that's the case, know that I'd die before I let that happen."

"That's what I'm afraid of. He's got the power of his family's cartel behind him. I almost lost you once already."

Her heart raced beyond control. Her vision went fuzzy. She hyperventilated.

"Breathe, just breathe, sweetheart," Hunter said calmly as he ran his hand up and down her back in a soothing manner.

Hunter edged back and held her gaze.

The intense look in his eyes let her know that no matter how hard she tried to convince him to walk away from her for his own safety, he wouldn't.

Her phone buzzed, drawing her attention, and with a bit of fear and reluctance, she snatched it off the table.

He's out. He's pissed as hell. You need to run! PB

The text proved her worst nightmare was about to come to fruition.

"Who's PB?" Hunter asked.

Before she could answer, her phone vibrated again.

I'm so sorry about everything. For Alyssa, for your parents, for you. This is all my fault. Please forgive me. PB

She swallowed hard. "Bianca. She always ended her texts with just PB, Princess Bianca."

"How does she have your number? I thought you and she didn't stay in touch?"

"I don't know. We don't."

The words played through her racing brain again.

He's out. He's pissed as hell. You need to run! PB

And what was she sorry for? What was her fault? She was just in the wrong place at the wrong time.

Katrina stared at the phone in her hand. How in the hell did Bianca have her number? Did she know where she lived as well? And run? She'd been running from her old life for a decade. Gave up what remained of her family and friends, and for what? Nothing. If Bianca knew where she was, then surely Sebastián knew where she was. Yet, in all this time, the entire time Sebastián was in prison, the Garcia family did nothing to her. Of course, shortly after Sebastián went to prison, his father hightailed it back to Mexico for some reason. His mom and sisters stayed in the States, but from the way Katrina understood it, Sebastián's dad relocated back to Mexico, and the rest of the family visited him there regularly. Maybe Sebastián's trial brought too much attention to the Garcia's business. Rumors had even surfaced that

221

during the time of the trial, the FBI, with assistance from the DEA, investigated Marco Garcia and the Garcia cartel. Which could explain why Marco returned to Mexico.

Bianca. All this time, her old friend knew her number and never reached out. It still stung that she deserted her immediately after Alyssa was murdered. More importantly, how did Bianca know Sebastián was pissed. Had they stayed in contact with each other?

Should she respond to the text? Ask questions?

Chapter Twenty-One

"You FUCKING BITCH," Sebastián yelled.

Spittle flew out of his mouth when he spoke, hitting Bianca in the face. Her gag reflex kicked into overdrive and her bound hands behind her back prevented her from being able to wipe her face. She tilted her head forward and to the side, hoping to use her shoulder to wipe the disgusting man's saliva off her cheek.

"Look at me!"

She ignored him and kept trying to wipe the spit off her face. If she didn't, she'd surely gag until she puked.

"I said, look at me!"

Bianca straightened in her hard metal chair and focused on the monster in front of her.

The blow to her cheek came fast and hard. Pain shot through her jaw. The second blow knocked her off the chair. Her head smacked against the cold, unforgiving concrete.

"Get up!"

She couldn't. Her hands were bound, her temples

throbbed, and her ribs still ached from when he'd thrown her to the ground and kicked her.

Using a fistful of her hair, Sebastián yanked her to her feet and slammed her back down onto the hard chair.

During the time Sebastián spent in prison, his physique changed. He was far more muscular than when they were in college, and his facial features had hardened. The tattoos on his neck, hands, and arms made him look as scary as he behaved. A few gray strands peppered throughout his slicked-back, jet-black hair. Weathered creases in his skin outlined his devil-dark eyes.

She'd once thought this man was magazine cover hand-some, but the hard prison years had changed that. Now, he looked like the thug he was. At one time, she'd even thought him nice enough to date. Her head fell forward. That was her first mistake. Allowing her to be wooed by him, even after what he'd done to Hannah.

Sebastián sucked her in, just as he'd done with her. Only for her, it was worse. He used her to get even with Hannah. It was all so clear now, but back then, it wasn't.

He promised her he'd leave Hannah for her, but he didn't. Though she shared Sebastián's bed, it was Hannah he paraded around in public on his arm. Why? She was far prettier than Hannah. Unfortunately, she was the easy one, and Hannah was the conquest. The one he could never win over. Maybe that's why he became so obsessed with her...because he couldn't have her. She wouldn't allow it. So, he tried and tried and tried to win her over, but to no avail. Even with his obscene amount of money, he was unable to secure Hannah. Hannah was too wholesome for a man like Sebastián. He knew it and didn't like it.

When Hannah dumped him, he went off the deep end, hence his decade in prison.

The first thing Sebastián did when he got released was knock on Bianca's door. She was unprepared because she didn't know he'd received an early out. Early release or not, it probably didn't matter. She knew this day would come. He'd get out and even the score with everyone. Even her, the person who helped him most, or at least tried to help, anyhow. Well, it wasn't like she'd had a say in the matter. Once she'd realized his true colors, she knew what he was capable of. If she hadn't done as he demanded, she'd be the one who was dead, not Alyssa.

Hot tears streamed down her aching cheeks. This was all on her. She allowed this to happen. Alyssa was dead. Hannah's parents were dead. Soon, Hannah would be dead, and if she didn't play her cards right, she'd be dead, too.

Bianca regretted every horrible decision she'd made when it came to Sebastián. The decision she didn't regret, though, was texting Hannah to tell her to run. Between the text and the flowers she sent to her, hoping she'd think they were from Sebastián, she hoped Hannah would get the severity of the situation and run.

Sebastián snapped his fingers in front of her face, drawing her attention.

"Where is she?"

"I don't know," she whispered.

Still, she tried to convince him she did not know of Hannah's whereabouts. If it hadn't been a chance sighting a few years ago, she wouldn't, but she did. She happened to be in Door County for a women's weekend when she spotted a familiar face on the Peninsula State Park beach. It was Hannah. No doubt. She followed her into the small store, ducking behind a rack to not be seen. When Hannah spoke to the woman working the cash register, Bianca knew for sure it was her, even though she was older now. The voice matched, her looks matched, her mannerisms matched. A sense of relief had washed through her, knowing she was still alive and well. When she had disappeared, Bianca was concerned that Sebastián's hired hand had done what he was supposed to in the first place. But that wasn't the case. Her old friend stood not ten feet away from her in the flesh. Now she could only conclude that Hannah assumed a new identity and went into hiding. That's why she'd lost track of her. Bianca fought the urge to speak to her. It was safest for everyone this way. She noted Hannah's license plate number when she pulled out of the parking lot, and when she returned home from her vacation, she sweet-talked a friend of hers into running the plate and learned her friend now went by the name of Katrina Holmes and lived in Green Bay, Wisconsin.

This choice of location didn't surprise Bianca. Close to where she was from, but far enough away to stay hidden. A city not too big or too small, and an area that provided quick access to the Northwoods that Hannah loved so much. Yes, this location made absolute sense to her.

"I know you know, and you have three seconds to tell me or else."

He didn't have to clarify what the 'or else' meant. She knew. He'd already tortured and killed the assistant district attorney. The proof was the woman lying on the cold cement floor not twenty feet from him. She supposed he'd left the body there to send her a message. He was serious about finding Hannah. Bianca squeezed her eyes shut to block out the unbearable reality surrounding her.

"Three..."

Bianaca's heart raced. This was it. This was how she was going to die. Would dying this way, not giving up her friend, erase all the bad things she'd done in her lifetime, especially when it came to Sebastián?

Death would set her free. Her secrets would haunt her no more.

She opened her eyes and met Sebastián's gaze.

"Two..."

She straightened her spine. She was ready.

"We got it!" one of Sebastián's thugs yelled as he stepped through the doorway of the abandoned warehouse.

He waved a cell phone in the air. Her phone. At first, she was mad she'd forgotten to take it on her run after work, but at two miles into the four-mile loop, it was of no use to worry about it. Rarely was a moment she didn't have her phone on her, but the events of the day had her so out of sorts she couldn't think clearly and forgot to grab it. Turns out, forgetting it was a good thing, since Sebastián nabbed her from the path. His not having access to her phone would ensure he wouldn't find out that she'd just texted Hannah. Knowing one day she'd probably need the number, she was glad she'd programmed it into her phone.

Her heart sank, and a lump the size of a golf ball lodged in her throat as she stared at her phone in Sebastián's hand. Programming the number in the phone hadn't been such a good idea.

An evil smirk rose on Sebastián's face, and his irises turned as black as his pupils.

Sebastián stepped around her and grabbed one of her bound hands, pried open her fingers from her balled fists, then pressed her thumb to the screen of the phone to unlock it.

He moved back to her sightline and studied her phone as he tapped the screen.

His hands stopped moving. The evil laugh that echoed

in the nearly empty room caused the eeriest of sensations to snake up her spine.

"Excellent work, Ramon," Sebastián said as he glanced at his thug.

He spun the phone around for her to see. The text to Hannah was on full display.

Bianca's mouth went dry.

"It looks like you are no longer needed, sweet pea. Where were we?" he asked as he yanked his pistol from his waistband.

She squeezed her eyes shut and braced herself.

"Oh, I remember."

Oh God.

"One."

Chapter Twenty-Two

Katrina's pulse pounded so loudly she couldn't hear herself think.

"We need to call the police," Hunter said.

"I know, but what are they going to do? It's not like they'll give me a bodyguard or something, and even so, Sebastián's resources are unlimited with his family business. I had no clue Bianca knew where I was. I'm worried about her. For her to send that message means she knows something, and she's probably in trouble."

She shook her head as if that would help her put her incoherent thoughts in order.

"What are you thinking?"

"I keep wondering what she meant when she said this was all her fault. What was? The fact that Sebastián knows where I work. How would she know that? I've been so careful not to make contact with people from my prior life. And how long has she had my contact information? And why hasn't she reached out before this? None of this makes sense."

Hunter reached down and gripped her hands.

"We'll figure this out. I will not let anything happen to you. I will protect you at any cost. You know that, right?"

Of course she did. He'd proven that years ago.

"That's what I'm afraid of. You nearly lost your life once already just from being in the wrong place at the wrong time."

She pulled her hands from his and crossed her arms over her chest.

"Don't pull away."

"I can't put you through this again."

His gaze intensified, and she wanted to pull hers away, but couldn't. She loved him and wanted to keep him in her life. She ripped her gaze away.

"I love you, Hannah."

Her heart beat erratically at his profession of love and use of her real name. There was no way she could walk away from him again. Her gaze floated back to him.

"I have an idea. First, we'll call the cops and get this on record. Second, let's bait him."

"What?"

The thought of intentionally calling attention to herself and Hunter scared the crap out of her.

"Let's see if we can't get him to do something stupid that gets him sent back to prison."

"Say that happens, that would only be a temporary result, and we'll be right back in this position when he gets back out."

"That could be true, but it beats the alternative, right?"

"I guess so. What's your idea?"

"We'll drive to the Green Bay Police Department and get a report on file. Then, you text Bianca back to let her know you're going to run and hide out up north for a while. If Sebastián is monitoring her phone or, unfortunately, if

Bianca is trying to draw you out for him, hopefully that will be enough information for him to figure out you're going to Yooper's Adventures."

So, a part of Hunter thought Bianca could be a willing partner of Sebastián's. She supposed this was a possibility, since her friend seemed to desert her a decade ago when she needed her most. In her heart, she wanted to believe Bianca was a good person. They were once friends. She couldn't be that poor of a judge of character, could she? Yes, she once liked Sebastián, so the answer was yes. In her own defense, though, she'd figured him out quickly.

"What do you think?" he asked at her lack of response.

"Let's start with the police. I'll mull the rest over. I don't want to put any innocent bystanders, meaning your uncle or clients, at risk."

"Fair enough. I'll call him to see what he's got going on this week. It's early in the season for camping and hiking, so maybe there aren't that many people there right now. Could be some there for fishing. We'll see."

"Okay."

"Give me a few minutes to pack a bag, and then we'll go to your place so you can pack, and then to the police department."

Katrina paced the kitchen and living room, waiting for Hunter's return.

When he entered the living room, he had a duffle bag slung over his shoulder, a large plastic case in his right hand, and a rifle case in his left. He stepped up onto the kitchen island and popped the case onto the counter, dropped the bag to the floor, and then opened the case. Inside were two pistols and ammo.

"Are you good with a .45 auto? Or would you rather a 9mm?"

He was dead serious and dead right. They'd need to provide their own protection. A 9mm is what she normally carried, but in this case, she wanted the .45. The bigger, the better.

She pulled one of the matching 45s from the case just to get the feel of it.

"This will work," she said as she put it back.

"I was hoping you'd opt for the .45, but I would have pulled a 9mm from the safe for you."

Hunter followed her as she drove back to her apartment. Paranoia ruled her drive. Not even sure what she looked for, she kept her gaze and senses on high alert.

She tucked her SUV into the garage and Hunter parked in front of the large door. He followed her into her apartment and waited while she packed. Then, they loaded into his truck and drove to the police department.

Even to her own ears, she sounded like a crazy person as she told her story to the officer. He was kind and took notes.

"I guess mainly, I just want this on record in case something happens. And I was hoping you would reach out to the Minneapolis Police Department and have them check on Bianca. You know, like a wellness check. Only I really don't know where she lives anymore, but I was hoping you could figure that out."

"The officer nodded. That we can do, but there's not much else we can do at this point."

"I know, and that is what I expected," she replied matter-of-factly.

There was no reason to bust the officer's chops, understanding how this story must sound, and the fact she had no actual proof Sebastián was after her, except for the flowers and the text from her old friend.

"It's not that I don't want to help you, but..."

She held her hand up, and he stopped talking.

"I know. I get it."

The officer held her gaze. "I am going to follow up about your friend."

"Thank you."

He looked and sounded sincere. She believed him.

After an hour at the station, she and Hunter exited the building and hopped into his truck. It was nine o'clock by the time they headed north on US-141. It was going to be a long drive to the U.P. in the dark.

"When should I text Bianca?"

"In the morning. I want to make sure we do this right. I want to talk with Chief Ricco to see what he thinks."

Chief Ricco. She thought of him, his department, and his wife often. They were all so kind and empathetic. Wholesome, small-town people who cared. Yet the man was all business when he needed to be.

"He's going to tell us this is too risky and forbid us to do it," Hannah said.

Hunter turned his head toward her for a moment before returning his gaze to the road.

"Probably, but you never know. He saw firsthand what happened ten years ago, so he may have a different perspective about the severity of this versus the officer in Green Bay."

"We'll spend the night at Uncle Lee's, then call the chief in the morning. Rather, we should go see him in person," Hunter said, then chuckled. "It's harder to say no when you're face to face."

"True."

"I suppose you'd better call Lee and warn him we're coming and why."

"I already did that when you were packing. He and Aunt Heidi are expecting us tonight."

After a couple of hours, Hunter pulled into the winding driveway leading to the office of Yooper Adventures and Lee and Heidi's house. Anxiety gripped her heart and squeezed.

"Just breathe," Hunter said as he reached over and took her hand.

Such a natural task seemed hard to do at that moment. The horrible memory of that fateful day hurt like hell and felt as fresh as it did on that day.

Hunter's grip tightened. "It'll be fine."

Though his words were meant to be reassuring, the hint of apprehension in his tone let her know he was worried too. But, this was the only way—the best way she could think of to protect herself and those she loved. Even if their plan worked, it was only a temporary resolution. How long would Sebastián go back to prison for? A tinge of guilt raked through her for trying to set him up this way, but the fact of the matter was, he would kill her and those around her, if she didn't do something.

As they approached Lee's home, the garage door opened, and Lee waved Hunter in. A thin woman of average height with short gray hair stood next to Lee and must be Heidi. She'd never seen the woman before.

She slid out of the vehicle and walked toward Lee and Heidi. Hunter hugged them both, then gestured to her.

"Uncle Lee, you remember Katrina?"

The man raised a brow and nodded.

"I changed my name after...the incident," Katrina added.

Lee pointed to his wife. "This is Heidi."

"Nice to meet you, dear. Can I help you with your things?" she asked.

"No, thank you. I just have one bag. I can get it."

She and Hunter grabbed their belongings from the backseat, including the pistol case, but not the rifle.

Once inside the modest log home, Heidi showed her to her room, upstairs beyond the open loft area. Hunter tossed his bag onto the bed in that room as she hoped he would.

"I'll let you get settled. We'll be in the kitchen. Do you want a nightcap?"

"More than you can imagine," Hunter replied with a hint of a forced smile.

The reality of what they were about to do seemed to settle in for him. It had taken its toll on her hours ago.

Katrina put her duffle bag on the floor next to a chest of drawers. She pulled out her toiletry bag, took it into the connecting bathroom, and set it on the small countertop. Then, she turned down the bed and followed Hunter down the steps and back into the open concept living room and kitchen area they'd previously walked through.

"Would you like a glass of wine or a beer?" Heidi asked.

"Beer, please," Hunter replied without hesitation.

"I'll take one, too," Katrina answered.

Lee and Heidi already had theirs cracked open and sitting on the kitchen island.

Nobody sat. They stood around the island in silence for a moment before Hunter filled them in on the details of how they'd come to be here. He'd informed them of some of the details over the phone before they arrived, but now he gave them the in-depth details. Now, two more people were involved. The tension in the room thickened. The thought of putting any of these kind people in danger made her sick, and the beer wasn't sitting well.

Lee nodded. "I understand why you want to do this. I really do, but are you sure?"

"I don't see any other way. I'm...we're open to suggestions."

"Heidi and I discussed this before you arrived. We understand you're stuck between a rock and a hard place, and we'll do whatever you need us to do."

"I don't want to put you in any more danger. Hence, why I asked to park in the garage. Just in case someone comes snooping around here, they won't see my truck."

Lee took a swig of his beer.

"You're family. Like a son to me. I will do whatever it takes to protect my family," Lee said firmly and then shifted his gaze to her. "You included."

Katrina's heart overflowed at Lee's conviction. She hardly knew the man, but believed him. At that moment, memories of her father bombarded her. This was something he would have said and done.

When Hunter's alarm sounded at six o'clock, she wasn't ready to get up. Worry prevented her from sleeping a wink. For a moment after she and Hunter had made love, she'd thought her sedated state would help her relax and fall asleep, but that wasn't the case.

With reluctance, she rolled out of bed and padded off to the bathroom. When she returned to the bedroom, Hunter was already dressed.

She threw on some clothes and followed him and the aroma of coffee to the kitchen, where Heidi and Lee sat at the table. A pile of pancakes and sausage filled a plate in the center of the table.

"Good morning. I hope you like pancakes," Heidi said.

The woman's warm smile comforted Katrina somewhat, but she wasn't sure if her swirling stomach could handle any food.

"You need to start your day with a hearty breakfast," Heidi added.

Katrina sat, and Hunter took the seat opposite her. He wasted no time filling his plate.

"The chief usually gets to City Hall about seven, so when we're done with breakfast, we can go see him," Lee said.

"You don't need to..."

"Yes," Lee said, cutting off Hunter's words.

There was no use arguing with Lee. His mind was made up.

Katrina looked across the table, beyond Hunter and into the living room. A large elk mount took up most of the area in the peaked area of the vaulted ceiling. It was a six-by-six.

Katrina looked at Lee. "Nice elk."

"You should tell Heidi that. It's hers. I could have never made that shot."

Heat rose in Katrina's cheeks. She just assumed it was Lee's.

Heidi's smile beamed. "Yes, you could have."

"She's too modest to tell you that six-by-six was shot at five hundred and seventy-five yards. She practiced and practiced before we went out to Colorado, and all the practicing paid off."

Lee winked at Heidi, who gazed at him lovingly.

"Aunt Heidi shows us all up. Hits the bullseye on the target all the time," Hunter added.

Heidi blushed. "You guys."

Heidi stood and cleared the table.

Katrina drained her coffee, then loaded the dishwasher.

"We'll take my truck to town. Keep any attention deflected that your truck may cause," Lee said.

Hunter ran back up the stairs and returned with the pistol case. Once in the garage, Hunter pulled the rifle case from his truck and put it into his uncle's. Lee loaded two more long guns into the back of his truck.

Good heavens, she hoped none of that was needed. But she knew differently.

Chapter Twenty-Three

KATRINA TOOK in the sights of Iron City as Lee drove. The small town was picturesque, like something out of a Hallmark movie. But for her, this little city was anything but that. She recalled frantically running down the street, tired and bruised, as she made her way to the city hall to get Chief Ricco to help Hunter. The memory of the horrible things that happened outweighed the kindness of the people who'd helped her, Hunter, and Bianca.

Lee parked in a stall on the street in front of City Hall. The building hadn't changed one iota since she'd last seen it.

"Wait!" Hunter said as she'd reached for her door handle.

"What?"

"You should text Bianca before we go in."

"I thought we were going to talk to Chief Ricco before we did that to see what he thought of our plan."

Hunter studied her for a moment. "If we do it before we go in there, the plan will be in place and he won't be able to talk us out of it."

That was true and manipulative.

Hunter's gaze hit the floor, indicating he was aware of that as well.

Lee and Heidi stared at her and Hunter from the front seat.

"I think you should. We need to stop this maniac before he hurts you or anyone else. Chief Ricco is going to tell you not to do it. That's probably what he should tell you. Sebastián shouldn't be on the street. He's dangerous. It's obvious he's coming for you. He needs to be stopped," Heidi said.

Katrina couldn't help but notice the surprised expressions Hunter and Lee wore when Heidi spoke. What was that about? Hunter had said his aunt was a quiet person. Was it her firm opinion about the matter that shocked them or the fact that she weighed in? It didn't really matter; the woman was right. It came down to her or him, and she wanted to live. Yes, she wholeheartedly believed she would die by his hand if she didn't do something.

Katrina pulled her phone from her pocket, called up Bianca's text, and hit reply.

I understand your warning and have already taken measures.

A reply came back so quickly one would have sworn Bianca, or Sebastián, was staring at her phone, just waiting for a communication from her.

I'm glad to know you're still safe. Wherever you are hiding, stay there. Don't go home.

Katrina's heart sank.

"Oh no," Katrina whispered.

"What's the matter?" Hunter asked.

"It's not Bianca."

"What?" he questioned.

"Look," she said as she handed him her phone.

"The reply text wasn't signed PB. The earlier ones were. That asshole did something to her!"

"All the more reason to get this done," Heidi said firmly.

"Maybe she just forgot to sign off the way she used to," Hunter stated.

"No. That wouldn't be like her. PB was her signature. Something's not right."

Katrina grabbed her phone back from Hunter and hit reply.

Will do. I'm back where I love to be. Except for one time, anyhow. You know the time.

She waited a few minutes for the reply that never came.

Sebastián now knew where she was.

The four of them slid out of Lee's truck and entered City Hall.

The woman who worked the front desk ten years ago greeted them and was easily recognizable. She had hardly changed at all except for the couple of creases formed at the corners of her eyes when she smiled. Using her hand, she flipped her long blonde hair over her shoulder when she stood. In that instant, the woman's name popped into her mind. *Mandi.* She confirmed her recollection with a glance at the nameplate on the counter.

"Good morning, Heidi, Lee, and Hunter. Long time no see," she said.

Mandi fixed her gaze on her and squinted. It was the kind of expression one used when trying to recall the name of a familiar face.

"I'm Hannah Rice. We met about a decade ago."

It felt strange to use her real name.

At the sound of her name, Mandi's eyes widened.

"Yes, I remember now. How are you?"

"Pretty good. You?"

Clearly a lie for the moment she was in, but a couple of weeks ago, life as she knew it was okay.

"Good. What can I do for you all?"

"We're hoping to see Chief Ricco. Is he in?" Hunter asked.

"He is. Hold on a sec."

Mandi spun around and took a few steps toward the doorway behind the reception area.

"Jack, the Samuelsons are here, and they have Hannah Rice with them. They'd like to see you."

"I'll be right there," the chief's familiar voice echoed out of the room.

A woman, Hannah recognized as Chief Ricco's wife, Clare, stepped out of the chief's office. A toddler was perched on her hip, and she held the hand of another young child who looked to be five years old or so. Cute kids. The little girl had the same shade of bright red hair as her momma, and the boy had dark hair like the chief's. They looked like the perfect little family.

Hannah recalled how nice Clare was to her and how the woman was able to calm her in light of all that had happened that day.

Clare caught her gaze and smiled warmly. "It's good to see you, Hannah."

"You, too, Clare."

"Well, I'll get out of here so you can talk to Jack," she said, stepping toward the exit.

The chief waved them into his office and motioned for them to sit at the rectangular table.

She glanced around the room. It was decorated exactly the way she suspected an office would be for a small town police chief in the Northwoods. A twelve-point buck mount hung on the wall with a stringer of perch on one side and a fan of turkey tail feathers on the other side.

Chief Ricco listened attentively as she and Hunter explained the chain of events that occurred leading to them sitting before him. The neutral expression Chief Ricco wore made it hard to know what he thought until she got to the part of how she texted Bianca, assuming it was Sebastián, and set him up to come after her up here. It was then that his eyes darkened and his facial muscles tightened. Still, he sat quietly until she and Hunter finished speaking.

"Well, if you are correct, and Sebastián understands the message, you've put us in quite the position," the chief said.

Though the man spoke in a normal tone, she felt scolded, and when Hunter's gaze hit the tabletop, she knew he felt the same.

Recalling his wife and two small children who'd just left the building made her feel guilty that she'd just endangered the chief and how this could impact his beautiful family. Her head hung.

"Hannah," the chief said, drawing her attention back to him.

"I understand the spot you're in. Unfortunately, circumstances like yours sometimes leave little recourse to ensure the victim's safety. I wish you'd come to me before setting this all in motion, but what's done is done. Now we just need to figure out our best course of action is from here."

Chief was clearly not happy about what they'd done, but he'd quickly switched gears to damage control.

"So, we're working with the assumption that Sebastián is really who you are texting with, and you've hinted that you are up here."

"Yes."

"There's a big assumption about where you are located here, though, right?"

"I guess."

"From what you've told me, back then and now, there's still no actual proof it was Sebastián who'd shot Alyssa and chased you and Hunter."

"It was him!" she said, cutting off the chief's words.

"You may be right, but what I meant was, was it really him or a hired hand?"

She dropped her gaze to the surface of the table again, but for just a moment before returning it to the chief.

"If I had to guess, a hired hand. Remember, he had an alibi during that timeframe. It wouldn't surprise me if he and his family paid for an alibi or threatened them, but he was behind it for sure. I just know it."

"I ask, because Sebastián may not know the exact location you referred to. If he is truly on his way here, I want to keep him away from the general public. I'd like to steer him toward a specific place, and maybe we can pick him up en route. Find out if Bianca is safe. It won't take but a few minutes for me to get his and Bianca's registered car information so we can be on the lookout, but still, there are a lot of roads in and out of here."

"If you stop him before he does anything, he'll just be set loose to..."

"I can't willingly let him try to kill you," the chief said firmly.

The thought of having to start all over with the hiding process made her sick. It was so hard to leave everyone behind and if this were the case, she'd have to leave Hunter, the man she loved, behind again.

Chief Ricco looked at Lee. "Do you have any clients on your property today?"

"No, and we don't have anyone scheduled until this coming weekend."

"Good."

"We need to make sure Sebastián, or whoever, gets to the right spot on your property. We can then monitor the roadway access points and the trail accesses."

The chief paused and frowned.

"What?" Lee asked.

"We don't have enough trained staff to cover all of those points."

"Heidi and I can cover two of them," Lee offered.

"I can't let you do that."

"We'll stay out of sight and watch from afar, and we can radio you if we see anyone."

The chief eyed his watch and looked a little defeated as he weighed that option. Probably realizing he had little choice. At this point, Sebastián would have received her text almost thirty minutes ago, and if he left right away, depending on where he actually was, it could be just a matter of a few hours before he showed up. If he was in Green Bay, it could be as little as two hours.

"I'll see if I can get help from the county sheriff's department. I'm sure Sheriff Anderson will lend a hand."

"We can..." Lee squeaked out before the chief held his hand in the air.

"No. We've got this. But, I will need your help to mark a map of all the access points."

Chief Ricco rose, walked over to the doorway, and leaned out of it.

"Mandi, call Dewey, Collins, and Hansen and tell them to get to the station ASAP. Then, get one of those large county maps from the records room and bring it into the conference room."

"Yes, sir."

The chief stood at the short end of the rectangular table.

"We need to send a text that doesn't sound blatantly obvious that we're onto him. It needs to push him to a specific location."

Hannah set her phone on the table. The room was silent. Chief Ricco was right. Since Sebastián was probably already en route, there was probably no stopping him, so they needed to manage this better.

Hannah's phone buzzed, and the screen lit up. She snatched it up and read the text.

I went to Lover's Leap Falls once. Sat on top of the falls and made myself sick thinking about what it must have been like for you that day. All the while, I was so close, lying on the beach out of harm's way. The dumb luck, I guess.

That text. It's like God was helping them play their hand.

Hannah handed the phone to the chief.

He read the message.

"How do you know it's him and not Bianca?"

"Bianca always signs with PB, Princess Bianca. The first couple of messages that came from this number were signed with PB. The last couple, including this one, were not."

"You're sure?"

"Yes."

"The appropriate response is pretty evident now," Chief Ricco said.

After discussing the wording for a moment, Hannah fired a text back.

I've only been there twice since then, until now. It's a bit cold for camping, but I'll make do.

"Mandi will take you to the conference room. I'm going to make a couple of calls, and I'll join you there in a bit," the chief said.

She, Hunter, Lee, and Heidi exited the office and waited for Mandi. When she returned to the front office area, she had a large paper map in her hands.

"Chief said to wait for him in the conference room," Lee said.

Mandi nodded and led them down the long, narrow hall to the conference room.

The horrid memory of walking down this same hallway felt as fresh as if it were yesterday. The reality of today enhanced the eerie sensation swirling in Hannah's stomach. Even with the danger, she was glad they were doing this today. She needed Sebastián to screw up, so he'd wind up back in prison. That would be the only way she'd be safe.

Lee took the map from Mandi and laid it out on the table. He, Hunter, and Heidi talked about the access points to Lover's Leap Falls. There were more than she'd realized.

Chief entered the room with three officers, one being Dewey, the older officer she'd met years ago. He grabbed a marker from the pencil holder on the table and began marking access points to Lover's Leap Falls. The group discussed each one and the level of access.

"I assume he'll go for easy access with a bit of cover," the chief said.

That made sense. Sebastián wasn't an outdoorsy guy, and he didn't know the area.

The most used access was the one they'd taken years ago from the campsite, but it required a canoe. The shortest access was the one she'd taken when she ran for help, but it wasn't a clearly marked trail. Once she'd gone off-trail, she simply followed the river until she reached a road. She doubted Sebastián would attempt this. There were two long, well-marked trails to Lover's Leap from two other campsites, and one long trail from a road on the opposite side of the river from where Yooper Adventures was head-quartered. But anyone could make their way through the woods from any point they supposed, but it would take someone with knowledge of the area and who wasn't afraid to deal with rugged terrain to do so. Sebastián was lazy. He'd opt for easy.

"Lee, I'd like you and Heidi to set up a tent with a few camping supplies on the Lover's Leap campsite. Make it look like someone is using the site. I want you to set it up quickly and then get out of there. Go home, but stay out of sight. If Sebastián winds up at Yoopers, I don't want you to scare him off. Call me if that happens. Can you do that?"

"You got it," Lee replied.

The chief pointed at the map. "Collins will post here, Dewey will take this trailhead, and Hansen here will cover the access from the campsites farther away. I'll take the Lover's Leap campsite. Sheriff Anderson will take the road access spot here, and his deputies will patrol the surrounding roads."

"What should I do?" Hunter asked.

"You and Hannah will be with me and stay out of sight and do as I say. Understood?"

Chief Ricco and Hunter eyed each other for a moment. "Yes."

Hannah supposed the last thing the chief needed was someone running rogue on him. At least she'd be involved.

The chief handed Lee a handheld radio.

"Let me know if you see or hear anything suspicious," the chief said.

Lee nodded.

Hunter followed Lee out.

"Where are you going?" Chief Ricco asked Hunter.

"I need to get something out of Uncle Lee's truck."

Hunter returned a moment later with the weapon cases, two camouflage, lightweight jackets, and a forest green backpack. She didn't recognize the jackets or the backpack. They must be Lee and Heidi's.

The chief looked him up and down but didn't say a word.

Chapter Twenty-Four

CHIEF RICCO GLANCED at his watch, then looked at Hunter.

"We'd better get moving and be ready for him in case he actually shows up here," the chief said.

"He will. I know it," Hannah replied without hesitation.

That's what scared Hunter. Without a doubt, he knew there would be some sort of altercation today. He'd helped to orchestrate it. Would it be what he and Hannah wanted? Still, it worried him. The last thing he wanted was for Hannah to be in harm's way, though he knew this was their best option. Get Sebastián to violate his parole and get him sent back to prison.

A touch to his arm drew his attention.

"Are you okay?" Hannah asked.

No, he wasn't, but he certainly wouldn't tell her that.

"I'm good. Just working through everything in my head."

The chief nodded.

"Let's go."

They loaded into Chief Ricco's SUV and he drove

toward the access point they'd use to get to Lover's Leap Falls and campsite. It was the same point Hannah had escaped the woods while being chased by the shooter—Sebastián. Though Sebastián provided an alibi that day, Hunter knew in his heart that Sebastián was the shooter. For a while, he'd thought maybe the shooter had been a hired hand, but now he believed Sebastián was the guy.

Chief Ricco tucked his squad SUV under the cover of the forest in a nearby driveway of a vacant property, and they exited the vehicle.

Hunter holstered his pistol and slung his rifle over his shoulder. Hannah holstered her weapon. The chief's lips parted as if he were going to speak, then he clamped them shut. He knew Hunter. He knew he'd be cautious with his weapons. The expression the chief wore still sent a message to Hunter to be careful.

As they neared the embankment, where Hunter had been told they'd carried him out of the woods on a stretcher, he took a moment to study the area. He had no memory of being hauled out of the woods or his ambulance ride. Though he'd heard the story enough from his brother and sister, it almost felt like he recalled it from his own memory bank. He remembered being shot at and leaping over the falls with Hannah tucked in his hold. He remembered being on the run, but at some point, his brain shut off. He woke up in the hospital, and Hannah was gone.

Once they reached the embankment, the chief climbed down. Hunter followed, then held a hand up to Hannah to help her. She didn't reach out to him. She just stood there, staring out into the woods. Her eyes looked glossy. Her skin was pasty white. Her body quivered.

"Hannah."

No response.

"Katrina."

Hannah stared into the woods, recalling that horrible day ten years ago. Her heart raced at the thought of placing herself in Sebastián's sights intentionally, but it was what she needed to do. It was the best way to deal with him. Draw him out, make him try something stupid to violate his parole, and get him back into prison. His being locked up was the only way to ensure her safety. She swallowed hard. He may have hired someone to take her out, but in any case, Sebastián needed to be removed from the public.

She heard Hunter say her name. *Hannah.* She missed using her real name.

"Katrina," Hunter said.

She looked at him. Those warm, dark eyes of his calmed her. She knew he'd protect her at all costs, just like he'd done once before. She didn't want him to get hurt again, or worse, die today. Maybe this was a bad idea, but she'd put the plan in motion, and there was no stopping it now. She could text Bianca, or most likely it was Sebastián and say she'd gone elsewhere. Throw him off their trail, but then she'd have to hide for the rest of her life.

She took Hunter's hand, and stepped down the embankment.

"It'll be fine. We'll be okay," Hunter said.

Hunter led them through the woods with a fast stride. When he intersected the actual trail they'd been on that fateful day, he paused and looked back at her.

She easily recognized this spot with the downed tree that was at the edge of a large hole created by the uprooted tree. This was the spot she'd stashed Hunter in to hide him from the shooter. Erosion had filled the hole in a bit, but it was still fairly deep.

Staring into the hole was like staring into a mirror of the past. Every detail of that day on top of Lover's Leap came into crystal clear view, making her nauseous.

She flashed her gaze around and could have sworn she heard the words, *I'm coming for you*, among the slight whistle of the breeze, just like she'd heard ten years ago.

Hunter scooped up her hand and held it reassuringly.

Honestly, she didn't think returning to this spot would be that hard, yet she should have known it would be similar to the two other times she'd visited Lover's Leap since the incident.

"We need to keep moving and get into position. And keep your eyes peeled," the chief said.

Now that they were on the trail, Chief Ricco took the lead. She followed him, and Hunter followed her.

It didn't take long to reach the pool of water at the bottom of the falls. She paused for a moment and stared at the waterfall. There seemed to be more water coming over the edge than she remembered from the past, but it was spring, so maybe the quick snow melt was feeding it.

Her gaze floated upward, running along the forty-foot falls she and Hunter jumped into. The memory of how he'd wrapped her in his protective arms warmed her heart. He'd taken the brunt of their fall. Sure, she had a few cuts and bruises, but he'd nearly lost his life, adding more injuries to his body after being shot.

The thick, thorny brush surrounding the pool wasn't as dense as it was that day in the middle of summer, but the spring foliage was entering full bloom now.

Hannah closed her eyes and blew out a long breath.

"Ready?" Hunter asked.

She opened her eyes and nodded, then she followed him to the path that led up the back side of the falls.

Once near the top, they all paused, staying just inside the tree line. The top of the falls was rocky and bald. She scanned the area, looking for any lurking dangers. When she looked at Hunter and Chief Ricco, they did the same.

The rush of the water echoed in the air, and her gaze latched onto the fast-flowing water that swept over the edge in a free fall, just like she and Hunter had done once. Only the water fared better than they had.

Chief Ricco radioed his men, "We're in position. Are you all in position?"

One by one, his men, the sheriff and his men replied. Everyone was where they needed to be.

"Any activity?" the chief asked.

Everyone responded acknowledging no activity.

Chief Ricco called out to Lee. "Is the campsite set up?"

"Yes, we just finished."

"Good. Keep your eyes peeled on the way back. Stay safe," the chief replied.

"My eyes are peeled," Lee replied.

My. Wouldn't it be *our eyes?* Hannah thought.

Now what? Should she stand on the bald rock like a sitting duck?

"Likely, he'll come up the trail. He doesn't know the woods, so that seems logical," the chief said.

Hunter nodded.

"We should go to the other side and stay tucked in the tree line. We'll still watch all directions."

She watched Hunter's nervous eyes scan the area.

"Due to the heavy, fast-flowing water coming in, I don't think there's an area shallow enough to walk through safely, without getting swept away, or an area narrow enough to leap over. We're going to have to cross over the exposed area and bridge for the best angle to watch the trail," Hunter said.

Chief Ricco nodded.

"I was thinking the same thing. We should still have plenty of time to do that before he arrives, that is, if he does, but let's move quickly," the chief replied.

It's not like the top of the falls was that large. It would only take them a minute or so to get to the opposite side of the river that fed the falls, but still, who knew?

"Let's go," Hunter said as he grabbed her hand and shot out of the tree line, over the rock, over the bridge, and to the tree line opposite where they'd been.

Her heart raced. Not from the distance they'd just run, but from the fear of the potential possibilities that could have prevented them from reaching the other side.

"Now we wait," the chief said as they stood next to each other, scanning the woods. The trees and foliage were thicker on this side, making it difficult to see far, but as Chief Ricco pointed out, it was likely Sebastián would use the marked trail.

"Just ran the plates on a passing car," one deputy radioed.

Hannah's heart leaped into her throat.

"Came back as Theresa Milborn."

"I know her. She's a resident of Iron City," the chief replied.

"I'm back at base camp. All quiet here," Lee's voice sounded over the radio.

I'm. Not we're?

Lee's choice of words didn't seem to faze the chief or Hunter. Was she overthinking this?

Two hours of mostly radio silence passed. An occasional

report of a passing car came through from the deputies and officers, but all the cars and occupants were known by Chief Ricco or his men. Maybe Sebastián wouldn't take the bait today.

Another hour of nothing except birds chirping. The temperature had warmed some, and the morning wind had settled. Hannah wanted to pull off the lightweight camouflage jacket that Hunter insisted she wear, but she decided to keep it on. Any cover was better than no cover.

Hannah's stomach growled. A glance at her watch informed her why. It was nearing one o'clock.

Hunter pulled three granola bars out of his backpack, handing one to her and one to the chief.

She kept her gaze on full alert even while eating. Hardly blinking, causing her eyes to become dry and itchy. She'd closed them for just a second when she heard Hunter's quick intake of breath.

Her eyes popped open and focused on Sebastián standing atop the bald rock. Her pulse pounded and her heart leaped into her throat at the sight of the gun he held, pointing to Bianca's head.

Bianca's cream-colored shirt was saturated with blood on the neckline. Her right eye was nearly swollen shut, and most of her face was the color of an eggplant. Dried blood streaked over her cheek. It obviously came from her disfigured nose. Her full upper lip was swollen. She looked exhausted as she stood limply, as Sebastián clutched her close to his side.

"Come out, come out, wherever you are?" Sebastián yelled.

Chief Ricco gripped her arm and put his finger to his mouth, telling her to stay quiet.

"I offer a fair exchange. You for Bianca."

That was bullshit, and Hannah knew it. He'd kill them both.

She and Hunter both looked to the chief for direction. He mouthed the word wait to them. Did he have a plan, or was he trying to think one up? She'd never expected to see Bianca with him. This was a game changer.

"I know you're here. I saw your campsite. You've got to the count of three before I blow your little friend's head off."

"Don't. Run. He'll kill us both!" Bianca yelled with slurred words.

Hannah sprang forward, but only made it one step before Hunter grabbed her upper arm so tightly it halted her.

Bianca slumped, and Sebastián yanked her back up, using her as a shield.

"One."

"Chief, do something," she pleaded.

He had his aim on her with his pistol, but Bianca was so close to Sebastián.

"Stay," he said before he stepped out of the tree line.

Sebastián's facial features hardened, and he tugged Bianca in front of him. Her body moved as if she were a ragdoll.

"Give me that bitch now," Sebastián yelled to the chief.

"No. Release Bianca. If you don't, you are not getting out of here alive."

"You won't shoot. You might accidentally hit her. How would that look? Cop kills victim."

Sebastián stood with only half of his face peering around Bianca.

He was right. There no way Chief Ricco could shoot.

Hannah wanted to leap out of the woods to end this madness. Hunter must have read her mind because his grip tightened on her arm. What they'd thought would be a good visual position was now the worst position they could be in. To get to Sebastián, they'd have to go through Bianca, and they couldn't do that.

Bianca went into a full-blown sob and kept slumping. Sebastián kept yanking at her. She gasped for air. Her face turned white as a ghost. The one eye Hannah could see rolled back into her head, and she collapsed to the ground. A shot rang out. Sebastián fell to the ground behind her. Chief Ricco crouched down and looked to the left, then back to Sebastián, then to the left again.

The chief sprang up and ran toward Bianca and Sebastián. Hunter flew by her side and did the same. She felt frozen in place. She didn't want to see another dead body on top of these falls, or anywhere else for that matter.

"She's breathing. Sebastián is dead," Hunter yelled to her.

Hannah leaped out of the woods and ran to Bianca.

Hannah crouched down next to her, placed her hand on her shoulder, and shook her slightly.

"Bianca, can you hear me?" Hannah asked twice before her friend's eyes fluttered open, the swollen one just a slit.

"Hannah?" Bianca whispered.

"Yes. You're okay. Sebastián is dead."

"I'm so sorry. This is all my fault."

"What?"

"I did this. I did all of this. I didn't want to. He made me."

"It's okay. I know."

"No. You don't. Even back then. Alyssa. Your parents. This is all my fault."

Bianca's words felt like a knife slicing her heart. Her friend had betrayed her.

Hannah looked at Hunter and Chief Ricco. Both men wore a shocked expression.

Bianca's breathing labored, and she passed out.

The chief called over the radio for evacuation help, then asked the million-dollar question.

"Who shot?"

One by one, the men replied. Nobody fessed up.

Chief Ricco glanced around.

"None of our men were in a position to see this far and shoot," the chief stated.

The probing look he wore basically asked her and Hunter if they knew who shot.

"I've got no idea. Nobody else knows we're here," Hunter replied.

Hannah nodded in agreement.

Chief Ricco shared a knowing glance with Hunter and he looked away.

Now she really wanted to know. Lee? Heidi?

Was this why Lee used the word my instead of we before, and I'm instead of we're? Was Lee letting the chief know Heidi wasn't with him—was in some sort of position?

Good heavens. Did Heidi do this? She recalled the elk story from earlier in the day. Lee beamed when he'd said Heidi shot that elk at five hundred and seventy-five yards.

Had Chief Ricco asked the men the question, already knowing the answer to keep the shooter a mystery? Had he and Hunter just held that brief conversation for her benefit? To keep her from knowing the truth when asked?

You know what, she didn't care who the shooter was, the demon was dead and wouldn't be able to hurt anyone else.

Chapter Twenty-Five

With Sebastián dead, there was no need for Bianca to confess her part in the murders of Alyssa and Hannah's parents, but she did. She'd written a full confession for the police. Filled in all the missing details. She told them how she and Sebastián had been secret lovers while he dated Hannah. How Sebastián had manipulated her into keeping him abreast of Hannah's every move. How Alyssa was not the target that day; Hannah was. How the guy from the gas station was the contract killer Sebastián hired. It all came out. Every horrible detail. Even the detail about Sebastián killing the gas station guy for screwing up. The man had still expected to be paid for killing Alyssa rather than Hannah.

As angry as Hannah was knowing her friend had betrayed her, she hoped Bianca's sentence would be a light one. Knowing firsthand how manipulative and unhinged Sebastián was, she believed wholeheartedly that Bianca felt Sebastián gave her no choice but to do what she'd done. He would have killed her if she hadn't complied.

Alyssa's parents were not as forgiving. After three years,

the case had been labeled as a cold case. For ten years, Alyssa's parents waited for answers, and now that they had them, they wanted Bianca to pay dearly for her role in the murder of their daughter. Even after all this time, when Hannah looked at Mr. and Mrs. Barnes, the pain in their eyes was unbearable. It broke her heart all over again, knowing that if not for her, her friend would still be alive. Alyssa's mom pulled her into a tight embrace and assured her she felt no ill will toward her, and then released her. The woman probably had no idea how much she needed to hear that.

Hunter gripped her hand as they walked out of the district attorney's office.

"Now what?" he asked.

"I'm exhausted. I want to sleep for a week."

Her exhaustion was no lie. It had been only two days since everything broke again on top of Lover's Leap Falls. It was a whirlwind during those two days. Getting Bianca the medical attention she needed. Talking to the authorities. Calling her brothers. Coming back home. Letting the world know they were out of hiding now that Sebastián was dead. She still carried a hint of fear that Sebastián's parents would retaliate, but the two had done nothing to her the entire time Sebastián was in prison, so she held hope they'd think better of doing something to her now. It was almost like they'd cut themselves off from their son back then. Maybe they did. Maybe the last thing they needed was the attention Sebastián brought to the family and the family business.

"Well, Hannah Rice, I think I can arrange that, and I know the perfect king-sized bed to do that in."

"Hannah Rice," she repeated.

"It's got a nice ring to it. Not that I didn't like Katrina

Holmes, but it wasn't the name of the woman I fell in love with."

Now that Sebastián was gone and she and her brothers returned to their former names, she'd go by Hannah again.

She turned toward Hunter and wrapped her arms around his neck.

"I love you."

He leaned forward, pressed his lips lightly to hers for a couple of beats before pulling away.

He arched a brow. "If you're not too exhausted, I know a lot of other things we can do in that king-sized bed that awaits us."

She pulled him to her and kissed him. This time, a bit longer. It about killed her to release him, but since they were standing on a sidewalk in front of the county building, she thought it best to back away from him.

"I'm up for whatever you have in mind."

Both his eyebrows wiggled teasingly.

"We've got a lot of lost time to make up for."

"Agreed. And the making up for it starts now."

What, there's a wedding???

Need more???

👉 You're invited - RSVP now for the wedding epilogue 🤍

Sign up for my newsletter to download the exclusive bonus epilogue and celebrate Hunter and Hannah's happily-ever-after commitment. Don't miss this special, heartfelt moment!

Sign up here: https://preview.mailerlite.io/forms/285170/162259133740876802/share

But wait, there's more!

Remember when you met Hunter's brother, Cap? Well things are about to get INTENSE for him. Don't miss out—watch for my newsletter to keep abreast of upcoming information regarding CURRENT TO TROUBLE, book 2, in the WILD HEARTS SERIES!

Also by Valerie J. Clarizio

Doing what I LOVE makes me productive😊

My book list is getting longer, so I needed to move it to my website! Cool, right?

To see a list of all my written works, please click the link below.

https://valeriejclarizio.com/printable-books-list/

-OR- scan the QR code below.

Enjoy this book? YOU can make a BIG difference!

Reviews matter!

Your honest review is one of the most powerful ways to help independent authors reach other readers. If you enjoyed this story, I'd LOVE if you would take a minute to review this book on your favorite platform(s). Your thoughts would mean the world to me. Reviews, even short ones, make a BIG difference. Even just clicking the ☆stars ☆ matter.

Click here for review platforms to leave your review and/or rating to help other readers discover TRAIL TO TROUBLE:

https://valeriejclarizio.com/book/trail-to-trou ble/

Thank you for your support!

Meet Valerie

Unlike many authors, I did not experience my love for reading until later in life. I cringed every time a teacher assigned a book report. I would have rather spent my time in six advanced Math classes versus one in English.

It wasn't until I was in my 40s that someone turned me on to this whole romance reading thing. You see, I was never a traditional college student. When I graduated high school, I knew I wanted to pursue a degree in Accounting, so I became a part-time student while working two jobs to make ends meet. That said, it took a while for me to work through the college coursework. First, I obtained an Associate Degree in Accounting from the technical college where I now teach part-time while working my full-time job as the Finance Director for the Wisconsin city in which I live.

After completing the coursework for my Associate Degree, I earned a Bachelor's Degree in Accounting, and then a Master's Degree in Business. \The day after I completed the coursework for my Master's, I came home from work, made dinner, ate, and then looked at my husband and asked, "What exactly do normal people do with their evenings?" I hadn't really had one of those in a couple of decades, and I wasn't sure what to do with myself. He looked at me, serious as a heart attack, and said, "Well, there's this thing called television. I'm about to watch a program now. Try it out."

The show was *Boston Legal*, and though it was awesome, it wasn't enough. I spent the next week cleaning every closet in my house before I didn't know what to do with myself again. I complained to a friend of my dilemma, and her resolution was to hand me a Janet Evanovich novel. I shook my head, declining the book, not wanting to read *anything*. She shoved the book back at me and demanded I give it a shot. I took it and read it in two nights. I was HOOKED!

I read through everything Evanovich had penned and then moved on to romance authors. I logged more than fifty books in that first year. They were a little easier reading than my Accounting and Finance texts. Then one night, I had a dream about a detective and a kidnapping. The next day I called my friend and told her I was going to email Evanovich with this great idea for a detective story to convince her to write it up. I know, right, like I'd get access to Evanovich. My friend replied, "Or you could get up off your butt and write it yourself." Hence, the birth of Detective Spinelli and that three-book series.

Truth be told, publishing Spinelli's story wasn't exactly that easy, but I got there, and now my bio includes how much I love to read *and* write. Particularly at my cabin in the Upper Peninsula of Michigan, where writing outside on the deck can be an adventure. I've seen deer, fox, turkeys, and eagles while penning my romantic suspense, contemporary, and time travel romance novels.

I've penned more than fifteen novels and novellas. I've hit the *USA Today* Best-selling Books List and have been designated as an Amazon top 100 author in Romantic Suspense, Suspense, and Mystery & Suspense. I've been ranked by

Amazon as a #1 Bestseller in Military Romance and Love & Romance. Additionally, I have been listed as a Barnes & Noble Bestseller and Kobo Bestseller. Persistence pays. 😊

A funny side note ... when I first told my family and friends that I'd written a book, most assumed it was an Accounting text. Little did they know.

My online home is: https://www.valeriejclarizio.com

You can also connect with me here:

Newsletter: https://valeriejclarizio.com/newsletter-signup-page/

Facebook: https://www.facebook.com/Valerie.Clarizio/

Facebook Street Team: https://www.facebook.com/groups/clarizioscronies/

Bookbub: https://www.bookbub.com/authors/valerie-j-clarizio

Instagram: https://www.instagram.com/valerieclarizio/

Tiktok: https://www.tiktok.com/@valeriejclarizioauthor?lang=en

Twitter (X): https://twitter.com/VClarizio

Amazon: https://www.amazon.com/Valerie-J.-Clarizio/e/B00A87RJVS

Printed in the United States of America

First published in 2025

Published by Valerie J. Clarizio, Trailhead Consulting LLC, 2025.

Title: TRAIL TO TROUBLE / WILD HEARTS SERIES / Valerie J. Clarizio

ISBN-979-8-9998103-0-4

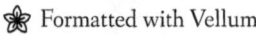 Formatted with Vellum